I0645802

Billionaire's Brothers

Julie L. Spencer

Spencer Publishing, LLC

Click or scan here to request a complimentary book when you join my newsletter.

Copyright © 2021 by Julie L. Spencer

All rights reserved.

No part of this publication may be reproduced, distributed, or transmitted in any form or by any means, including photocopying, recording, or other electronic or mechanical methods, without the prior written permission of the publisher, except as permitted by U.S. copyright law. For permission requests, contact Spencer Publishing, LLC.

The story, all names, characters, and incidents portrayed in this production are fictitious. No identification with actual persons (living or deceased), places, buildings, and products is intended or should be inferred.

ISBN: 978-1-954666-02-3

www.AuthorJulieSpencer.com

Contents

Note to Readers:

The entire Sayid Family Saga is written in the Contemporary genre. That means they all have cell phones and private jets and superyachts. Even though the saga spans multiple generations, each story is designed to take place in modern day. None of the stories are historical fiction or futuristic. For any similarities to historical events, I have taken extreme artistic liberty. Send me an email when you figure it out! -Julie

Another Note to Readers:

Falling in love is the greatest feeling in the world. That's why I write romance and love stories. The day I met my husband I looked across the room at him and knew I was going to marry him. I didn't know his name (it's Clayton), I didn't know how old he was (nine months older than me), or if he was dating anyone (he was). All I knew was I was going to marry him. Almost twenty-five years later we're still on our honeymoon. Because that is my experience with falling in love, my characters tend to fall in love just as quickly. Love grows over time, but sometimes you look at someone and just know they are your person. You can call it Instalove, Love-at-First Sight, whatever you want. I pray that everyone in the world experiences the kind of love I feel every time I look into the eyes of my eternal companion. God bless you, my friends. Stay safe! -Julie

Part One: Contested Crown

Prince Marcos Sayid

As told by Prince Marcos Sayid, brother of Crown Prince Jared Sayid, son of King Sayid, who was in his forty-second year at the time the story begins...

Chapter One

Brother of the Crown

"**F**antastic wedding." Marcos held up his glass of Scotch, toasting with Nick's brothers while they lounged in chaises by the outdoor pool.

The older Cohen brothers—Liam, Lyle, and Sam—had already tossed back a few drinks each. Nick's younger brother, Jacob, was not yet eighteen and was sipping a soda.

"I'm glad it's over," Liam grumbled. "I haven't gone that many hours without a drink in years." He downed another large glass of Scotch and laid his head back on the lounge chair, eyes closed and probably not long from needing an escort to his suite for the night.

Nick and Adele had decided not to serve any alcohol at their wedding because Liam had made a complete fool of himself at a wedding less than a year ago. But when the bride and groom snuck away, presumably to head up to their hotel suite, they left the rest of the bridal party to fend for themselves. By eleven-thirty, Marcos suggested that the guys find the tiki bar near the pool.

Since Nick was upstairs doing what Marcos wished he could be doing, he wouldn't fault Marcos for having a little fun of his own. They'd attended prep school together, gotten into a little trouble over the years, and were best friends. He was happy for Nick but a little jealous.

Marcos joked about being an eternal bachelor, but that was mostly just to anger his father.

As Nick's best man, Marcos had nearly upstaged the groom, because he was required to wear his crown while attending formal social events. If the occasion warranted a tux, it required at least a simple band of gold around his head.

Marcos wished he could remove his crown. It had been a long day, and he had a headache. Nothing that a little Scotch couldn't absolve. He held up his nearly empty glass and lifted his chin to the bartender, requesting that someone bring him another.

There were still quite a few people mingling after the wedding reception, probably seeking out the same thing the guys were, the open tiki bar and a place to kick back and loosen their ties and remove their sport coats. Marcos and the Cohen brothers had even gone as far as removing shoes and socks and rolling up the pant legs of their tuxes.

Marcos was eyeing the pool and its promise to wash away the oppressive heat that never seemed to dissipate in the City of Dubai. That would require the removal of his tux and crown, and that would require traipsing all the way up to his suite and requesting his advisor to assist him. Way too much work just to cool off. He downed the last of his Scotch as a waitress handed him another.

Because he wasn't the crown prince, Marcos had very little responsibility except that of a dignitary, schmoozing the world on behalf of the royal family that stayed mostly within the palace walls.

His brother, Crown Prince Jared Sayid, had been expected to marry at the ripe old age of sixteen, as was tradition, and produce an heir as quickly as possible. Before his eighteenth birthday, the virile little twerp had gotten his young bride pregnant and then sought comfort in the arms of other women, usually much older women.

As the family's ambassador, Marcos vowed to be a better example than his older brother, which required him to stay relatively sober and chaste. That forced him to maintain a certain level of discipline.

Other than young Jacob, who didn't really count, Marcos was the only guy in the group neither married nor in a committed relationship. He could probably have his pick of the single women at this outdoor bar. But that would require getting up from his chaise, and his feet hurt from standing all day.

No, he was happy right here, with his drink and his friends.

Until a small group of ladies passed by close enough to catch his attention and up his heart rate. In addition to wedding attendees, guests of the estate mingled in the bar and pool area, including women. Several of them giggled and waved coyly. A blonde in a little black dress held his gaze like a deer caught in the headlights of his imported Bentley.

She was so distracted by their intense connection that she walked right into the pool—

And landed with a giant splash.

Chapter Two

Rescuing Lyla

Marcos didn't hesitate for a second, not considering his attire, his crown, or his dignity. He jumped in after the blonde, vainly attempting to save the damsel in distress.

The young lady's head popped out of the water, barely sputtering, and definitely not drowning.

"Are you okay, miss?" Marcos asked. The pool was shallow enough for her to touch the bottom, but just the same, he wrapped his arm around her waist.

She draped her hands around his broad shoulders and laced her fingers together behind his neck. "I think I'll be alright," she said, a hint of humor and sarcasm tingeing her statement. "Just the same, I'm glad a strong man jumped in to save me."

Was she flirting with him? Definitely.

"Well, it was my fault you fell," Marcos said, smoothing her long hair across her shoulders. "It was only fair that I should rescue you."

Their eyes met and neither looked away. Marcos had the overwhelming desire to kiss this girl he didn't even know.

"What's your name?" he whispered.

"Lyla," she whispered. "And yours?"

"Marcos."

"It's really nice to meet you, Marcos."

"The pleasure is all mine, Lyla." He loved the way her name rolled off his tongue.

"Prince Marcos," Collins called from beside the pool. "Are you quite alright, Your Highness?"

"I *was* doing just fine," Marcos grumbled, glancing up at his trusted advisor. Although the same age, Collins seemed older and more mature. Apparently, he wasn't astute enough to realize Marcos would want a minute alone while holding a beautiful woman. He spoke through clenched teeth, "Thank you very much."

Lyla giggled. "Prince Marcos, huh? I guess that would explain the crown." She raised her hand to touch his crown, but Marcos grabbed her wrist gently.

"No one's allowed to touch my crown save my advisor and my wife."

"You're married?" Lyla pushed him away, with disgust lacing her voice.

"No, no, no, not married." Marcos reached for her again. "Please don't leave. I just meant, until you're my wife, you can't touch my crown."

"*Until* I'm your wife?" Her jaw dropped, and she raised her eyebrows. "Isn't that kind of presumptuous of you? You think just because you're a prince you can snap your fingers and demand a woman marry you?"

"Of course not," Marcos insisted. "I would never presume such a thing. A man could only get so lucky to marry a woman such as yourself." He moved a step toward her again, pushing against the resistance of the water between them, wishing to have her back in his arms.

"What makes you think you'd be lucky to have me for a wife?" she asked, splashing away from him. "You know nothing about me. And don't you dare say it's because I'm beautiful. Believe me, I've heard it all before."

"Have you?" Marcos couldn't hide a grin. "Well then, I'll try to find some other word to describe you."

"Oh really?" She was still moving away from him, staying barely out of reach as he continued stalking her, purposely keeping a few inches slower rather than catching her. "Let's hear your descriptive words, *Your Highness*."

"Let's see... feisty... wet... clumsy."

"Clumsy?" She stopped and folded her arms across her chest.

"You *did* fall into a pool after all," Marcos said, lithely slipping himself close to her and wrapping both arms around her waist. "Would you please stand still long enough for me to rescue you... princess?" He added the last word as a reverent whisper.

"Princess, huh?" Lyla gulped as she slipped her arms around his neck.

"You like the sound of that?" His husky voice was suggestive.

"I'm undecided."

"How about if we get dried off, change into clean clothes, and I'll buy you a drink and woo you into the wee hours of the night, sitting *beside* the pool rather than *in* it, and by the time you fall into the softness of the pillows in your hotel suite you will have... decided."

"Hmm... I suppose that is a decent plan." While she spoke, Marcos slid through the water with Lyla in his arms as if he'd truly rescued her from imminent drowning.

He carried her all the way up the steps leading out of the pool and set her onto her bare feet. Marcos raised his eyebrows. "Where are your shoes?"

"Bottom of the pool, I think." She glanced over toward the deep end and bit her lower lip.

Marcos waved for a pool attendant and spoke with authority, "Fetch the lady her shoes, won't you, kind sir?"

"Of course, Your Highness." Without hesitation, the young man trudged down the steps into the pool, fully clothed, and walked toward the deep end, eventually ducking under the water and popping up a moment later holding two black stilettos.

By the time the pool attendant returned to the deck, Marcos had waved over his advisor, Collins, and requested a one hundred dirhams note to give to the man for his service.

"Here you are," Marcos said, handing the boy the hundred dirhams note in exchange for the dripping shoes. "Why don't you take the remainder of the night off, get yourself into some dry clothes and have a drink on me."

"Thank you, Your Highness." The young man lowered his head in a brief bow. "It was no trouble at all."

Marcos turned back to Lyla, ceremoniously handing her the shoes. "I believe these belong to you."

"Why, thank you, Your Highness," she drawled in a fake Southern American accent. "I think I'll trade these in for some sandals or, better yet, some fluffy slippers."

"What do you say we meet back here in twenty minutes, clad in robes and fluffy slippers, and spend the remainder of the night discussing our many future adventures."

"I cannot wait to see you in fluffy slippers." Lyla bit her lip playfully.

"The feeling is mutual." Marcos touched her knuckles to his lips and then backed away slowly, releasing her fingers at the last possible second. "Until we meet again, princess."

"Likewise, my prince." Lyla nodded regally as they parted.

Marcos could hear her giggling with her friends, and he offered a mock salute to Nick's brothers and then strode, with purpose, away from the pool deck toward the waiting elevator. When they were almost to his suite, Marcos grumbled to Collins, "Assist me in removing my crown and fetch me some Tylenol. I have a splitting headache. Oh, and get me the tackiest fluffy slippers you can find."

Chapter Three

Return to Madain Saleh

"W ho would be calling this late at night?" Marcos grumbled. His heart sank when he saw the number on his caller ID and feared that something had happened to his father. Rarely did he get a call from the palace and never this time of day.

He'd removed his soaking wet tuxedo and was sitting at his dressing table in a dry T-shirt and boxers while Collins carefully removed his crown.

"Damian? Is everything alright?" Marcos touched the screen to set the call on speaker phone so that both he and Collins could hear the king's most trusted advisor.

"Your Highness, there's been an accident," Damian said. "You need to come home immediately."

"Has my father been injured?" Marcos waved his hand in annoyance, indicating that Collins should hurry up his ceremonial removal of the crown. Collins quickly had the band of gold off his head and into its velvet and mahogany box.

"No, sir, your brother, Jared. He was riding his motorcycle again and slid on some loose gravel." Damian became choked up and paused. His voice cracked when he said, "Your Highness, they don't think he's going to make it."

"I'll be there as quickly as I can." He glanced up at Collins, who already had his cell phone to his ear and was ordering the helicopter to come immediately.

Having ended the call, Marcos hurried into the closet and pulled on a pair of comfortable jeans and slipped a hoodie over his T-shirt. Almost as an afterthought, Marcos grabbed a piece of hotel stationary and scrawled a quick message.

Princess Lyla, my brother was in an accident on his motorcycle, and I'm heading home to Madain Saleh. Please text me your number so I can contact you in a day or two. I'm sorry to cut our night short. Yours truly, Prince Marcos

He scribbled his phone number, tucked the note in his pocket, along with his wallet, and rushed to meet Collins, who brought one leather satchel with him, which Marcos knew contained his crown.

"The pilot said he'll be on the helipad in less than ten minutes, Your Highness. Let's head down."

"I need to stop at the bar first," Marcos insisted.

"Your Highness, this is no time to go to the bar. They can provide you a drink once you're aboard the plane. The airport is only a few moments away by helicopter."

Marcos pulled the slip of stationary from his pocket. "You idiot, I just need to drop off this note for my future queen."

Collins snickered in spite of the seriousness of the situation. "Presumptuous, much?"

"Completely," Marcos stated. "Now let's go."

They hurried to the elevator and rushed out to the tiki bar where they found Nick's brothers still lounging by the pool. Marcos explained the situation and handed the important note to the only Cohen brother who was sober, young Jacob.

"Be sure she gets this," Marcos told him.

"You have my word," Jacob said.

Collins pulled at Marcos's arm gently but insistently, and they ran toward the back of the resort where they could already hear the whir of the helicopter approaching the helipad.

As they lifted into the sky, Marcos pressed his face against the window, longing to see the pool and catch a glimpse of Lyla and her long blonde hair. The rotating blades of the helicopter carried him the opposite direction, and Marcos swore under his breath. He knew that ghosting Lyla was the least of the horrors this night would bring.

Chapter Four

Your Future King

"My prince, I'm here, brother." Marcos hurried to Jared's bedside and grasped his hand. Between the helicopter and private jet, he'd managed to make it home to Madain Saleh in just over nine hours.

"Marcos," Jared choked out in a raspy voice. "We don't have much time."

"I'm here now. I'll sit with you through the night."

"Hear my words," Jared demanded in a much stronger voice than Marcos would have thought possible considering his obvious pain.

"Forgive me, my prince." Marcos lowered his eyes obediently to the man who was slated to be his king.

"No, *you* forgive me," Jared pleaded. "I have made some poor choices, and I need you to forgive me so that you can lead my people."

"I forgive you, my prince," Marcos said. "What would you have me do?" Lead his people? Is that really what he'd said? Marcos lifted his eyes and met his brother's gaze.

"My wife is not fit to raise our future king," Jared said. Marcos agreed but didn't vocalize his concern. "Do you understand what I'm saying?"

"I understand." Marcos nodded with increasing confidence. "I will lead our people as best I can."

"I fear you may need to flee this land," Jared said. "My wife will fight you on my decision."

"How am I to lead if I flee the country?" Marcos was confused.

"As long as father is alive, you won't be needed here."

"Good point," Marcos said.

"You need to get married," Jared insisted, cringing in pain. "The Crown needs a father *and* a mother to raise him."

"I'm starting to understand the desire to settle down." Marcos chuckled, thinking of the spunky blonde who'd already texted him to offer her condolences. "I think I can accommodate you on that request."

"Promise me one more thing." Jared gripped Marcos's hand with more strength than he'd thought possible.

"Anything, my prince," Marcos promised.

"Raise him as your own," Jared said.

"You want me to raise your son?"

"Your future king..." Jared's weak voice trailed off.

Marcos froze as realization entered his heart. Jared wasn't asking him to assume the role as Crown; he was asking Marcos to raise the future Crown, his five-year-old son, Omar.

"No," Marcos whispered, not sure his brother could hear him anymore. "He's not of age. When you die, whether that be tonight or ten years from now, unless your son is of age, I inherit the title of Crown. I will help raise him, but not as my future king."

Jared never responded with words or even a twitch of a muscle to indicate he'd heard his younger brother's declaration. His breathing grew more and more labored as the night wore on.

Clutching his older brother's hand, Marcos kept vigil through the long night, and by the time the sun rose, Jared no longer had a heartbeat.

Marcos pried his hand from within Jared's clutch and rose from his chair to inform the king that his oldest son had died.

Chapter Five

Funeral

There was no discussion of the contested crown during the three days of preparation for the funeral. Jared's widow, Princess Tayma, faked just enough tears to make her grief believable to anyone who didn't know her. She clutched Omar as if he was her most treasured possession even as Omar cried for his nanny. She also stayed close to the king's side. Marcos narrowed his eyes, wondering what she was up to.

The funeral procession was formal and attended by most people in the kingdom. Some in attendance seemed genuinely grieved by the loss of their prince, and Marcos knew Jared had been beloved by his subjects. He really had been a good Crown and would have made a great king.

Some who attended the funeral were either there out of curiosity or were reveling in the pageantry of seeing the royal family outside the palace walls, which was rare. Marcos couldn't remember the last time they'd ever been out together.

His father, King Sayid of Madain Saleh, led the procession, with Marcos on his right and Princess Tayma carrying little Omar to the King's left. His mother, Queen Salaina, walked a few paces behind her husband. That was one tradition Marcos intended to put to rest as soon as he was in charge. His queen would walk beside him, as an equal.

When the internment had been spoken, and the family began the procession back to the palace, one young lady broke away from the crowd and knelt near Jared's tomb, sobbing into her hands. No one else seemed to notice, and Marcos casually left the procession and returned to stand beside her.

Marcos stood close enough that the woman was able to lean her head against his leg for support. He reached down and patted her on the head and then spoke words she probably wouldn't hear from anyone else, "I'm sorry for your loss."

"Jared will be missed," she sobbed, probably not realizing she was talking to his brother. No woman in the kingdom would be so bold as to call the crown prince by his first name unless she had a *very* familial relationship with him. Even then, never in the presence of royalty.

"By all who knew him," Marcos agreed and then patted her on the head again and turned to walk away. He paused for one more acknowledgment. "Take all the time you need."

At that, the young lady, probably in her early twenties, gasped and looked up at him, horror crossing her face at the bold way in which she'd spoken to the prince. "Your Highness?"

"I will forget we had this conversation," Marcos stated.

"Thank you, Your Highness." She lowered her gaze and twisted her hands in her lap, wringing a white handkerchief over and over.

Marcos started to leave again but stopped and took a deep breath, steeling himself for whatever the answer might be. "Are there any other... family members I should know about?"

"No, Your Highness, we were careful."

"I don't need to hear details," Marcos halted her sternly. "Please just let my brother's memory rest in peace."

"Yes, Your Highness," she whimpered.

This time Marcos didn't hesitate but walked briskly away from the woman. No man was perfect. Even a man as good as his brother, Jared. Marcos vowed never to do the things his brother had done.

Chapter Six

Contested Crown

"**F**ather, the Crown should not be contested," Marcos insisted. "The title is mine in the absence of my elder brother."

"Not if he has an heir," Princess Tayma argued. "My son is the rightful Crown."

"Omar is *five* years old," Marcos said. "He is not of age and could *not* rule if the king were to die."

"Planning my demise so soon, my youngest son?" King Sayid chuckled.

"You know that's not what I meant, Father. Please, hear my reasoning."

"I hear you, Marcos," Sayid said. "My biggest concern with you is that you'll never marry and produce an heir of your own. You're twenty-three already and haven't even considered taking a bride."

"But, Father, I have considered marriage." Marcos jumped on this chance. "I met a woman, and I'm quite enthralled with her. I would very much like to marry her." He didn't point out that he'd met Lyla four days ago and didn't even know her last name or where she lived or if she had any royal bloodline.

"I'll believe it when I see it," Tayma said, sticking her nose in the air. "Produce an heir, and then we'll talk."

"*You* are not in charge, princess." Marcos sneered at her.

"That would be Your Highness, thank you very much." Tayma crossed her arms and lifted her chin higher.

"I outrank you by blood and status, *Tayma*." Marcos emphasized her given name to purposely knock her down a notch. "I'll call you whatever I darn well please."

"Children, would you please stop fighting," Queen Salaina cut into the conversation.

"Sorry, Your Grace," both Marcos and Tayma said and then lowered their gazes. The only person above the queen was the king, and even Sayid often took direction from his wife. She didn't speak often, but when she did, her words were powerful.

Marcos took advantage of this diversion and knelt at his mother's feet, pleading to her maternal nature. "Your Grace, what is your opinion on the matter of naming the Crown?"

"I'm not allowed to have an opinion, son." She held out her hand for him to grasp. He was unsure if he was acting as a loyal subject or devoted son.

"Of course, you are, Mother." Marcos glanced toward the king, wondering if he'd be reprimanded for speaking to the queen so informally. Seeing no objection in Sayid's eyes, Marcos took his plea to a higher level of informality. "Father values your counsel."

"I want to hear more about this future bride of yours," Salaina cleverly changed the subject. "What's she like? How has she captured the heart of my young prince? She clearly has; I can see it in your eyes."

"She's beautiful, Mother." Marcos sighed and settled on the top marble step. His parents' thrones sat at the highest point in the room. "But she doesn't like to be *told* that she's beautiful. She liked it when I called her feisty."

"Oh, you've got it bad, my son." Salaina chuckled.

"Oh brother, this is ridiculous," Tayma grumbled. "I'm outta here. I'll see you at dinner."

"Princess Tayma," Sayid commanded. "You have not been dismissed."

"My apologies, Your Majesty." Tayma curtsied and lowered her gaze.

"I have not made any decision," Sayid said. "I will take both of your testimonies into consideration and consult my advisors. The choice I make could have generational implications. I will not take my responsibility lightly."

"Yes, Your Majesty," Tayma said softly.

"You are dismissed."

"Thank you, Your Majesty." Tayma hurried out of the throne room, and the tension seemed to lift from Marcos's shoulders.

"As I was saying, her name is Lyla, and she has long blonde hair and crystal-blue eyes, and she fell for me quite literally when I rescued her from drowning."

"Where is she from? What is her lineage?" his mother asked.

"I'm pretty sure she's not a princess, if that's what you're asking." Marcos's eyes crossed with unfocused dreaming, and he laughed to himself. "Although she kind of liked when I called her my princess."

"Reeeally?"

"How about this, Mother? I'll send her a text to ask if she can provide her lineage, and we'll discuss her some more at dinner."

"You are dismissed, my son."

"Thank you, Your Grace." Marcos bowed to his mother and then turned to the king with expectant eyes. "Your Majesty?"

"You're dismissed, son."

"Thank you, Father." Marcos bowed to this man who could reprimand him for the casual manner in which he'd been addressed multiple times today. Marcos hurried from the room, pulling his cell phone from his pocket and typing out a quick message.

My parents want to know everything about you. Do you have time to talk?

They'd texted back and forth several times in the past few days since he'd left Dubai but had not spoken. Marcos looked forward to hearing Lyla's voice.

Chapter Seven

She Hung Up on Me?

"Marry you? Are you insane?" Lyla screeched into the phone.

"I need to produce an heir as quickly as possible, and you are the most logical woman for the role of queen," Marcos said.

"Logical? Produce an heir? You *are* insane!"

"No, wait, Lyla, let me explain," Marcos said, gathering courage. "I was intrigued by you from the moment you fell in that pool and wrapped your arms around my shoulders. The water droplets clinging to your eyelashes, the way your hair became darker when it got wet. The way you challenged me on everything I said. I can't wait to hold you in my arms again."

There was silence on the other end of the phone.

"Did you hang up?" he asked.

"No, I'm still here."

"Speaking of, are you still at the resort in Dubai? I'd love to come visit with you, and we can plan our future together."

"I'm still at the resort, but, Marcos, we don't even love each other," she said.

"Love grows over time."

"I feel like you're just trying to hire me for sex."

Marcos scoffed. "Trust me, if I were just hiring you for sex, it would be a lot less expensive than a royal wedding."

"How dare you!" The line went dead.

"She hung up on me?"

"You offended her in so many ways I can't even count them all," Collins told Marcos.

"You weren't supposed to be listening to my conversation," Marcos said.

"You pay me a large sum of money to stand beside you through all your waking hours," Collins said. "It is my job to listen to your conversations."

"You will *not* stand outside my door once I'm married," Marcos insisted, pointing at Collins with mock anger.

"I'll be on the opposite side of the palace, pretending I don't know what you're doing."

"Good, because just the thought of you listening gives me the creeps."

"How about if we hop onto a jet and go find your princess, apologize to her profusely, convince her to marry you, and bring her home to your palace," Collins suggested. "Then I can have a night off once in a while."

"You'll have *every* night off if I have any say in the matter."

"You won't have any say in the matter if you don't convince her to marry you, so let's go."

"Fire up the private jet, my eavesdropping advisor."

Chapter Eight

First Kiss

"There she is Collins." Marcos pointed at a small round table where Lyla and two other women sat in the open patio area between the pool and the tiki bar. "What should I do?"

"You flew all this way. Maybe you should walk over and talk to her."

Marcos took a deep breath and started forward. "Wish me luck."

"I'm coming with you, Your Highness. It's what you pay me for." Collins fell into step a little to Marcos's right and one foot behind. "Besides, her older friend is smokin' hot. You're introducing me as your wingman, not your advisor."

"Then I'd suggest you stop calling me 'Your Highness' and start calling me Marcos."

"I can do that, Your—uh, okay, that's going to be more difficult than I thought. How about you refer to me as merely your trusted advisor."

They were halfway across the patio, and Lyla hadn't noticed him yet.

But her friend did, and she tapped Lyla on the arm, pointing at Marcos and Collins.

A strange expression crossed Lyla's face. Confusion? Anger? Awe? Frustration? Exasperation? "You've got to be kidding me," Lyla said.

"Ladies, mind if we pull up a chair and buy you a drink?" Marcos asked boldly. He swung an empty chair around from the next table, straddled it and leaned his arms against the back, directly across from Lyla so he was able to look her in the eye.

Collins also pulled up a chair but sat in a more conventional manner.

"What are you doing here, Your *Majesty*?" Lyla asked with a sneer.

"Your Highness, actually," Marcos corrected her. "Your Majesty would be my father, the king."

"What?"

"You're offending her again," Collins stage-whispered.

"Ya think?" Lyla's eyes widened.

"I realize my proposal over the telephone was in poor taste, so I have come to formally request your hand in marriage," Marcos said. "May I be introduced to your father?"

"No!"

"No, I cannot be introduced to your father?" Marcos asked. "Or, no, you won't marry me?"

"Both," Lyla said. "We are not in love, and I will not marry a man just so he can produce an heir. I really don't care if you lose your stupid kingdom. I will *not* marry you, Your *Highness*."

"At least you got my title correct that time, Your Highness. You might want to get used to your new title as well."

They had drawn the attention of every patron in the bar and adjoining pool deck, and Lyla's friends were snickering, the older of the two actually snorted and then laughed out loud. She cleared her throat and said, "I need another drink."

"Allow me," Collins said and waved a hand to the waitress.

Marcos didn't release Lyla's gaze and raised his eyebrows when he caught the tiniest hint of humor behind her fiery expression. He allowed a playful smirk to spread across his face, and he could tell she was cringing, trying to force herself not to answer his grin. Finally, she cracked and broke eye contact as she laughed into her hand, trying to cover her traitorous smile.

Not waiting for her to change her mind, Marcos rose quickly from his chair and stepped around to her side of the table, holding out his hand in invitation. "Would you come for a walk with me? Just around the pool deck, in full view of your chaperones, of course."

"My chaperones?" Lyla glanced at her two friends, both of whom were barely stifling laughter. Lyla took a deep breath and growled and then finally slipped her hand into his and allowed him to help her to her feet.

The momentum of standing led her right into Marcos's waiting arms, and he took the opportunity to wrap one arm around her waist, keeping her hand in his other. Not wanting to continue their conversation in front of all their friends, Marcos backed away from the table, pulling her with him. She didn't resist.

"Dang it, you smell really good," she muttered. "Why do you smell so good?"

"Probably because I'm not drenched in pool water," Marcos said.

"The night is young. I could still push you in."

"True, but then I wouldn't smell nearly as good."

"You've got a point," she said.

"My brother died," Marcos said suddenly, feeling the need to explain himself, as if she didn't already know.

"I'm glad you were you able to get home in time to say goodbye," she said quietly. He dropped his arm from her waist but continued to hold her hand as they began a leisurely stroll in the gardens beside the pool, out of earshot but within sight of their friends.

"Yes, I spent the night at his bedside." Marcos had to stop when his voice hitched. "I held his hand..." He didn't have to finish that part of his sentence.

"I'm sorry for your loss."

"Thank you," he said. "I'm sorry I was rude, crass, brazen, and a presumptuous jerk. And for standing you up."

"Well, you had a valid reason for leaving the resort, but I'm curious to know if there is any excuse for your behavior the past twelve hours."

"Yes, there is actually." Marcos turned and pulled her other hand into his, looking down into her eyes. "My brother's widow is trying to convince my father to name her five-year-old son as the next king."

"He'd probably do a better job of running your country than most politicians in this world."

"Valid observation," he said. "But just the same, I've been a little out of sorts arguing with my family. I'm sorry if my grief, anger, and lack of a full night's sleep—for I don't know how many days—has led me to say or do things I wouldn't normally."

"Like call up a woman you hardly know, insult her repeatedly, and sit on an airplane for eight or nine hours so you can insult her some more and then take her for a stroll in the gardens behind your friend's resort."

"Exactly." Marcos nodded.

"What is it you're hoping to accomplish?" Lyla asked.

"I'd like to make you my princess," Marcos said and then lifted her hand to his lips and kissed her knuckles.

Lyla let out a little sigh that was almost a whimper. "Why me? You know nothing about me."

"I know how good you feel in my arms." Marcos took a step closer and pulled her to him, their faces now inches apart. "I know I've thought of little else but you since the moment I saw you, even *before* you fell into the pool."

"I haven't been able to get you off my mind either," she admitted, gazing up into his eyes.

"Would you mind very much if I kissed you?" Marcos whispered, his face lowering closer and closer to hers. "If I ask really, really nicely?"

"What if I say no?" Lyla asked, biting her lower lip.

"You've said no to me quite a few times today." Marcos pulled her just a little closer and inched his face lower.

"I'm getting good at saying no," she whispered.

"How about we make a deal." Marcos pulled back just slightly and cocked his head to the side. "When you kiss me, if you feel absolutely nothing, I'll walk away and never bother you again."

Marcos leaned closer and kissed Lyla's neck just below her earlobe and then moved to the other side and kissed her there as well. She moaned softly and closed her eyes, leaning closer.

"But if you feel the way I think you're going to feel," Marcos whispered, his lips close to hers again. "Then consider my proposal, and I will spend every night for the rest of our lives making you feel as good as you feel *right now*."

Without waiting for any more invitation than that, Marcos brought his lips to hers with feather-light pressure, allowing her the choice to complete the kiss... or not.

Lyla reached into Marcos's hair, and she pulled him to herself, kissing him with all the wild passion she possessed.

He forgot, or ignored, all the people who were probably watching them, and kissed her with his whole being, holding nothing back.

He'd never given himself to a woman before, but he suddenly realized how much he was going to love being married. He understood how a man could be tempted to quench this passion before a proper wedding, because he wanted every part of him to become one with every part of her.

His body was in physical pain, and he felt tears prick the corners of his eyes as he stopped himself from kissing her further, and further. *Oh my gosh.* Marcos didn't want to cry in front of her, or any of the people watching them, but he felt so dang vulnerable.

He closed his eyes and pressed his forehead to hers, breathing so heavily he was almost panting or hyperventilating. He didn't trust himself to speak, so he just held her.

"Are you averse to flying to America?" Lyla whispered. "Because that's where my dad is."

"Yes!" Marcos called into the sky. "I mean, no! No, I'm not averse to flying. Yes, I'm glad you're going to introduce me to your father. My private jet is waiting at the airport. Would you like to take a limo over there? Or shall I order the helicopter to come pick us up?"

"Well, I can't leave tonight," Lyla said, placing her hand on his chest playfully. "But soon, okay? Within the next few days."

"Okay, I can be patient." He gulped. Sort of. He'd try to be patient.

"Would you be willing to get married in America so my family and friends can all come?"

"Of course," Marcos said. "No problem. My parents could probably even come to the wedding. My father will want to arrange a meeting with your president while he's there, but that can be done sometime after the wedding while we're on our honeymoon."

"The... president? Of, like, the United States?"

"Oh, I'm sorry. Do you live in another part of America? I always forget there are several continents that are all called America, right? Northern, Southern, Central? Is that right? Where do you live? I forgot to ask. My apologies."

"No, I mean, yes, I live in the United States," Lyla said. "In New York City, actually. That's not too far from our nation's capital, Washington, D.C. Your father should be able to get down there to meet with the—uh—president."

"Wonderful," Marcos said. "It's settled, then. Would you like me to wait until your father offers his blessing first? Or would it be okay to give our audience a satisfying conclusion by allowing me to lower myself to one knee and formally asking for your hand?"

"You are the strangest man I've ever met, Your Highness." Lyla leaned her head back and laughed.

"Thank you, Your Highness." Marcos picked up both her hands in his and kissed them gently and then continued to hold them as he lowered himself to the ground. Ignoring the dew that soaked into the knee of his slacks, he kissed her hands again and smiled up at her. "Lyla—oh crud, I have no idea what your last name is—will you do me the honor of becoming my wife and princess?"

"Yes! You silly man! Get up here and give me another kiss!"

Marcos stood and lifted her into his arms. As he swung her around, they both smiled and laughed and listened to the people in the bar clapping and cheering. He stopped spinning, rested her back on her feet, and, before kissing her again, asked, "What is your last name?"

"Donovan," Lyla said. "For now."

"Lyla, Princess of Madain Saleh," Marcos said reverently. "I cannot wait to marry you."

"Kiss me once more, my prince," Lyla teased. "Before I bid thee goodnight, lest we get ourselves into trouble."

"I wouldn't dare," Marcos said playfully. "I've heard everyone in your country has a shotgun, and I'd like to meet your father without him holding one to my head."

"You're so funny, Marcos." Lyla stopped and cocked her head to the side. "Am I allowed to call you Marcos?"

"My darling, you can call me anything you want," Marcos's voice was husky, every emotion close to the surface.

"Okay... Marcos," she said. "Are you going to kiss me now, or what?"

Marcos drew his hands up her neck and cradled her face as Lyla closed her eyes, surrendering to one more sweet, soft kiss. He pulled away after just a few short seconds, and they both opened their eyes, staring into one another's souls.

"I look forward to falling in love with you, my princess."

"Goodnight... my prince." Lyla slipped from his arms and held his hand in hers until the last possible second as she backed away from him, leaving him standing alone in the garden as she glided back to her friends.

Marcos watched as they gathered their purses and phones and beach towels and sweatshirts and other belongings and started toward the elevator to head back up to their suites.

Before entering the elevator, Lyla turned one more time and waved lightly to Marcos. He sighed with cheesy, blissful happiness as she stepped into the elevator and disappeared.

Chapter Nine

Game of Chess

W hen the head of state from one country visited another country, it was customary to have a formal meeting between the two heads of state. Marcos's father, King Sayid of Madain Saleh, arranged to fulfil that requirement before traveling to New York City.

Marcos had no desire to detour through Washington, D.C., or meet the president of the United States. He was ready to meet his future in-laws. He commanded the limo driver to take him straight to Lyla's parents' historic residence on Manhattan's Upper East Side, not far from where the royal family would be staying at the Baccarat Hotel.

Because his parents had yet to arrive in New York City, Marcos was able to stay under the radar and arrived at the Donovans' front door without incident.

Lyla and Marcos had been texting and video-chatting and calling multiple times a day, trying to get their story straight so that her parents would believe they met and fell in love over the course of the whole two weeks Lyla had been in Dubai rather than her agreeing to marry him after spending five minutes together in a pool.

There was nothing fabricated about their chemistry. From the moment Marcos stepped into the foyer, their bodies were like magnets. Their fingers intertwined and barely let go long enough for Marcos to shake Lyla's dad's hand.

Marcos tried to rein in his speech and cadence to not sound haughty. He wanted Wesley and Rebecca Donovan to feel at ease and agree that their daughter was making a good choice.

The big question remained unanswered, and Marcos knew they'd have to address the inevitable over dinner: what's the rush? Why were they in such a big hurry to get married? He and Lyla had decided honesty would be best in this instance, so Marcos didn't wait for someone else to broach the subject.

After eating the obligatory first several bites of his filet, he dabbed his mouth with a cloth napkin and rested it in his lap before reaching for his glass of red wine. He hoped he'd waited long enough into the meal and then took a deep breath.

"I need to explain something to you, Mr. and Mrs. Donovan," Marcos started.

"Please, you're welcome to call us Wesley and Rebecca," Lyla's mom said with a warming smile.

"Thank you, Rebecca." Marcos nodded regally to the woman who would soon be his mother-in-law. "I want you to know that I fell hard for your daughter. Infatuation at first sight, you might say. We realize *love* grows over time." Marcos chuckled and cleared his throat.

Lyla reached for his hand and gave it a squeeze, encouraging him to continue.

"But we don't have a lot of time," Marcos continued.

"What do you mean by that?" Wesley sat forward, leaned his elbows on the table, and clasped his hands over his plate. His furrowed brow showed suspicion.

"My brother died suddenly a few weeks ago," Marcos said. "In a motorcycle accident actually."

"Oh, my goodness," Rebecca said, leaning forward and placing her hand over the top of Marcos's in a comforting, motherly gesture. "I'm so sorry."

Marcos wondered what it would have been like to have a mother growing up rather than a prim and proper queen and several nannies. "Thank you."

"What does that have to do with you marrying our daughter?" Wesley asked, pursing his lips.

"Well, because my brother, Jared, was the crown prince, his son would be next in line for the throne, but my five-year-old nephew is too young to be named Crown. My father would like me to have an heir before naming me Crown."

"I'm confused..." Wesley cocked his head to the side. "You just need my daughter so you can have a baby?"

"Not just a baby, sir. An heir."

"And you think my daughter is the *proper* woman for the job?"

"Daddy..." Lyla glared across the table at her father.

"I would like to hope that marriage will not be a *job*." Marcos turned himself toward Lyla and rested his hand against her cheek lightly, ever so slightly rubbing his thumb on her cheek, wishing he could kiss her. His voice lowered in reverence, speaking directly to Lyla's heart even as the words were initially intended for her father. "I will treat your daughter like the princess she is, and the princess she will become."

Lyla sighed, and her eyes glazed over. She turned her face toward his hand and kissed his palm. Marcos almost lost control and pulled her into his arms right there at the dining room table.

"All right. You've convinced me," Wesley said. "You have my blessing."

"Thank you, sir. I wouldn't have wanted to go forward without your blessing," Marcos said sincerely and then turned to Rebecca. "I'm sorry that we're not giving you much time to shop for dresses, and I apologize that you may have to choose a dress off-the-rack rather than custom-made, but you have my fortune at your disposal. Please, spend as much as necessary to provide Lyla with a gown fitting a princess."

"That's very kind of you, Marcos," Rebecca said. "We wouldn't expect you to pay for our daughter's wedding dress. Nor expect something custom-made." She coughed lightly.

"Under normal circumstances, you would have plenty of time to prepare for these things. I just want you to know that you have my support." Marcos turned to Lyla. "Would you like to accompany me tomorrow to pick out wedding rings? Or would you prefer to have a jeweler bring a selection here so we can avoid drawing attention to ourselves?"

"We will need to get used to being seen in public," Lyla said. "No time like the present to start. There are lots of famous people in this town. We might just be like any other shoppers."

"Not discounting that viral video that plastered your names and faces all over the free world," Rebecca said with a chuckle.

"Yeah, we may have gotten carried away with that kiss." Lyla shook her head and giggled.

"My fault," Marcos said. "I got caught up in the moment."

"Okay, can we talk about something else besides kissing my little girl and"—Wesley visibly shuddered—"having babies with her."

"My apologies, sir." Marcos cleared his throat. "How about those Giants? Yankees? What sports team am I supposed to know about?" Marcos asked Lyla through the side of his mouth. She giggled.

"I'm more of an academic myself," Wesley said.

"Oh, thank goodness," Marcos said with a sigh. "I know *nothing* about sports."

"Do you play chess?" Wesley raised his eyebrows.

"Absolutely."

"Perfect," Wesley said. "Let's finish this lovely dinner my wife prepared and head into the lounge."

"I'll drink to that," Marcos said, holding up his glass of wine. They all raised their glasses in a subtle toast, and Marcos winked at Lyla. They'd gotten through the hard part. The rest was just wedding planning, and Marcos suspected Lyla and her mother had already begun picking out flower arrangements.

Chapter Ten

Meeting the King

K ing Sayid of Madain Saleh arrived at the Baccarat Hotel, with his queen and entourage, to very little fan fair. He was a private man who mostly stayed within the walls of the palace in his tiny kingdom.

Marcos was ready to greet his father, wearing a formal suit and simple crown, his fiancée at his side wearing an evening gown and sparkling diamond ring.

The crystal chandeliers and lighting, together with the black-and-white motif of the reception room, offered an elegant backdrop for the royal family to meet their future princess and her parents.

"Your Majesty." Marcos offered a formal bow to his father. "May I present Miss Lyla Donovan and her parents, Wesley and Rebecca Donovan?"

Marcos had coached the Donovans' in advance that it was not necessary for them to bow to his parents because they weren't subjects. They were to merely offer their hand, palm down, for the king to choose how he would prefer greeting them. When greeting each of the ladies, he pulled their hands to his lips for a kiss, and when he came to Wesley, the king shook his hand like any two men greeting one another.

The opposite was the case when greeting the queen. She presented her gloved hand to the Donovans', palm down, and gave each of the ladies' hands a friendly squeeze, like kindred spirits. Lyla also chose to offer a subtle curtsy to the woman who would soon be her mother-in-law. Wesley kissed the queen's hand in much the same way the king had kissed his wife's and daughter's hands.

Formalities aside, the king and queen retired to their suite for an hour or two to get settled and dressed for dinner. Marcos and the Donovans were led to an informal sitting room where they were served light cocktails and hors d'oeuvres.

"Thank you for humoring them," Marcos said, sitting on a settee next to Lyla, draping his arm around the back of the sofa. "You'll get to know them better at dinner."

"They seem lovely," Rebecca said, reaching for a plate.

"Your mother is elegant," Lyla said. "And formal."

"That she is." Marcos chuckled. "She is a queen first and a mother second. I know she loves me, but... I had several nannies."

"Is that what"—Lyla gulped and lowered her gaze to her hands folded in her lap, which were shaking. She suddenly lifted her chin and locked her eyes with his—"is that what you want for your wife?"

"Just the opposite." Marcos placed his hand on top of hers, hoping to calm her nerves. "I want you to walk by my side as an equal. And I want to help raise our children. Together." He gave her hands a light squeeze and winked.

"Maybe," Lyla suggested, a playful gleam in her eye. "We could just have a nanny to change the diapers."

They all chuckled at that, and Marcos decided to change the subject. "How did the shopping go this morning?"

"We found the most elegant wedding dress with dozens of tiny buttons made of pearls with loops of silk thread to hold each one in place," Lyla said, pulling out her cell phone. "Here, I'll show you some pictures."

"You most certainly will not, young lady," Lyla's mother said, snatching the phone away. "The groom is not allowed to see your dress before the wedding."

"Oh my gosh, that is so old fashioned, Mother." Lyla shook her head, then turned back to Marcos. "Anyway, we were lucky to find something off the rack that needed very little alteration."

"What about in your country, Marcos?" Wesley asked. "What would a wedding be like in—how do you pronounce the name again?"

"In modern days the pronunciation has shortened from the more formal Mada'in Saleh. Most people eliminate the extra syllable in Mada'in and pronounce it Madain."

"And why have we never heard of your kingdom prior to now? Why isn't it on the map?"

"Oh, it is," Marcos said. "If you know where to look. Because we are completely contained within the country of Saudi Arabia, most people just consider us to be part of that country. But we are a sovereign nation, neither subject to nor controlled by the Saudis. We are quite dependent on their protection, however."

"Understandably," Wesley said.

They were interrupted by the hotel staff presenting them with samplings of the meal that would be presented the night of the wedding, including a few bites of an elegant cake that melted in Marcos's mouth.

By the time the king and queen returned from their suite prepared for dinner, Marcos and the Donovans were no longer hungry. They went along anyway. Meals were rarely intended for satiating a person's appetite but rather as an opportunity for diplomacy.

That night was no exception. The king started most discussions with a question for Lyla or the Donovans. Marcos played mediator, helping lead the conversation toward an answer that would be comfortable for everyone, addressing potential concerns before they were even voiced. He was a gifted diplomat and had seen more of the world than everyone else at the table combined.

He felt confident he could pull this wedding off. He was hopeful anyway.

Chapter Eleven

Royal Wedding

Most royal weddings have more than ten people in attendance. Most royal weddings require greater than a three-week planning window. Most royal weddings take place in the royal family's country of origin.

Marcos and Lyla wanted to legally and formally join their lives just so they could go on their honeymoon to Cancun. The more time they spent together, the more fun they had.

As little as they knew of one another, their families knew even less. Neither set of parents were aware of how little time the kids had spent together before agreeing to marry.

Keeping the secret was half the fun. Marcos and Lyla spun tales of walking in the garden at the resort, without mentioning they'd only taken *one* walk. They described sitting together at a table with their friends at the tiki bar, without mentioning they'd only been at the table for less than two minutes. They described playing in the pool, without mentioning they'd both been wearing formal attire or that the encounter had lasted fewer than eight minutes.

As far as their parents were concerned, they'd had a whirlwind romance, lasting almost two weeks. The more time they spent telling stories, the more it felt as if they had indeed spent weeks together.

Collins stood up with Marcos, and Lyla had her two best friends, Deb and Cory, as her bridesmaids. Add two sets of parents and one Aunt Carol, and there were more hotel staff than wedding attendees, including the bride and groom.

When Marcos saw Lyla standing at the top of the curved staircase, his breath caught. The wedding planner had staged her dress to rest in an elegant flair on the patterned carpet. Lyla's instructions were to stand there, holding the elegantly simple bouquet of cascading, inverted calla lilies, and glance demurely down at her groom. Marcos was led to the bottom of the short flight of stairs after she had already been placed so the photographer could capture the moment when he saw his princess for the first time.

Most of the pageantry of the wedding was to create photographs featuring the prince and his bride, the king and queen, the bride's parents and the tiny wedding party. Every little step of the ceremony was carefully and meticulously staged to provide the perfect collection of photographs.

The Mayor of New York City officiated, and King Sayid offered a solemn coronation afterward, placing an elegant little crown atop his new daughter-in-law, proclaiming her as Princes Lyla Sayid of Mada'in Saleh, using the traditional pronunciation.

There was nothing more beautiful than when she rose from her formal curtsy and lifted her eyes to meet Marcos's gaze. For the second time that evening, Marcos's breath caught. Emotion choked off whatever words he could have used to describe her beauty.

As if speaking to a room full of attendees, the mayor pronounced them husband and wife, and the king announced them as their royal highnesses, and Marcos didn't need permission to know what came next.

He gently pulled Lyla into his arms, being careful not to crush her dress or mess up her makeup, and kissed his bride. Again, mostly for the pageantry and photo ops. The real kissing would take place later that evening when the cameras were gone—

When the parents were gone and the friends were gone and the staff was gone and doors to their presidential suite were closed.

Collins was the last person to say goodnight to the bride and groom because he had one last duty to perform. He was to instruct Lyla in the proper procedure to formally remove Prince Marcos's crown.

As Marcos was seated at the dressing table in their private suite, still in his tux, he watched in the mirror as his most trusted advisor reverently explained each step of the procedure.

When Lyla's hands lifted the crown from his head, their gazes met in the mirror, and the moment was almost spiritual. Her eyes fluttered with unshed tears until one tear slipped down each of her cheeks.

Marcos was reminded of that moment the day they'd met when he'd caught her wrist before she reached for his crown. His prophetic words telling her she couldn't touch his crown *until* she was his wife had come full circle.

Lyla carefully placed the crown in its velvet and mahogany box and tucked the box in its leather satchel.

In continued reverence, Marcos rose from the settee, and Lyla took his place. A smaller velvet and mahogany box lay open to receive the princess's crown. Marcos lifted the gold band inset with diamonds off his bride's head and placed it in the box. The small box nested atop the box where his crown was stored, and he closed the leather satchel.

Marcos performed one last ceremonial and symbolic action by lifting the leather satchel from the dressing table and placing it in Collins's hands for safe keeping.

"Your Highness," Collins said with a subtle bow and then turned to Lyla and bowed to her as well. "And, Your Highness. I will see you back at the palace in Madain Saleh. Enjoy your honeymoon."

With that, Collins strode from the suite, pulling the door closed with a soft click.

Chapter Twelve

Wedding Night

"How is this supposed to work?" Marcos gulped. Nothing in movies and television had prepared him for this moment. Standing there, together, alone in their honeymoon suite. He wasn't sure of the next step.

His best friend growing up was even more inexperienced than he was. His brother had gotten married when Marcos was fourteen and in boarding school. The idea of asking his father about sex was ludicrous. Collins had never been married. Nick's brothers had been less than good examples of healthy relationships.

"They make it look so easy in the movies," he said, adding a nervous chuckle to the end of his statement. He rubbed his sweating palms down the front of his pants.

"Who makes what look easy?" Lyla asked, pulling her long curls over one shoulder. "Can you help me with these?"

All down the back of her elegant wedding dress were dozens of tiny buttons made of pearls. Without considering the implications of what he was doing, he stepped forward and deftly unhooked the top pearl from its latch of silk threads, then the next, and the next. "The wedding night."

"Oh, please don't tell me you've never..." Lyla chuckled and snorted.

Marcos pulled his hands away from the delicate pearl buttons and took a step back, every vulnerable experience of his life paling in comparison to this moment. She was laughing at him. His new bride was laughing at him on their wedding night. He shoved his hands into his pockets, still wearing most of his tux other than the jacket, which was now draped on the back of a chair.

Lyla turned halfway, the train of her dress reaching across the floor like an alluvial fan, the silk clinging to her hourglass shape as the bodice twisted like an elegant winding staircase of tiny pearl buttons, the top three of which were now unlatched, presumably waiting for his fingers to return and finish the job.

Her porcelain face, so subtly brushed with simple, conservative tones hung in resigned confusion. "Oh my gosh... you haven't."

There wasn't a question or a hint of humor. Marcos raised his chin with resolve, no longer embarrassed. More offended that she would assume he had. "I would never dishonor my wife by giving myself to another woman."

"You've never even been tempted?" Lyla asked, her expression softened from confusion to awe.

"Not until I met you." Marcos lowered his gaze, embarrassed by how much he'd been tempted by her the night he proposed. After a shaky breath, he steeled himself to meet her gaze again.

"But you promised you'd spend every night for the rest of our lives making me feel good," she reminded him, a coy smile playing on her lips.

"And I fully intend to keep my promise." His voice had lowered to a husky whisper. "I'm just not entirely sure how to shift from restraint to abandon."

"I'll just have to teach you, then." Lyla's dress coiled around her legs as she turned and practically fell into his arms, tripping over the train.

"How?" Marcos chuckled, catching her.

"How what?" Lyla giggled, looking up at him with flirting eyes.

"How are you going to teach me?" Marcos asked. "You've never been married before, have you?"

"Oh, Marcos." Lyla gulped. "You don't think... You do, don't you?"

Marcos's heart plummeted into his stomach when he realized the implication of what she was saying.

"Marcos, you never asked any questions before you proposed to me," Lyla said, no apology in her voice. "You said the only thing that mattered was how we felt in each other's arms."

"I never dreamed that you..." His voice trailed off, realizing this was partially his own fault. He should have learned more about her before marrying her.

"He and I were living together," Lyla said, her arms folded across her chest. "Right up until he saw the videos on social media of you and I kissing in the gardens at the Cohen's resort, and then me accepting your proposal."

"Wow." Marcos wasn't even sure what to say to that.

"Maybe I got caught up in the moment. Maybe I couldn't get you off my mind from the first time you looked me in the eye. Maybe we were meant to be together. I don't know."

"I always assumed the woman I married would be... I guess those were naïve, childish expectations."

"Would you like me to offer you an annulment?" Lyla challenged.

Marcos raised his gaze back to hers in shock and confusion. "Why?"

"Since you need a princess who is a virgin to produce an heir, and I am obviously not."

"That is not what I'm saying, Lyla," Marcos backpedaled. "The admission merely took me by surprise."

"I'm not going to apologize to you or try to be something I'm not."

"I would not ask that of you," Marcos said, remembering how he'd felt a few moments ago when she'd learned the truth about his past, or lack thereof. Vulnerable. He'd felt nervous and vulnerable.

Marcos stepped around behind Lyla again and calmly reached for the next pearl button.

"I owe you an apology," Marcos whispered.

"Why?" Lyla asked in a soft voice.

"I'm sorry if I made you feel anything less than happiness and love after the promise I made." He continued loosening pearl buttons, distracted by the milky-white skin of her exposed back.

"The expression on your face right after you kissed me for the first time..." She hesitated, and he almost held his breath, anticipating what she was about to ask. "What were you thinking about?"

"I was thinking about... *being* married to you." He resumed unbuttoning her dress, tempted to rip the remaining pearls from their confinement. "How I wished we were already married so I could take you up to my suite."

"And what would you have done with me once we were there?" she whispered as the last pearl slipped out of the little silk clasp.

Marcos's fingers trailed up Lyla's exposed back and very gently slipped the silk wedding dress over her shoulders. The heavy fabric collapsed in a heap around her feet, revealing white lace undergarments. He lowered his lips to her neck and whispered close to her ear. "I would have done whatever my body instinctively wanted to do."

Lyla slowly turned around so she was facing him, her gaze meeting his. Marcos's hands slipped around her waist, the softness of her skin more enticing than the silk wedding dress had been. "Show me."

"Show you what?" Marcos could barely breathe, nerves and anticipation battling in his chest.

"Show me what you wanted to do that night," Lyla said. "Now that we're married, you don't have to wait a minute more to have me in your arms. Show me."

Marcos hesitated for a few more seconds, then lifted his new wife into his arms and carried her to the bed.

Chapter Thirteen

Honeymoon

They planned to honeymoon in Cancun, but after careful research, Marcos found an all-inclusive resort down the coast in a little town called Puerto Aventuras. The resort was named Barcelo Maya Palace, which Marcos thought was fitting for a prince and his new princess.

They didn't disclose their titles when reserving a suite. But checking into the resort required presenting identification. He'd hoped to remain anonymous for a few days to be alone with his bride but cringed when he reluctantly handed over his passport and diplomatic identification.

The desk clerk's eyes grew large as she examined the card and started typing his information into the computer.

Marcos leaned closer and insisted in a firm tone that she not mention his title in her reference. "Por favor no incluya mi titulo en tu notas. Señor sera suficiente."

"Sí, Your High—uh, señor." She handed him back his identification.

"Gracious," Marcos thanked her.

"Señora?" the clerk nodded to Lyla.

"Sí, gracious," Marcos said.

"El conserje lo acompanara a su suite." She handed their key to the concierge and nodded regally.

Marcos held his arm to escort Lyla to their room and slipped a hundred-peso note into the young man's hand after he carried in their luggage.

The door barely closed behind the concierge, and Marcos pulled Lyla into his arms hungrily, ready to pick up where they'd left off in New York City. Or more accurately where they'd left off in the private suite to the rear of the jet they'd chartered from New York to Cozumel.

Now that he knew what he'd been missing all these years, he had no desire to do anything that didn't involve kissing his wife.

They eventually ventured down to one of the six restaurants at the resort and took several walks on the sandy, white beaches but mostly stayed in their suite and ordered room service.

On the tenth day after arriving at the resort, Marcos's cell phone rang. He rarely received phone calls unless there was an emergency or diplomacy assignment. He wasn't keen on either of those circumstances but was pleased to see Nicholas Cohen's name on the caller ID.

"Nick!" Marcos answered with enthusiasm. "How's married life treating you?"

"I could ask you the same thing, Your Highness," Nick said. "I understand congratulations are in order."

"Married life is heaven, if that's what you're asking." Marcos traced his fingers along Lyla's spine, loving the graceful way her body was sprawled on the bed at his side. "I'm assuming that's why you called."

"I called to inform you that I'm thoroughly offended you didn't invite me to your wedding, considering you were my best man a mere three weeks prior." Nick chuckled on the other end of the line. "Is it true you met her the night I got married? My older brother regaled me with the tale when I called to check in."

"Your older brother tells stories," Marcos said. "And to my great pleasure, I will confirm that they are all true. And it would have been easier to invite you to my wedding had you not been on your honeymoon."

"Would you agree"—Nick lowered his voice in conspiracy—"that marriage is by far the best earthly experience possible?"

"Wholeheartedly," Marcos said. "Why on earth did we wait so long?"

"I have no excuse save my own idiocy," Nick said. "But until recently, you hadn't met your bride. Tell me her name. I can't remember what Sam told me."

"Princess Lyla of Madain Saleh," Marcos said regally. "Formerly of the Donovan family in the kingdom of New York, which I have learned is in the northern American continent."

"I would very much like to meet this princess of yours," Nick said. "Would the two of you be available for dinner this evening?"

"Not unless you want to fly to Cancun." Marcos chuckled.

"I'd much rather take the ferry from Cozumel," Nick said. "Considering Adele and I are standing on the deck awaiting our departure."

"What are you doing on Cozumel?" Marcos sat up in bed, pulling the sheets with him by mistake and becoming momentarily distracted when the sheets slid off his wife's lower backside. He wondered if his hunger for her would ever be fully satiated. He reluctantly lifted the sheet over her sleeping form, recognizing her need for rest.

"We've been honeymooning here for a month," Nick said. "But alas, our time on the island has concluded, and our trunks are now aboard this ferry and will be transported to our new suite, which, coincidentally, is one floor down from yours."

"You're coming to Puerto Aventuras? Today?"

"We will be there in less than two hours," Nick said.

"I'm not getting out of bed that soon, so you'll have to wait to see us until the dinner hour," Marcos said.

"Understandable," Nick said. "I'm sure we'll need a siesta between now and then as well."

"Nick!" Adele was in the background chastising her new husband.

"Feel free to call me when you've awoken from your… nap," Marcos said, "and we'll arrange to meet you downstairs. There is a fabulous French restaurant here at the resort, which is ironic considering we're in Mexico."

"I do love good French cuisine," Nick said. "Anyway, the boat is preparing to depart, and my wife is eyeing me with disdain for sharing private details about our plans for the afternoon. Ow! Quit smacking my arm. Turn around is fair play, you know."

Adele was giggling loud enough for Marcos to hear her through the phone, and he could imagine the tickle war Adele had instigated.

"I'm going to hang up now, Nicholas. Call me later."

"Goodbye, Your Highness." Nick had laughter in his voice as the line went dead.

"Who's on the phone?" Lyla slurred through a sleepy yawn, lifting her head.

"Nick and his wife are on their way from Cozumel and will be joining us for dinner," Marcos said. "Wanna take a bubble bath with me in the Jacuzzi tub?"

"Umm hmm," she mumbled. "But sleep first."

"I could use a few moments of sleep, myself," Marcos said.

Lyla rolled over into his arms and snuggled close. Resting her head in the crook of his arm, she whispered, "I love you, Marcos."

That was the first time she'd vocalized her feelings for him. He'd mentioned on the day he'd proposed that love grows over time, and no truer words could be spoken. "I love you too, my princess."

Chapter Fourteen

Nick and Adele

"**H**elp me understand this," Adele said, setting aside the iced horchata she'd been sipping. "What is your official title, and what am I supposed to call you? Your Grace?"

"Please, just call me Lyla." The subtle blush on her cheeks reminded Marcos how uncomfortable she still was with everything that involved his status.

Marcos was nervous to bring Lyla home to Madain Saleh and glad they'd chosen to take a few weeks alone on the other side of the world where they could get to know one another as husband and wife before assuming their positions as a prince and princess.

"Our kingdom is not the same as a monarchy in Europe," Marcos explained to Nick's wife. "Our hybrid traditions date back a thousand years and have been adapted through the centuries as times have changed. I'm pretty sure my ancestors didn't conduct diplomatic meetings by video conference on their smartphones."

"No, I suppose not." Adele's brow creased. "I still don't get it though."

"Lyla will be referred to mostly as Her Highness," Marcos explained.

"Then why do you sometimes call me Your Grace?" Lyla asked with skeptical teasing.

"When you are my queen, that will be your title." Marcos lifted Lyla's hand to his lips and winked at her playfully.

"I have a question," Nick said, leaning forward. "You're not having some weird Freudian obsession about your mother when you call your wife Your Grace... are you?"

"Thank you for placing that disgusting thought in my head, Nicholas." Marcos shoved his best friend's shoulder. "I'm merely looking forward to becoming king someday."

"That's why he married me after all," Lyla said, feigning haughtiness. "So he could obtain the title of Crown Prince."

"I don't get it," Adele said. "I thought Jared was the crown prince."

Marcos's heart plummeted when he realized they hadn't heard. Laughter faded from his smile and Lyla took his hand for comfort. He swallowed hard. "You haven't heard the news?"

"What news, my friend?" Nick's brows creased.

"Jared lost control on his motorcycle and didn't live another twenty-four hours." Marcos's voice caught. "The accident happened the night of your wedding, actually."

"Oh my gosh, I'm so sorry, Marcos," Adele said, scooting her chair closer to her husband. "His wife and their little boy must be devastated."

"Princess Tayma is not capable of raising our future king." Marcos raised his chin and set his jaw. "Jared told me himself. He asked me to raise their son in his stead, and I have refused to recognize my five-year-old nephew as my future king."

"If not him... then who?" Nick asked, cocking his head to the side. "You?"

"As my father has rightfully acknowledged, we are in uncharted waters with this regard," Marcos said. "Never before in the history of our kingdom has the crown prince died prior to the king. As the only prince who is of age, I have claim to the crown, and Tayma has challenged my claim. She insists her son is the rightful Crown."

"But he was next in line... right?" Nick asked.

"Next in line is not the same as Crown." Marcos shook his head definitively. "The named Crown must be of age and sound mind, capable of taking on the role of king in his absence should the inevitable occur."

"And that would be you?" Nick asked.

"Correct." Marcos nodded.

"What's that got to do with Lyla?" Adele asked.

"His daddy wants him to have a baby before naming him Crown," Lyla teased.

"I believe the words he used were a *wife* and an *heir*," Marcos clarified. "We have taken on that challenge and will work hard to complete the task. It's a difficult job but someone has to do it."

"Frequently." Lyla faked a cough, and they all laughed.

"Neither of us are complaining," Marcos said with a grin.

"Well, we wish you luck in your endeavor," Nick said, raising his glass of hibiscus aqua fresca in a toast. "May the best man win in his race to produce an heir."

"Excuse me," Adele cut in. "I believe the women are those who will produce the heirs. Am I right, Lyla?"

"Absolutely," Lyla said. "Although you've had a three-week head start. I'm not sure it's a fair race." Lyla pouted and batted her eyelashes at Marcos.

"We're just going to have to work overtime to catch up," Marcos stage-whispered to his wife.

"On that note, I think it's time to call it a night, don't you?" Nick suggested. They all laughed again but didn't linger too many more minutes at the restaurant.

The night was young, and Marcos intended to take full advantage of the moonlit romance of Puerto Aventuras before returning to the real world and flying back to his kingdom, his new princess in tow.

Chapter Fifteen

Jared's Widow

"It doesn't matter how many little princes you and your new princess pop out. My son was still the first born and has a claim to the title." Jared's widow didn't wait for Marcos and Lyla to get unpacked before she stormed into their personal bedroom suite, asserting her dominance and making it very clear she wasn't backing down.

While Marcos and Lyla had been on their honeymoon, Princess Tayma had continued to spend a great deal of time with the king and her young son Omar, feigning affection in order to gain favor.

"I don't need an heir to claim my title," Marcos said with disdain. "As much as I love my nephew, he will never be my king."

"Mark my words, *Marcos*," Tayma said, purposely degrading him with her use of his given name rather than his title. "I will convince your father to name Omar as Crown even if Lyla is pregnant."

"*Her Highness*, as you will call her, is not required to be with child for me to claim my title either. And you would do well to remember your place, princess."

"That's *Your Highness* to you, Marcos," Tayma said flippantly.

"I will afford your title the respect it deserves when you have earned that respect," Marcos said. "Now leave my residence before I have you arrested."

"As if." Tayma flipped her long braid over her shoulder, then glanced dismissively at the woman challenging her position. She said with a sickly sweet voice, "It was a pleasure to make your acquaintance, *Lyla*." Tayma lifted her chin and marched from the room.

"Gee, she's friendly," Lyla said with a chuckle. "I understand now why you were stressed to the point of breaking when we first met. She brings out the worst in you."

"I apologize that you had to see that side of me," Marcos said. "I will do my best to rein in my anger when dealing with the princess."

"She's a handful," Lyla said. "What did your brother ever see in her?"

"Her title," Marcos said. "Theirs was an arranged marriage."

"Oh." Lyla wrinkled her nose. "I'm glad you weren't Crown back then."

"Me too. It is tradition that the crown prince marry at the age of sixteen."

"Sixteen?" Lyla's jaw gaped. "How old was the princess?"

"Eighteen, I think." Marcos shrugged.

"Dang, she had to marry a little boy. No wonder she's cranky."

"How are you holding up?" Marcos asked. "Are you completely overwhelmed? I haven't even presented you to the king and queen yet."

"Do you always refer to your parents that way?" Lyla asked.

"I slip occasionally, but it's a good habit to get into just to maintain their status as a rule of thumb, and then we don't make mistakes in front of the staff or members of the community."

"Good point, I guess." Lyla slumped into a chair, defeated. "To answer your question, yes, I am overwhelmed. But I'm a big girl. I can handle it."

"What do you think of your living quarters, Your Highness?" Marcos spun around, holding out his arms to show off the grandeur in which she would be living.

"Love the Persian rugs," she said with a teasing grin. "Hate the sand."

"I will ignore your comment about the sand, since we met in Dubai. If you hadn't wanted to live within the blazing desert, you wouldn't have come to the Middle East." Marcos lay himself down on the large Persian rug in the middle of their bedroom and propped himself on his elbow, wagging his eyebrows at her.

"I was on vacation, Your Highness. If you remember correctly, it was never my intention to get married at all." Lyla stalked forward like a lioness on the attack.

When she got close enough, Marcos grabbed her playfully and rolled her onto the carpet, growling and tickling her neck.

"Stop!" Lyla cried out. "You're gonna make me pee my pants."

"Not on the Persian rug, woman." Marcos pulled back but kept a gleam in his eye. "This thing cost more than my Range Rover."

"I guess you better stop tickling me, then." Lyla relaxed into Marcos's arms, and he lowered his face to hers for a lingering kiss.

"Your Highness, is everything all right?" Collins came rushing into their bedroom suite, the door of which was still wide open from when Tayma stormed out. "Oh! I am so sorry!" Collins started backing out of the room, with his hand covering his eyes.

"Collins, stop," Marcos called. "Come back. We were just goofing around." He sat up and offered a hand to Lyla.

"Yes, His Highness was just showing me the... lovely furnishings in my new bed chambers. Isn't that right, darling?" Lyla raised her brows and batted her eyelashes at Marcos.

"Her Highness is quite fond of Persian rugs," Marcos explained to his advisor, and he and Lyla both cracked up.

"I'm sorry to have disturbed your... uh... tour of her new chambers," Collins said. "I'll just pull the door closed on my way out."

"Wait, no, please." Marcos scrambled to get off the floor and helped Lyla up as well. "I need your help."

"How can I be of service, Your Highness?" Collins lowered his head in a respectful bow.

"We are expected to make an appearance before the king and queen, and then to have dinner with them," Marcos said. "I will need to be dressed for the occasion, as will Her Highness. Have we secured a lady for her? And have her belongings been delivered?"

"Yes, Your Highness," Collins said. "The princess will find that her things have been arranged in her closet and can be rearranged to her liking. Shall I send up her maid?"

"Uh... in a few hours," Marcos said. "We just arrived and will need some time to... uh... rest after our long flight. Traveling... ya know." Marcos's attention was drawn once again to his wife, who raised her eyebrows and smirked.

"May I now be excused and pull the door shut on my way out?" Collins asked, a hint of desperation at the end of his question.

"Please do..." Marcos's gaze never left his wife's as he pulled her gently in the direction of their large, marble bathroom. He barely registered the main door to the suite latching quietly as he raised his brow suggestively. "Bubble bath?"

"Heck yeah," Lyla said, pulling closed the door to the spacious bathroom, offering that little extra degree of privacy.

An audience with the king and queen could wait. They had more important things to do first.

Chapter Sixteen

Welcome, Your Highness

"Your Majesty and Your Grace, may I present His Royal Highness, Prince Marcos, and Her Highness, Princess Lyla," Damian, the king's most trusted advisor, called out to the nearly full throne room.

Marcos stepped from the foyer, with Lyla's hand in the crook of his arm, both dressed in formal wear and their crowns, as were the king and queen.

This was to be an unveiling of the new princess to the royal court, and Marcos wasn't sure Lyla was ready.

She held her head high and kept her expression stoic as Marcos had coached her, perfectly adhering to the traditions his parents would expect.

Over the next few days, she would be gradually introduced to the remainder of the kingdom, first by hosting a less formal party on the patio that spilled out into the square so Lyla wouldn't have to travel beyond the patio to be seen.

The following day, Marcos would take her into town and introduce her to the local establishments, like government offices and his favorite restaurants.

Next, she would be led on a tour of the hospital to check in on the subjects who were currently unable to attend any of the other activities. At that time, she would be introduced to the doctor who would presumably be her obstetrician, should she need one, and Marcos hoped she would.

Marcos felt a tiny bit embarrassed that his physical relationship with his new bride was a topic of national interest because her conceiving a child would likely produce the next-in-line to the Crown.

But tonight was all about meeting the dignitaries. The leaders of the government at all levels, the leaders of the military, all locally appointed officials. There were no elected officials as there would be in Lyla's home country because Madain Saleh was a monarchy rather than a democracy.

He wasn't sure if Lyla had taken that into consideration when she agreed to marry him or if the idea was disagreeable.

The court also included the queen's sister and brothers, the king's sister, and several aunts- and uncles-in law, along with multiple cousins he'd never have time to introduce before the end of the evening. Lyla would get to know them in time.

Marcos and Lyla walked the length of the room along a perfectly pre-served Persian runner, which almost caused Marcos to break his stoic expression as he thought of their kiss from earlier in the afternoon.

Before ascending the three marble steps to the elevated platform at the center of the far wall, Marcos paused and held his hand along Lyla's lower back, encouraging her to take a half step forward as if he was physically presenting her as the new princess.

"Your Majesty"—Marcos bowed his head briefly—"and Your Grace, may I introduce my wife, Her Highness, Princess Lyla of Mada'in Saleh."

Lyla curtsied and bowed her head as he'd coached her, instinctively mastering the show of respect to her new in-laws.

"Welcome, Your Highness." King Sayid nodded regally and held out his hand.

Marcos took that as the invitation to approach the thrones and led Lyla up the stairs to where she held her hand out to the king. He didn't kiss her hand as he'd done when first meeting her in New York, just held hers clasped within both of his.

When Lyla stepped over to greet Queen Salaina, Marcos heard his moth-er whisper, "I can't wait to give you a hug and welcome you to our family, but that will need to wait until we are out of the public eye."

"Likewise, Your Grace," Lyla said quietly and curtsied again.

After they greeted the king and queen, Marcos and Lyla descended the steps once more to where Princess Tayma sat with her young son, Prince Omar standing at her side, regally holding up his little head as if waiting to relax his stance once given permission. He'd been trained well.

Marcos was having none of it. He crouched lower and held out his arms. "How's my favorite nephew?" he asked with a grin, completely ignoring Tayma.

Omar released a big smile and ran into his uncle's outstretched arms. Marcos lifted him to eye level, and Omar wrapped his legs around Marcos's waist and his arms around his neck as if he wanted a piggyback ride. Maybe that was just what this party needed in order to relax and enjoy the evening.

"Your Highness, may I introduce your new nephew, Prince Omar of Madain Saleh," Marcos said, meeting his wife's gaze. "Prince Omar, this is Princess Lyla, your new aunt."

"It is an honor to meet you, Your Highness," Omar stated in his most grown-up voice and bowed his head regally to Lyla.

"Likewise, Your Highness," Lyla said, returning his nod.

"Ahem," Tayma said, still sitting on her throne. The chair was much smaller and less regal than the king's and queen's, but a position of honor in its own right.

"Your Highness, you remember Princess Tayma," Marcos said through clenched teeth and then lowered his voice. "From when she so rudely interrupted our homecoming."

"It is an honor to be formally introduced, Your Highness," Lyla said with a small curtsy and subtle nod of her head.

"Likewise... Your Highness," Tayma said with a fake smile and sarcasm lacing her voice. "Welcome to *our* kingdom."

"Come, allow me to introduce you to my cousins," Marcos said, shifting Omar to his back for a piggyback ride. "I'm sure you'll have plenty of time to get acquainted with the princess."

Marcos lifted Lyla's right hand into the crook of his left arm, a subtle reminder that it was not appropriate for her to shake hands with her subjects but merely acknowledge them with a slight nod of her head.

Lyla must have been nervous, but she never showed the slightest sign of apprehension. Marcos couldn't have been prouder of his wife. He winked at her and pulled her gently from one member of court to another, all the while carrying his five-year-old nephew on his back.

Chapter Seventeen

Ancient History

"**I** don't like you," Tayma said through clenched teeth and a fake smile.

"No way!" Lyla turned to her with an equally fake smile, sarcasm dripping from her words. She laid her hand on Tayma's forearm as if they were engaging in girl talk. No one outside a ten-foot radius would have a clue they weren't the best of friends, and no one could hear them except Marcos and Collins. There were bodyguards between them and the rest of the market square. "And here I thought we were finally having a breakthrough."

"Not a chance." Tayma lifted a long pink scarf off a vendor's table and held it up to Lyla's face as if to check whether the scarf was her color. "As long as there's the possibility that you could have a son and he might challenge my little prince, you will need to sleep with one eye open."

"Is that a threat, princess?" Lyla asked with a cheerful laugh, glancing behind to offer Marcos a smile. He knew she was biting her tongue about the things she wished she could say to Tayma.

"That's a promise," Tayma said, draping her arm through Lyla's as they walked along the dusty town square. Although paved roads and concrete sidewalks attempted to provide a sure footing, the constantly blowing sand swept the pavement clean even as the next layer of sand was deposited.

Marcos wasn't thrilled with the direction this conversation was turning, but he wanted to give the women space to get to know one another. He held back and raised his eyebrows to Collins.

"On it," Collins mumbled, pulling out his cell phone, no doubt ordering additional security for Lyla.

He knew Lyla wasn't happy here in his kingdom, if that's what it could be called. The only real benefit Madain Saleh offered to the world was a very deep and very refreshing natural aquifer in an otherwise barren desert wasteland.

Dating back well over two thousand years, this was the only stop between Tabuk and Medina before there were cars.

The original lonely castle still stood, worn by the elements and now used mainly as a historic marker where foreigners came to take pictures with the hieroglyphics and view the ancient tombs.

No longer used for its original purpose, the stone structure had been replaced by a state-of-the-art palace with modern facilities and high-speed internet.

Marcos sensed he and Lyla wouldn't live here much longer. She wasn't thrilled about the linen scarves wrapped around her head, neck, and shoulders as protection from the elements. She hated the sand and despised her sister-in-law.

He had already begun devising plans on how to get her out of the desert while still maintaining his title and attempting to keep his promise to his older brother.

Princess Tayma wasn't giving up, and he wanted to demand she go home to her own kingdom and assert her dominance on someone other than his wife. Sharing her name, Tayma was a beautiful kingdom oasis dating back to the sixth century before Christ. A kingdom the princess should be proud to call her own. Yet here she was in Madain Saleh, causing more trouble than she was worth.

But she had a little boy who she insisted was next in line to the throne. Marcos wouldn't put it past her to go to extreme measures to keep that status quo, and he intended to get his wife out of her line of fire.

If only he hadn't promised his brother to help raise his nephew, he'd be free to travel the world with his bride. If only...

Chapter Eighteen

The Lady Bountiful

"**S**he's a masterpiece, Nicholas." Marcos leaned against the sparkling brass railing of the *Lady Bountiful* the night before its maiden voyage.

With plenty of room for a farewell party of this size, the yacht was a full 200 feet in length, had four decks above the waterline, two decks below, a helipad, two VIP suites in addition to the owner's suite, a pool and Jacuzzi, a movie theater, a massage parlor and beauty salon, a playroom, a bar, and a library.

Marcos was a billionaire and a prince, but this felt like a step above luxury. If Nicholas was talented enough to envision the design of this beauty, Marcos couldn't wait to see what he came up with next.

"Thank you, Your Highness," Nick said. "I'm glad you and Lyla could make it all the way down here to see us off."

"Anxiously awaiting the opportunity to join you on the high seas." Marcos spoke through a fake smile, attempting to hide his plans from anyone who might suspect he was plotting an escape from the desert paradise he called home.

"What's holding you back from leaving now?" Nick asked.

"Got any extra yachts lying around?" Marcos raised his eyebrows.

"Workin' on it. We could always charter one."

"I want my first child to be born in Madain Saleh," Marcos admitted the real reason for his delay.

"Is Lyla...?"

"Not yet." Marcos shook his head. "Adele?"

"We suspect," Nick said softly. "But we're not telling anyone yet."

"She's not gonna handle the rough seas very well if she is," Marcos said.

"We realize that," Nick said. "But this is the best time to leave, and the trip will only last a month."

"Can't you just fly?"

"And miss the maiden voyage of the *Lady Bountiful?*" Nick asked playfully. "Not a chance."

"Okay, okay." Marcos held up his hands in surrender. "Good luck handling a wife with morning sickness on a yacht for twenty-nine days."

As if on cue, Marcos's own wife, Lyla, jumped up from the chaise lounge where she was chatting with Adele and ran to the side of the boat right next to Marcos. She hung over the side of the railing and threw up the expensive appetizers they'd enjoyed all afternoon.

"You were saying?" Nick asked, wrinkling his nose. "I'll go get your wife a water bottle and washcloth. Good luck to you as well, Your Highness." Nick patted Marcos on the shoulder as he hurried away.

"Thanks," Marcos said with a grimace, rubbing his wife's back as she heaved over and over. Marcos wasn't sure whether to be sad the party was over for the night or excited that this might be a sign of new life. He chose excitement.

Chapter Nineteen

Prince Benjamin

"P ush, Your Highness," the doctor said. "I need you to push."

"Aghhhh!!!" Lyla cried out as beads of sweat dripped down her forehead. She squeezed Marcos's hand so hard he thought the bones would break. Her blotchy face was pinched in agony.

"What are you doing to her?" Marcos demanded. "Can't you see she's in pain? Why is this taking so long?" Marcos's stomach clenched in panic.

"Your Highness, if you are not able to maintain calm, I will pull rank and ask you to leave the delivery room," the doctor said.

"Don't you dare leave," Lyla cried, gripping his hand even tighter. "You did this to me. You're the one who needed to produce an heir, now you're going to stay right here until... iiiiiiiow!"

"You're doing great, Your Highness," the doctor called out. "One more big push and we're going to meet our new prince. One more push. You can do it."

Lyla's whole face and body grimaced and morphed into a shout of pain and before the doctor could finish his sentence, a burst of energy seemed to power through Lyla's body, and her shoulders relaxed into Marcos's arms. It was over.

The anguish of the previous six hours seemed to disappear in the tiny wail that replaced his mother's cries of pain.

"Benjamin," Marcos whispered in awe, gazing at the perfect little person the doctor held in his hands.

"Your Highnesses..." the doctor said ceremoniously. "You have a son." He reached over Lyla's hospital gown and laid the squirming, shrieking, slimy boy onto his mother's chest. Marcos's hand took over, holding the tiny little man in place, his other arm draped around his wife's shoulders.

"Look what we made, Lyla," Marcos whispered. "We made a boy."

"We sure did." Lyla lifted her face to Marcos's and shared a kiss.

Chapter Twenty

Nothing Sexier than a Diaper Change

"We're buying a yacht!" Marcos announced, bursting through the doors of their bedroom suite.

"Shh... I just got Benjamin to sleep," Lyla whispered, pulling the blue blanket closer around their baby's head, covering his little ears.

Marcos padded softly across the floor as quietly as he could and leaned down to kiss Benjamin's forehead and then shifted his focus to kiss Lyla gently.

Benjamin was nestled against her breast, his tiny mouth twitching in a half-smile as if he'd just fallen asleep mid-suck. He'd never looked more beautiful. His mother had never looked more beautiful.

"Want me to take him to his crib?" Marcos whispered.

"I suppose." Lyla shifted forward and gently rolled Benjamin from her arms into Marcos's. He had never felt more love for a creature than he did for this tiny bundle and the woman who nursed him day and night. He thought the love they shared as husband and wife couldn't be topped until they created life together and his whole world shifted on its axis.

As Benjamin's face pulled away from Lyla's breast, his little mouth moved as if begging for more. "I know how you feel, little man. I can never get enough either." Marcos winked at Lyla.

"You, silly guy," Lyla whispered, tucking herself back into her maternity bra. Benjamin was only four weeks old and the doctor hadn't officially given them permission to resume a physical relationship. He hadn't specifically forbidden it either.

Marcos didn't want to push his wife toward anything she wasn't ready for, but he missed having her in his arms. At the moment, he was holding something much smaller in his arms. He rocked his son gently while staring down into his little face and then carefully rolled him into the waiting crib. He propped Benjamin on his side with a rolled up receiving blanket and tucked a larger blanket around the sleeping baby.

Then he just stood there, gazing down at his son, the most incredible creation he'd ever seen.

"He's beautiful, isn't he?" Lyla whispered at his side.

Marcos shifted and wrapped his arm around her, pulling her close. "Almost as beautiful as his mother."

"His mother is curious to know more about this yacht she's supposedly purchasing," she said in a low voice.

"Oh, that's right," Marcos said, pulling her away from their sleeping baby. "I got a little distracted. Remember how Nicholas and his family bought a ship building company in Dubai?"

"How could I forget? I must have puked over the side of the deck a dozen times while we were onboard for their inaugural sail party."

"You gotta admit that was a fun way to find out you were pregnant." Marcos chuckled.

"Fun... right, that's exactly what I was thinking. Good thing I didn't have much left in me when I puked on your shirt while you were carrying me off the boat."

"There are easier ways to get me out my clothes, you know?" he said in a husky voice, pulling her close.

"I haven't gotten you out of your clothes in quite a while," she said, reaching up and playing with his collar.

"Five weeks, three days and"—he pulled away slightly to glance at his watch—"thirteen hours. Not that anyone's counting."

She tossed her head back with a soft laugh, her eyes gleaming up at him. "You know, Benjamin just had a bath and a feeding and a diaper change. He'll probably be asleep for a couple of hours."

"There's nothin' sexier than you talkin' about a diaper change to get your man in the mood," Marcos said playfully.

"Well, gosh, if you're not in the mood," she said, pretending to pull away from him.

"Woman, don't tease me." He pulled her back into his arms but handled her delicately, lifting her face to his with feather-light touches. The fragile way she'd gradually recovered from having the baby made him want to take their time and be careful.

Gone was the reckless abandonment from the early days of their marriage. This was a different kind of passion. A slow-burning love that reached into the depths of his soul, and Marcos wanted to treasure every moment of it.

He forgot everything he'd planned to tell her and lost himself in their kiss, wishing he could pull her over to their bed but not wanting to rush her. He just held her and kissed her, letting her set the pace.

When she finally pulled away and looked up at him, her eyes betrayed the passion he felt from her kiss. She whispered, "I could use a bubble bath."

She didn't have to drop any further hints. Marcos lifted her hand to his lips and held her gaze as he backed into the adjoining bathroom, pulling her gently with him.

Chapter Twenty-One

Through the Eyes of a Princess

"Finish telling me about our new yacht," Lyla said.

"I commissioned one to be built for us." Marcos sighed with contentment, loving his wife's head resting on his bare chest, as she drew slow circles on his abdomen. The blankets and sheets that once covered the bed in perfect order were tangled and wrapped around their legs. "We can sail back to the spot where we honeymooned. Or anywhere else in the world. Although I'll be sorry to take you away from this beautiful desert you love so much."

Lyla snorted in sarcastic laughter. "You mean the non-stop sandstorm that creeps into every crevice of my being? Including my mouth! Yeah, I'll be totally devastated to leave the desert."

"Oh, my darling, thank you for sacrificing all your hopes and dreams to come here and help me save my kingdom."

"Doesn't every little girl dream of marrying a prince?" she asked, lifting her head to smile up at him.

"I don't know," Marcos said with a soft laugh. "I've never been a little girl."

"Maybe we should try for a little girl, and then you can view the world through the eyes of a princess."

"I can accommodate you on that suggestion."

She giggled and resumed drawing circles on Marcos's abdomen.

"You're distracting me again." Marcos closed his eyes, willing his body to relax so he could have a conversation with his wife. "I'll never finish the story."

"I'll stop." She sat up halfway, but he pulled her right back down.

"I'll finish my story, just don't stop touching me. I've missed this."

"Me too," she whispered. "I thought you'd never want me again."

"Why would you think that?" This time it was his turn to sit up halfway, trying unsuccessfully to get her to look him in the eye. "Talk to me, babe. What did I do to make you feel that way?"

"It's more what you *didn't* do," she said. "I thought maybe you saw me more as the mother of your child and less as your lover."

Marcos rolled her over and propped himself on his elbow, gazing down into her face. He ran his fingers through her damp hair, letting the rich smell of Jasmine oil engulf his senses. He kissed her lightly and continued.

"Lyla, my darling, just the opposite is true." He kissed the top of her head and pulled her a little closer. She snuggled into his arms and sighed. "You holding our baby in your arms is the most beautiful thing I've ever seen. The passion I feel for you now transcends anything I've ever felt before. I just didn't want to pressure you. Trust me, I want you."

"Could you, maybe... not wait another five weeks to let me know that."

"I promise, my love."

Marcos leaned forward, sealing his statement with a lingering kiss.

Chapter Twenty-Two

Poisoned Soup

"Does this soup smell funny to you?" Lyla held out her bowl, and Marcos sniffed. He wrinkled his nose. Although the spacious dining room off the main kitchen was large enough for the whole family to gather around the imported mahogany table, her question was barely acknowledged by anyone other than Marcos and Collins.

"Don't eat it if it smells funny," Marcos said, leaning down to sniff his own food. It definitely smelled different. He was instantly on alert and glanced at Collins and then picked up Lyla's bowl. "Would you take this and see if you can find Her Highness a new bowl of soup?"

Translation: have this tested for anything meant to make Lyla sick. Marcos didn't ask the kitchen staff to bring more food; he asked Collins, the only person he knew he could trust.

Too many little coincidences had happened over the past two months since Benjamin had been born, like the poisonous snake curled up under his crib or the bar of soap in their bathroom that had an irritant on the surface that made them break out in hives.

"Maybe Lyla's pregnant again," Tayma said, batting her eyelashes. "That would definitely make her think her food smells funny."

That garnered the attention of Queen Salaina. "Oh, how exciting. I've always hoped for lots of grandchildren." Her usually proper demeanor relaxed for just a moment, and she slouched forward to reach for Lyla's hand, squeezing affectionately.

"It smelled funny to me as well, Tayma," Marcos said, ignoring his mother. "Maybe you'd like to switch bowls with her?"

"I've already finished mine." She held up her nearly empty bowl. "But thank you for the offer."

Marcos narrowed his eyes at her, and she smirked. He was on to her game, and she knew he was aware that she was behind these little pranks. They wouldn't be so funny if Lyla or Benjamin got seriously ill or worse.

"Your Highness," Collins said softly, standing near Lyla's side. "I've personally prepared you a new bowl of soup." Collins raised his eyebrows at Marcos, subtly telling him in their non-verbal communication that he'd take the other bowl to be tested.

"Thank you, Collins." Lyla leaned over the steaming soup and sniffed. "Much better." She lifted her spoon and made a show of approving the first bite.

Marcos continued to glare at his sister-in-law throughout the rest of the meal.

"To answer your question, Tayma"—Lyla set her spoon on the saucer where her soup bowl rested—"I don't think I'm pregnant, although we have talked about wanting a little girl someday."

Marcos lifted Lyla's hand and kissed the back. "A little princess."

"You'll have to let us know as soon as you find out," the queen said. "I'm so excited for you. You're our only hope for more grandchildren, you know."

"Can't my mommy have any more babies?" Omar asked. Now six years old, he was still innocent enough to not realize the underlying implications of his question.

"Your father died, remember?" Tayma said in the condescending voice she faked when talking to her son. "Having babies requires a mommy and a daddy."

"You can find a new daddy," Omar said.

Tayma laughed and patted Omar's head. "Someday you'll understand."

"Maybe you should go home to your own kingdom and find some unsuspecting second cousin or something," Marcos said. "You're still considered royalty over there in Tayma, right princess? You could marry a different prince."

"I'm not going back to my *former* kingdom, thank you very much." She lifted her chin. "Madain Saleh is my kingdom now. And my son, Omar, is the only prince who matters."

"What about my cousin, Benjamin?" Omar asked, looking up at his mom. "He's a prince too."

"But he's not the *first*-born prince," Tayma said, wrapping her arm around his shoulder. "You are."

"On that note," Lyla said, pushing back her chair. All the men at the table, including the king, stood when she did. "I think it's time for me to nurse *my* little prince. If you'll excuse me."

Marcos stepped aside and tucked his own chair up to the table, not having finished his meal. "I'll come with you, darling. I wouldn't want you to walk alone."

"Thank you." Lyla tucked her hand into the crook of his arm, and as they stepped away from the table, King Sayid sat down and resumed eating.

Marcos decided it was time he had a talk with his father. Tonight.

Chapter Twenty-Three

This Palace Has Many Eyes and Many Ears

"We need to leave, Your Highness," Collins said, pulling the double doors to their suite shut behind them. "There have been too many incidents. The three of you aren't safe here."

"What happened?" Nasrin asked as Lyla took Benjamin from her arms. The young lady hired to be Lyla's assistant and trusted advisor had gradually taken on the role of nanny as well.

Lyla still insisted on being Benjamin's primary caregiver but welcomed the extra set of hands especially during times when she was expected at dinner with the royal family. Marcos suspected tonight was the last time Lyla would be told when and where and with whom to eat a meal. She strode over to her favorite intricately carved rocking chair she'd convinced him was required for young mothers and draped a silk scarf across her shoulder to cover any exposed parts while she nursed their baby.

Collins and Nasrin were so frequently in the royal suite that no one was fazed by nursing and diaper changes and cleaning baby spit up off the polished marble floor. Collins had even been known to change a diaper or two and was always on hand to fetch whatever the ladies needed, even if that meant making a run to the market. Marcos suspected Collins and Nasrin had grown affectionate toward one another, but no one had come right out to admit anything.

Each of them had a suite of rooms on opposite sides of Marcos and Lyla's to have them easily accessible should they be needed. But the four of them frequently found themselves congregating in the chic sitting area centrally located near the nursery.

"There's no way I can have that soup tested here in the kingdom because I don't trust *anyone*." Collins paced the marble floor, avoiding the largest of Marcos's prized Persian rugs, visibly distraught.

"I want to speak to the king tonight," Marcos said, collapsing onto the brocade sofa near where his wife fed Benjamin. "But I suspect his answer will be dismissive. He doesn't seem to see any faults with Tayma."

"May I speak frankly, Your Highness?" Collins stopped pacing. His expression was one of fear that he would be chastised for whatever he was about to say.

"Of course," Marcos said. "I value your counsel."

"I suspect they're having an affair."

"What?" Marcos sat forward and glared up at his advisor. "The king? And Princess Tayma?"

"And I think the queen is aware."

"How do you know of such things?" Marcos rested his elbows on his knees and bowed forward, gripping his hands into his hair as if he could pull the words he'd heard back out of his mind.

"The palace has many eyes and many ears," Collins said.

"I agree with your advisor's assessment, Your Highness." Nasrin stepped closer to Collins, lifting her chin with confidence. "There is talk."

"And you've only now decided to tell me this?"

"Prior to this evening, my suspicion was a hunch. After what happened tonight, I'm quite confident."

Marcos felt his heart plummet. He didn't want to think of his father that way.

Lyla piped in her opinion. "Did you notice how none of them acknowledged my concern about the soup? And then changed the subject, allowing Tayma to steer the conversation away from my concern about being poisoned?"

"Poisoned?" Nasrin rushed to Lyla's side, kneeling next to her chair and placing her hand on Lyla's arm. "Are you feeling okay?"

"Don't worry, I didn't actually eat any of the soup." Lyla patted Nasrin's hand. "I found the remainder of the conversation fascinating though. Only in a monarchy are a couple's marital relations a topic of national interest."

"Your Highness, if I may return to my original concern." Collins nodded briefly to Lyla and then turned to Marcos. "How soon can we leave?"

"We can stay in Dubai until our yacht is ready," Marcos said, standing.

Marcos glanced around at his posh surroundings with its gilded tapestries and pure gold accents on hand-carved furniture with the finest craftsmanship he desired. He reminded himself his money could recreate the luxury he had come to expect.

He brushed the backs of his fingers across Lyla's cheek. "You two please stay with Lyla and Benjamin while I go claim an audience with the king. Depending on his reaction, we'll leave quietly in the next day or two."

Marcos didn't wait for anyone's answer, just strode from the room and pulled the double doors to their suite closed on his way out.

Chapter Twenty-Four

An Audience with the King

M arcos snuck through the quiet hallways as if he was afraid to get caught requesting an audience with his father. The hour was not late, and he'd never had to hide his actions here in his own home.

The light coming from under his father's door indicated that someone was inside the office. Marcos rapped his knuckles lightly and waited.

"It's open." King Sayid's muffled voice gave Marcos permission to enter. His office held all the grandeur of any head of state. Marcos was curious if the Oval Office in America or the Queen of England's office was as pompous as his father's. Dark masculine wood furniture accented the off-white sculptured carpet and drapery, gold fixtures, and lighted water feature that trickled down the north wall as if an infinity pool spilled from the ceiling.

"Your Majesty." Marcos bowed in respect upon stepping into the ostentatious room. "May I have a moment of your time?"

"Of course, my son." The king rose from the desk and came around to offer a leather chair. "You are welcome any time."

"Thank you, Father." Marcos sat in the proffered chair and rubbed his sweaty palms across his pant legs, forcing himself to breathe evenly. The king sat opposite him on the matching chair.

"What's on your mind, Your Highness?" Sayid asked formally.

"The future of our kingdom, Your Majesty." Marcos took courage and answered in a similar tone. "I want you to name me Crown. Immediately."

"What brought this on suddenly?" his father asked, cocking his head to the side. "It's only been a year since your brother died. There's no hurry."

"I sense there is urgency," Marcos said. "Especially in light of what happened this evening."

"What happened this evening?" Sayid spoke dismissively and brushed a fleck of lint from his slacks.

"There was another attempt at harming my wife," Marcos said, not coming right out and saying he suspected Tayma of foul play. He was still reading his father's reaction.

"I'll start an inquiry to see if we can figure out who's behind these... attempts."

"That's not good enough, Father," Marcos said. "It's time you made a firm declaration and named me Crown. The kingdom deserves to know your intention for your successor. Jared reminded me on his deathbed that as long as our father is still alive, I will not be called upon to lead. It is my hope that you will lead our kingdom as long as humanly possible. But the people need to know who will follow you. I am the only viable candidate for Crown, and it's time you state that as a declaration."

"You're right, son." King Sayid pursed his lips, and his gaze strayed to the far corner, unfocused and sad. "I think... naming you Crown feels like admitting that my Jared is no longer with us."

"I miss him too, Father." Marcos felt emotion prick his eyes, and he forced himself to maintain his dignity. "But we will carry on his legacy as he would want us to."

"You will do a fine job, serving in his stead."

"Thank you, Father." Marcos bowed. "When should we schedule my coronation?"

"I'll check with my advisors and determine the appropriate date for a national holiday."

Before they could discuss the issue further, the door to the king's office burst open, and Princess Tayma strode into the room. "Finally. I couldn't find either of his nannies and thought I was going to have to put Omar to bed without any help. But thankfully I found them both on the back patio, smoking, and I insisted that they come inside and do their job—" Tayma stopped short when she realized the king was not alone.

Marcos stood slowly and held his chin high, narrowing his eyes at his sister-in-law.

"What is *he* doing here?" Tayma asked, stepping closer to the king.

"We were just discussing my coronation," Marcos said. "Since your *husband* died over a year ago, and it's time we got on with naming his successor."

"My husband's successor is Omar," Tayma said confidently.

"I'm talking about the *king's* successor," Marcos said. "A crown prince does not have a successor."

"Minutia." Tayma waved her hand dismissively. "My son is next in line. Nothing more needs to be discussed."

"How about if we discuss how your presence in this meeting is not required, and you can show your way out the door," Marcos said.

"I already had plans with—eh, a meeting scheduled with—the king prior to your arrival. It is you who needs to leave."

"So, it's true?" Marcos asked. "The rumors... are true?"

Sayid shoved his hands into his pockets but didn't bother answering. He held his head high as if he had nothing to apologize about.

"The kingdom seems to be running shy on princes, so you're just gonna dig your claws into the king?"

"That's an interesting way to view the situation." Tayma smirked.

"Does Mother know about this?" Marcos asked his father. "Your... queen."

"Your mother will always be the queen, son. Even when I take a second wife."

"You plan to make her a *wife?*" Marcos nearly yelled at his father and pointed at the princess. "She's your *daughter*-in-law!"

"Your mother's not able to have any more children," Sayid said, his voice calm with reason. "She completely understands my position."

"Until the princess decides to poison her also," Marcos grumbled. "Then Princess Tayma will take her place as the queen of Madain Saleh. Is that how this will work?"

Tayma stepped over to rest her hand on the king's arm and turned to Marcos with a smirk.

"Will her children call you *grandfather?*" Marcos sneered.

"That's enough, son." Sayid's voice was calm but firm.

"You're right. It is enough. My wife and I are taking a holiday to visit Nicolas and his family. Let me know what date you decide for my coronation."

With that, Marcos strode confidently from his father's office, disgusted.

Chapter Twenty-Five

My Brother's Crown

"Take only what you absolutely need," Marcos said, reaching into his spacious walk-in closet and flicking on the light switch. He turned back to the main sitting room. "It must appear to the royal family and staff as if we are merely going on a holiday to visit Nicolas and Adele and that we'll return soon."

"And that is not reality?" Collins gulped.

Marcos stepped closer to his trusted advisor and put his hand on Collins's shoulder. "I will understand if you don't want to uproot your life here and follow me to Dubai, and Cancun, and wherever fate leads us after that."

Collins glanced over Marcos's shoulder to where Lyla and Nasrin stood near Benjamin's crib. He cocked his head slightly, and there was a subtle question in his eyes. Before Marcos could fully register what had happened, Collins met his eyes again. "We will come with you."

"We?" Marcos understood the non-verbal communication he'd witnessed was between Collins and Nasrin. "I'm glad to hear that." There was double meaning to his statement.

"I will follow wherever you lead, Your Highness." Collins bowed his head.

"As will I," Lyla said, stepping up beside him and slipping her hand in his.

"And I," Nasrin stated, sidling up next to Collins, who wrapped his arm around her shoulders.

"I don't know how soon we'll return." Marcos heard the vulnerability in his own words. "I don't know how soon the king will schedule my coronation, if he will schedule it at all. I have little confidence in his ability to keep his word as long as Princess Tayma is controlling him."

"Then we will wait, Your Highness," Lyla said. She didn't often call him that unless she was teasing or in the presence of others. He looked down at his wife in wonderment. She wasn't teasing. "Let's go on a second honeymoon... and stay for a really long time."

"Could we, maybe, go on a *first* honeymoon?" Collins asked, looking down at Nasrin. "If we're going to be traveling together... perhaps we should travel as husband and wife."

"I would really like that," Nasrin answered, tucking herself into Collins's arms.

"We can arrange for an officiator when we get to Dubai tomorrow," Marcos suggested. He wrapped his arm around his advisor's shoulder, and Lyla wrapped hers around Nasrin's.

The four of them stood in a loose circle, ready to take on the world, or perhaps escape from the world. Together.

"Let's finish packing," Marcos said as they dropped their arms and stepped away from each other.

Marcos hesitated, then turned to Collins, an idea forming in his thoughts.

"We have one more item to acquire, and I'll need my advisor to assist me with the acquisition." Knowing his father was otherwise occupied at the moment, they would have easy access to his safe.

"What is it, Your Highness?" Collins asked.

"My brother's crown."

Epilogue of Part One
The Princess of the Desert

"Prince Marcos Sayid of Madain Saleh," Nick called out from the shore as Marcos's new yacht, *The Princess of the Desert*, docked. "Welcome to Puerto Aventuras."

Their captain had sailed smoothly through the canals to the marina since Marcos didn't yet own a home with its own boat slip.

Nicholas had already begun quietly shopping around for the prince and his family to purchase a home close to his. But for now, they planned to stay at the Cohen's compound where there was plenty of room, since Nick and his brothers had gotten married and dispersed, off to create their own lives.

Adele had given birth to a beautiful baby girl, just two months ahead of young Prince Benjamin. Alexandria and Benjamin were destined to grow up as best friends, maybe more if their families had any say in the matter.

The prince's arrival marked the beginning of a dynasty. The Cohen family who had fled Jerusalem to avoid an accusation of murder, and the Sayid royal family fleeing from a civil war and a contested crown, joined together in the beautiful community of Puerto Aventuras.

Nicholas borrowed his father's magic wand and bought homes and land and businesses up and down the coast between Cancun and Puerto Aventuras and south almost to Tulum. He was heralded as a savior to the impoverished communities. He took everything he'd learned from their father, buying failing businesses and helping the former owners get back on their feet, teaching them skills to help them flourish. He built and improved resorts and other tourist attractions always a step ahead of the trends. Marcos served by Nick's side, pooling resources and connections until their power was unparalleled.

Prince Marcos continued his insistence that he was rightful heir to the throne of Madain Saleh even as two generations were born... and King Sayid continued his reign.

Part Two: The Crown Prince

Prince Elmer Sayid

As told by Prince Elmer Sayid, son of Prince Omar Sayid, grandson of Crown Prince Jared Sayid, great-grandson of King Sayid, who was in his eighty-third year at the time Prince Marcos Sayid passes away...

Chapter Twenty-Six

The New Princess

Two Generations Later...

"I don't want to meet the baby," Eli whined, resisting, but only a little. "I don't want to have anything to do with her." He had made up his eight-year-old mind. He was too young to be an uncle.

His seventeen-year-old brother, Jared, was too young to be a father. But the crown prince of the Kingdom of Madain Saleh was required to marry at the age of sixteen and expected to produce an heir immediately.

Jared Sayid, named after their deceased grandfather, had no argument getting married at sixteen and frequently shared details with Eli that his little ears didn't want to hear.

Born Prince Elmer Sayid, Eli was just glad he hadn't been born first. He was quite content hanging out with his friends in the homeschool that had been established for the children of the palace. His father, Prince Omar, was a cold man who was all business and Eli had no problem avoiding him unless otherwise required.

"I'll come with you to meet the baby princess, Eli." Savannah took Eli's hand and pulled him toward the door of the playroom. Savannah, the daughter of the king's captain of the guard, was his best friend, and her younger brother, Kadin, followed them around like a puppy dog.

They never treated Eli special because he was a prince. Most everyone at the palace brushed him aside. Because he was so far removed from the title of Crown, he was of little importance.

Being the lesser prince never bothered him until now. He was free to run and play and have fun with his friends while his brother had to learn how to run their kingdom. Not that Jared took his duties seriously.

Jared loved being Crown Prince for the perks. He was treated like a god and fawned over. As if that weren't enough to be married to an eighteen-year-old princess, Jared hadn't attended the birth of his daughter because he was drunk and in bed with one of his many lovers.

And now Eli was expected to smile and pretend he was happy for his brother and congratulate him and profess his undying devotion to the baby princess who had just shoved him even further away from any claim to the title of Crown. Not that he cared.

"I'll come with you too, Eli," Kadin said. He grabbed Eli's other hand and tugged.

Eli couldn't resist them both. He dragged his feet all the way to the nursery where two nannies were already employed round the clock to care for the baby.

Jared would never lift a finger to change a diaper or feed the little princess, and likely his young bride wouldn't either.

Princess Linah wasn't exactly the mothering type. She had been selected and arranged to marry Jared based on her lineage, beauty, and connections in Jordan.

"There you are. It's about time." Jared's brow creased when Savannah pushed Eli in the door of the nursery. "Can we get this family photo done already? I have other plans."

What's her name? Eli almost asked, but thankfully bit his tongue. Highlighting Jared's behavior in front of the entire royal family wouldn't gain favor for either of them.

Jared stood dutifully behind and to the left of his wife, who sat regally, holding a little pink bundle. Their great-grandparents, King Sayid and Queen Salaina, took their place of honor at the far left of the group. The king's second wife, Princess Tayma, stood next to Eli's father, Prince Omar, with their mother to his right.

Eli didn't know where he fit in this crazy group. He was the only male in the room not wearing a crown because he wasn't old enough, and his status had now been downgraded below that of his infant niece. Why even pose for the photograph?

As he took his place to the far right of the group, Eli glanced at his two best friends, the only people that he knew cared about him unconditionally, and found them both making funny faces at him.

The smile that lit Eli's face at precisely the moment the photographer took the group photo of the Sayid Royal Family had nothing to do with happiness in his family and everything to do with his goofy best friends.

Chapter Twenty-Seven

A Diamond Befitting a Queen

I wish you were here. Eli hit send on his text, then added a follow-up. *The palace is pandemonium, scrambling to get ready for our stupid American cousin to arrive. Whatever.*

Wish I was there too. If I could skip my midterm, I'd fly home today. Savanna's text brought a smile to Eli's countenance. *Is this kid even a cousin? Isn't he your dad's uncle's grandson or something?*

You have a good memory. You should do well on your midterm tomorrow. Although both twenty-three years old, Eli had stayed in the kingdom to work with his father, Prince Omar, and his great-grandfather, King Sayid, while Savannah headed off to Ariel University in Jerusalem. She only had a few semesters left to complete her degree in Molecular Biology.

If only the test was on the history of Madain Saleh, Savannah texted. *Seriously, I am really sorry for your family's loss.*

Thanks. My dad and the king are both pretty upset. You'd think they would have gotten over Prince Marcos by now. I mean, he ran out on the family forty years ago.

That's harsh, Eli, Savanna chastised him. *Prince Marcos was the king's son, and your dad's only uncle. They loved him.*

I know, I know. They never gave up hope he'd come home someday. I've heard the rhetoric all my life. Sucks that the first time I'll meet him is in a coffin.

You can ask your cousin all about him.

Speaking of my cousin, he texted, *your brother just walked in the door and is giving me that look. Guess it's time to go pick up my cousin from the airport. Wish me luck.*

Cut him some slack, Eli. Prince Marcos was his beloved grandfather. Just think, maybe you and this kid will become friends. His name is Prince

Marcos also, right? Named after his grandpa. Just like your brother. Runs in the family.

Just so you know, you and I are not naming our first child after my father. Not happening. I'll let you pick the name as long as it's not Omar.

I hope this conversation implies you're finally going to pick out a diamond and get down on one knee, she said.

I told you, I'm not marrying you until you finish your undergrad and come home to stay. I can't move to Jerusalem while my kingdom is in such turmoil and I'm not forcing you to quit school to come home.

Well, I'm coming home for the funeral in two days, and I expect to return to the university with a diamond engagement ring at the very least.

Okay, okay, I'll go talk to my grandma and see if I can raid her jewelry closet, he said.

In that case, I want her hundred-year-old chocolate pear-shaped diamond with the thick band. Savannah's text made her intentions clear.

Eli leaned his head back and laughed heartily for the first time in several days. Everything had been somber since the announcement that his father's uncle had died. Savannah was a welcome reminder that life would go back to normal someday.

I'll see what I can do. Eli hit send.

"What's so funny?" Kadin asked, still standing in the doorway to Eli's sitting room, arms crossed, controlled impatience gracing his rehearsed expression. His dark hair and copper skin were accented with strangely mysterious eyes. Couple his good looks with the fact that he was an advisor to a prince, and twenty-two-year-old Kadin Dumont could claim any female under the age of thirty that he wanted. Maybe even older than thirty.

"Your sister is picking out engagement rings long distance," Eli answered, still grinning.

"Who's the lucky guy?"

"Shut up," Eli grumbled, pushing himself off the sofa where he'd been lounging and texting his girlfriend. "You know darn well she's marrying me."

"Whatever you say, Your Highness."

"What's that supposed to mean?" Eli stood to his full height, not quite towering over his advisor and best friend but tall enough that Kadin had to look up to meet his gaze.

"Maybe you should propose one of these days." Kadin raised his eyebrows. "What are you waiting for?"

"I don't want her to quit school for me," Eli grumbled, his shoulders slouched.

"She won't. I know my sister well. Nothing's going to stop her from getting her degree. But I also know it's time you gave her a firm commitment."

"I know." Eli huffed and almost stomped his feet on the way into his dressing room. He sat down hard on his dressing stool and looked up at Kadin in the mirror as he approached from behind.

"What's the real issue?" Kadin asked softly, laying his hands upon Eli's shoulders and meeting his gaze in the mirror.

Eli didn't want to admit out loud his real concerns about marrying Savannah, especially to her brother.

Her bloodline had never been a concern while they were growing up. Savannah and Kadin never treated Eli like a prince, and he never treated them like children of the staff.

But the reality was, Eli was expected to marry someone with royal blood. If he were Crown Prince, his spouse would have already been chosen for him years ago. He worried about the fallout if he chose a bride outside of a royal bloodline.

"She's not a princess." Kadin's statement wasn't really a question.

"You know *I* don't care about her bloodline," Eli said.

"Then why do you let your father and great-grandfather dictate who you marry?" Kadin lifted his hands from Eli's shoulders and stepped away, entering the walk-in closet. Eli could hear the gears clicking as Kadin opened the safe and brought out the leather bag that contained Eli's crown.

As official advisor to Prince Elmer, Kadin was keeper of the crown. There was no higher honor outside the royal family than the person who watched out for his prince, stood by his side, acted as his eyes and ears, a de facto bodyguard and companion.

In a way, Kadin had been training for this job all his life, following Eli around with a level of hero worship that came with being one year younger and always in his shadow, but always beside him, willing to stick up for him or kick a bully in the shin to defend him. Not that anyone on the playground would have dared bully a prince. The bully would be expelled from the school, banished from the palace, and his parents would likely lose their jobs. The sentiment was the same. Kadin would always be there for his prince.

Kadin rested the leather bag on Eli's dressing table and lifted the velvet box from within. Opening the lid revealed Eli's simple crown, not as elaborate as his older brother's or father's or great-grandfather's.

Eli's was not nearly as elaborate as the crown that had been missing for forty years and was about to reappear, resting on the head of Eli's cousin.

The crown. The crown that represented the king's successor. The crown that had once rested atop Eli's grandfather, Jared, back when he was Crown Prince. Before his life ended in a tragic motorcycle accident.

That was the event that spiraled their kingdom into turmoil and split their family in two. Two opinions. Who was next in line if the Crown died before the king? Such an event had never occurred in the history of their kingdom.

Eli's father was only five years old when his father died, not old enough for a coronation, not old enough to be a successor should the king die. In the absence of his older brother, Prince Marcos insisted the title should be his. Eli's grandmother insisted the title belonged to her son. The rest is legend and rumors. Poisoned food, dangerous snakes that just happened to slither into Prince Benjamin's nursery, threats, illicit affairs, manipulations, fleeing for safety. Eli didn't know what to believe.

One thing was certain; this cousin arriving from America claimed the title and wore *the* crown representing the king's successor. What did that mean for the remainder of the royal family? How would his father and older brother react? That evening's reception could be a bloodbath if they weren't careful.

Eli watched as his advisor lifted his simple crown out of the velvet box and raised the band of gold above Eli's head, then with reverence, lowered the crown. Almost like a comfortable glove, the crown fit into place, and Eli felt whole and at peace.

He raised his chin and was transformed into Prince Elmer Sayid of Madain Saleh. Whatever else happened that day, Eli knew his worth inherently was within his blood. His mind returned to the discussion with Kadin about marrying his sister.

"You know"—Kadin rested his hands upon Eli's shoulders again—"regardless of her bloodline, the moment you marry Savannah, she *becomes* a princess. Think on that, my prince."

Kadin had a point. Their wedding would be accompanied by a coronation at which time Prince Elmer Sayid would rest a beautiful crown of gold on his bride and name her his princess. The thought brought a smile to Eli's face, and he nodded.

"Come on, Your Highness." Kadin patted Eli on his back. "Let's go retrieve your cousin from the airport."

Chapter Twenty-Eight

Overconfident

"Fancy private jet." Kadin barely moved his lips, almost in full advisor mode, but not yet within earshot of anyone.

"Nice of them to keep us waiting this long," Eli complained. His cousin's plane had landed ten minutes prior, and Eli and Kadin were baking in the desert sun. Although both were wearing formal linen robes meant to wick away heat and sweat from the body, nothing could tame the sun beating down. But Eli was determined to be the first person his cousin saw upon arriving on the tarmac, to make it clear one of the royal family had come to retrieve him rather than a driver.

Eli's first thought as Prince Marcos appeared in the open doorway of the private jet was that he was very young, and uncomfortably regal as if this was new to him. What could he expect? The kid had grown up on the American continents. There was nothing regal about America. Haughty, but not regal. A hint of a smile played on his face when noticing Eli, and then he descended the stairs with confidence.

Too much confidence.

The amount of confidence that dared him to wear his full crown as he arrived in the kingdom, as if asserting his position and dominance. This guy didn't realize he was about to enter a lion's den. Eli had two choices; let him get eaten alive or teach him how to tame lions. He'd rely on first impressions to decide how to proceed. He stepped forward and extended his hand, one of the few people in the kingdom equal enough to do so.

"Greetings, my cousin. I'm Eli."

"Mark." Prince Marcos reached for his cousin's hand.

Interesting. Of course, Eli had done the same thing in using his nickname upon introduction.

The young prince cocked his head to the side and creased his brow. "What's your real name?"

"Elmer," Eli said through clenched teeth, wondering how he'd react and which of the American cartoon jokes he'd spout.

"I can see why you go by Eli." Mark chuckled, not skirting the humor.

"Yeah, what were my parents thinking?" Eli fought a smirk and leaned his shoulder against the black Hummer limo. Being a wealthy prince had its advantages. He traveled in style.

"Who is your father?" Mark asked, probably familiar with Jared, and their father, Omar, and the king, but not remembering the lesser prince of the family.

"Crown Prince Omar Sayid of Madain Saleh," Eli said, raising his chin slightly, almost challenging Mark to question his father's claim to the crown. Not sure what made him slip his father's title before his name, Eli somehow wanted to remind Mark that most of the royal family and subjects in the kingdom recognized Omar as Crown.

When Mark's grandfather left the kingdom forty years ago, he'd abandoned all claims. Stealing his brother's crown didn't give him the right to wear it.

Although the title had been passed from his grandfather, Jared to Eli's father Omar, and now had been conferred upon Eli's brother, Jared, Eli inherently wanted to make the distinction to his haughty American cousin.

Mark didn't bat an eyelash or alter his stoic expression. "My grandfather spoke highly of his nephew. Will I have the opportunity to meet him?"

"Absolutely," Eli said. "We have a planned reception for you this evening."

"I'm honored," Mark said, then stepped aside and waved another young man forward. "This is my advisor, Alexander Cohen-Stephenson."

Eli fought to maintain his own stoic expression. The Cohen family were practically royalty in the Middle East even though they made claim to no physical kingdom. Almost like being a Kennedy in the United States. If Mark's advisor was a Cohen, that elevated his status considerably.

"Pleasure to make your acquaintance, Alexander." Eli greeted Alexander in a similar casual style as he'd greeted Mark, minus the handshake.

"Likewise, Your Highness." Alexander nodded respectfully.

"And this is my advisor, Kadin," Eli said, indicating his best friend. Mark smiled and stood erect as Kadin bowed his head regally.

"I'm honored to meet you, Your Highness," Kadin said.

While they were yet speaking, several gentlemen were busy lowering a casket from the jet, and Eli turned reverently to watch as the late Prince Marcos Sayid was brought to the ground and rolled carefully into a waiting hearse.

"Come," Eli said, opening the door to the waiting limo. "Let's escort Prince Marcos home."

Chapter Twenty-Nine

The Hand that Rocks the Cradle

T he forty-five-minute drive through the dusty mountainous canyons and open desert gave them an opportunity to discuss all whom they would meet upon arriving at the palace.

"My father was seventeen when my older brother, Jared, was born," Eli explained, wondering how much his cousin knew about the royal family.

"Seventeen?" Mark's jaw dropped. Apparently not much.

"It is tradition and expected that the Crown Prince be married at sixteen," Eli said, thankful once again that he hadn't been born first. Now, at twenty-three years old, Eli was finally committing himself to the love of his life rather than being forced to marry a stranger back when he was a teenager.

"Man, I'm glad I didn't grow up in Madain Saleh," Mark grumbled.

Eli almost chuckled, wondering how this conversation would have been different if Mark *had* grown up in the kingdom. Would he have been recognized as Crown? Or would the title be as disputed as it was today?

"How old was your father when *you* were born?" Mark's brow creased.

"I wasn't born until he was twenty-six, which meant I became an uncle at the ripe old age of eight." Eli fought the urge to sneer, even now remembering his discomfort at watching his older brother forced into adulthood at such a young age.

"Huh?"

"Yeah, my brother had his daughter when he was seventeen," Eli said. "She is by far the most spoiled little fifteen-year-old princess you'll ever meet. Takes after our grandmother, the lovely and charming Princess Tayma." Eli realized how much sarcasm dripped from his words.

"I take it you don't like your grandmother," Mark said.

"Forgive me, Your Highnesses," Alexander interrupted. "But isn't she the reason your grandfather fled this land with your father in his arms because she tried to poison him?" Alexander raised his eyebrows. "Are you sure we're safe here?"

"My initial reaction to your question is that none of us are safe as long as she is pulling strings in the background." Eli chuckled nervously, realizing the truth of his statement. "But the reality is my niece and grandmother are both such flighty airheads, to borrow some American slang. I don't think poisoning you would even cross their minds, especially if they don't see you as a threat." Eli fought the urge to raise his gaze to the brazen adornment on Mark's head. Might as well throw it out there. Mark was playing with fire showing up at the palace wearing *that* crown.

"That's... reassuring." Mark gulped and glanced at Alexander.

Threats aside, Eli's grandmother was the main catalyst for almost every problem their kingdom faced, and Mark would be in her sights before he stepped from the limo. Her first husband had barely been interred when she insisted her five-year-old son be named Crown. The notion was preposterous.

Not able to sway the king, Tayma seduced him instead. Before the year passed, she had him in her bed, and shortly thereafter, the king had taken her on as a second wife. The scandal was unfathomable to someone as committed to purity as Eli. He would never compromise a woman in such a way. Or himself for that matter.

"Oddly, my best advice is for you to flirt with them," Eli said, realizing the hypocrisy in his words.

"What?" Mark's jaw dropped.

"Stoke their already inflated egos. My grandmother is an immature sixty-six-year-old but thinks she's thirty-five and regularly takes much younger men as her lovers," Eli said.

"Yeah, that ain't happening," Mark said, eyes wide and appearing disgusted at the thought.

"Nor do I recommend it," Eli said, backpedaling. "But appeal to her youthfulness and treat her as a peer, then ask her about her lovely granddaughter."

"The fifteen-year-old?" Mark gulped, looking mildly nauseated by this whole conversation.

"She has yet to choose a husband," Eli explained. "A wealthy distant cousin, who also happens to be a prince whose roots trace back to Madain Saleh with only one generation removed? Yeah, you are perfect."

"P-perfect?" Mark placed one hand on his stomach, and Eli wondered if they'd need to pull the car over. Better offer clarification.

"I'm not saying you actually entertain the notion. I'm just giving you pointers on how best to survive the next few days.

"Gee, thanks." Mark gulped. "I'll take all this into consideration."

"Oh, and Alexander." Eli turned to Mark's advisor, needing to address one other issue. "When advising your prince, pull him aside and stage-whisper in his ear rather than interrupt his conversation. You will be seen as a highly revered advisor with an impressive bloodline who elevates Prince Marcos's status even loftier by mere association."

Alexander sat up straighter and lifted his nose with an air of snobbery. Yeah, he wasn't grasping the point Eli was trying to make.

"Perfect. Your acting skills are superb," Eli said. "But remember to stay one step behind and to the right and never attempt to be his equal."

Alexander's shoulders drooped. "Gee thanks."

"I'm just helping you guys out," Eli said with a sigh. "I want you to enjoy your stay here. You can laugh about it later. Oh, and by the way, I am not your equal either. My status in our royal family is almost a step down from Alexander's as your advisor."

"You're kidding," Mark said.

"Not at all," Eli said with resignation. "I was told by my father's advisor that I should be walking to your left and one step behind Alexander."

"Wow... okay," Mark said. "Interesting."

"Here we go," Eli said as the limo came to a rolling stop before the main entrance of the palace. "Do *not* get out of the car until my father's advisor opens the limo door for you, which he will, rather quickly, I might add."

"Okay..."

The door to the limousine opened, and Ahmed offered his calculating fake smile and bowed regally. "Prince Marcos Sayid. Welcome to Madain Saleh."

Eli waited while Mark and then Alexander stepped from the limo. He and Kadin exited the vehicle as Ahmed introduced himself.

"I am Ahmed bet David, advisor to Crown Prince Omar Sayid of Madain Saleh." The man bowed his head respectfully, if briefly. To his credit, Mark didn't react to Ahmed's emphasis on the word *crown* with the mention of his prince.

"Allow me to present my advisor, Alexander Cohen-Stephenson," Mark said, holding his hand out to his right as if displaying Alexander proudly.

"Cohen?" Ahmed raised his eyebrows. "Any relation to the late Levi Cohen?"

"I am his great-grandson by lineage of Nicholas Cohen," Alexander said.

"A respected businessman in his own right," Ahmed acknowledged.

"Thank you, I agree." Alexander maintained his air of aloof haughtiness.

Eli struggled to keep a straight face, remembering how he had complimented Alexander on his acting skills.

"I trust that you will enjoy your *visit* to *our* kingdom." Ahmed's subtle emphasis on the words *visit* and *our* were a little too obvious.

"Your cousin, His Highness Prince *Elmer*, will escort you to your suite," Ahmed said. Eli nearly rolled his eyes at the derogatory way Ahmed emphasized his given name. "We have arranged to have a grand reception for you this evening and formal attire is expected."

"Naturally," Mark said, then took a step back and nodded to Eli. "I will follow you, Your Highness."

Eli pursed his lips and tried to hide a grin. He raised his eyebrows at his cousin as he led the way into the palace. Way to stick it to Ahmed, asking Eli to lead the way. He was almost certain Mark had done that on purpose.

"We've maintained your grandfather's suite, and you'll be honored to be the first person sleeping there since he left," Eli said, leading them in much the same way a tour guide would explain a museum exhibit. "His Majesty, King Sayid, never gave up hope that his son would one day return to occupy his suite."

"His Highness, Prince Marcos, regretted on his deathbed that he hadn't taken the time to do so," Mark said. "Perhaps that's one of the reasons he requested I return his body to our homeland."

After multiple twists and turns and ascending two sets of grand staircases, they finally stopped in front of a set of ornately carved double doors.

"Here we are," Eli said, opening the doors to reveal an elegant sitting room.

Mark drifted slowly to the obviously more masculine of the two dressing tables and glanced in the mirror. The way Mark stood behind his grandfather's chair reminded Eli of how Kadin stood behind Eli's chair, attending to the care and management of the crown.

Suddenly Mark turned to Eli. "Is your father's advisor having an affair with Princess Tayma?"

"How on earth did you pick up on that?" Eli folded his arms and leaned against the door frame. The kid had only been in the kingdom ten minutes and hadn't even met the princess. Yet he had already made that connection.

"The hand that rocks the cradle," Mark said, his face a mixture of awe and alarm.

"I'm not following you." Eli creased his brow.

"There's an American saying about how the hand that rocks the cradle is the hand that rules the world," Mark explained. "Who is actually ruling our kingdom?"

Good question. "I'll be interested to hear your take after you've been here a few days," Eli said, creasing his brow. "Having an affair is one thing, influencing matters of state... I'm going to need some time to process that." Tayma and Ahmed had been having an affair for several years, and Eli suspected she controlled both sides of the crown; the king and his successor, whoever that turned out to be.

"Sometimes it takes an outsider's perspective to see what's right in front of our eyes," Mark said, turning back to his grandfather's suite. "What time shall we make our appearance at the reception?"

Eli took that as his dismissal and pushed away from the doorjamb. "The reception begins at seven o'clock, so I'd suggest arriving at about twenty minutes after the hour."

"Thank you, Your Highness," Mark said sincerely, stepping over and affectionately placing his hands atop Eli's shoulders. "You have been a wealth of knowledge."

"Glad to be of assistance, Your Highness," Eli returned the sentiment. "I'll see you at the reception."

Eli took his leave and strode down the hall, with a crease in his brow and a heavy heart. An outsider's perspective indeed. Where would this new enlightenment lead him? He picked up his pace, wondering where his advisor had disappeared to upon arriving at the palace.

Chapter Thirty

The Royal Family

T he red carpet stretched from the entrance of the throne room to the far wall, the center of which included a raised platform of marble where three thrones sat. Several lower levels of raised platforms sat to the right of the king, each with thrones, all of which were occupied by various members of the royal family.

As Eli took his place on the lowest of the platforms, he scanned the room.

Small groupings of dignitaries stood around, unaware they were being watched. The leaders of the government at all levels, the leaders of the military, all appointed officials of the monarchy, descendants of the queen's sister and brothers, the king's sister, aunts, uncles, and a myriad of cousins.

Formal dress was in the eye of the beholder when the people of Madain Saleh gathered for a reception. Some men were in business suits or military uniforms, others wore ornate robes made of colorful linens. Only a few men wore tuxedos; most opted for formal suits. Some women wore floor-length evening gowns and jewels while others were shrouded from head to toe. Most fell somewhere in between, and all of them seemed comfortable in their chosen attire. Eli appreciated the diversity of his kingdom.

A tiny hint of commotion caught Eli's attention as his cousin stepped into view at the entrance of the throne room, Alexander at his right. Mark didn't show any signs of nervousness, although the scene must have been intimidating from his point of view. He had the serious disadvantage of everyone knowing who he was and why he was here.

The young man appointed to be caller at the entrance to the throne room spoke with clarity that resounded through the excellent acoustics. "Your Majesty and Your Grace, may I present His Royal Highness, Prince Marcos Sayid, and his advisor, Alexander Cohen-Stephenson."

Murmurs preceded them as they walked the length of the room, and as Mark got closer to the royal family, his gaze quickly swept from the top platform down the line. When he met Eli's gaze, he smirked.

Eli was glad to have given Mark the lowdown on what to expect. This whole evening could have been a disaster otherwise.

At the base of the marble steps leading up to the platform, Mark lowered to one knee, as did Alexander.

"Your Majesty"—Mark bowed his head briefly—"and Your Grace. It is with regret that I bring you the news that your son, His Highness, Prince Marcos Sayid of Mada'in Saleh, has passed away. I have brought him home so that he might be returned to the soil from which he came."

Eli raised his eyebrows at Mark's use of the ancient pronunciation of their kingdom, which was rarely used other than the most formal declarations. The observance spoke volumes as to Mark's commitment to their land.

"Welcome, Your Highness," King Sayid nodded regally and held out his hand.

Mark and Alexander stood and ascended the marble steps to approach the thrones and stood before the king. "Your Majesty, I am your great-grandson, Prince Marcos Sayid, son of Prince Benjamin Sayid and grandson of the late Prince Marcos Sayid. May I present my advisor, Alexander Cohen-Stephenson."

King Sayid lifted a hand to introduce the women who sat on either side. "May I present, Her Grace, Queen Salaina of Madain Saleh, and my second wife, Princess Tayma."

"Your Grace, I'm honored to finally meet you." Mark bowed to his great-grandmother and pulled her hand to his lips in a kiss of respect. Alexander appropriately held back and didn't step forward to greet the king or queen, merely bowed his head and maintained his stance behind Mark.

Mark stepped to the other side of the king's throne and similarly greeted their great-grandfather's second wife, forgoing the bow of respect he'd given the queen. Eli fought the urge to chuckle at the omission. "Princess, it is a pleasure to make your acquaintance."

Liar, Eli thought but held his peace.

"May I present my son," the princess practically purred at Mark. "His Highness, *Crown* Prince Omar Sayid of Madain Saleh." Her emphasis on the word crown was even stronger than that of her son's advisor, Ahmed, who stood dutifully behind Omar's throne, a defiant lift to his chin.

"Your Highness," Mark said to Eli's father, with an added level of respect and admiration. "Your uncle, His Highness Prince Marcos, wished for me to convey to you the extreme amount of love he held for you throughout the remainder of his life, and the regret that he felt in never having the opportunity to see you again before he died."

Eli fought the urge to glare at his grandmother, knowing she was the reason why his father never had a chance to say goodbye to his beloved uncle.

"Thank you, Your Highness," Eli's father said with real sadness in his voice. "I remember him fondly as well. I regret not having him here as I grew up." He seemed to pause and compose himself, then lifted his chin and straightened his shoulders.

"May I introduce my sons, Prince Jared and Prince Elmer."

"Prince Elmer was of great assistance to me this afternoon when he escorted me from the airport." Mark nodded to Eli's father, then stepped down to extend a hand to Jared. "Pleasure to meet you, Your Highness. You simply must introduce me to this lovely young lady at your side."

"May I introduce my daughter, Her Highness, Princess Nimrah," Jared said, as if he were a doting father who loved his little girl.

"A princess befitting such a strong name, I'm sure." Mark took her hand, and his eyes seemed to smolder with calculated attention. Perfect. He was playing his part well. Maybe Mark's inevitable rejection would push Nimrah off her high horse if that were possible. Eli wanted to be around to see her stumble.

Chapter Thirty-One

I Will Stand Beside You

"How did I do?" Mark asked Eli in a hushed tone.

Eli felt he could speak frankly to his cousin as they stood near one corner of the throne room, waiting for the meal to commence. Alexander and Kadin hovered just far enough away to provide a screen of privacy. "Better than I could have predicted. Nimrah has already requested the seating arrangement be reorganized to have you at her side. Her *right* side, of course."

"Of course," Mark sneered. "I will be sure to offer her my undivided attention."

"Don't get caught in her web, my cousin," Eli warned, knowing how persuasive Nimrah could be. She had more than one man within the palace walls wrapped around her finger, not that any of them would be suitable as a husband. For that, she needed a prince or dignitary. If given the opportunity, she would sink her claws into Mark. "And do *not* go anywhere alone with her."

"If she tries anything, I'll make mention of my intended bride back in the States," Mark said. "The daughter of a powerful U.S. senator."

"I'm not sure that's wise either." Eli pursed his lips in thought. "At least not until the last day you're here. Flirt with her tonight, then stay regrettably busy meeting with the king and other princes over the next few days." Eli had already been told that he was expected to be available in his office by late morning because the king planned to personally take Mark on a tour of the palace.

"Sounds like a plan," Mark said. "I look forward to that anyway. Any advice about my audience with the king?"

"Do *not* bring up your suspicions about the likely affair between his second wife and his grandson's advisor," Eli said.

"I wouldn't dream of it," Mark said. "And what should I know about your older brother?"

"Jared is next in line behind my father, although Nimrah calls the shots in that family."

"Seems a lot of power bestowed upon a fifteen-year-old girl," Mark said, creasing his brow.

"There has never been a Crown *Princess* in the history of our kingdom, and Princess Nimrah seems to think that should be remedied." Eli allowed his gaze to drift in the general direction of where Nimrah was entertaining a small circle of other teenage girls. They frequently giggled and turned to look at Eli and Mark, probably hoping to catch the attention of the mysterious twenty-year-old prince from America.

"Have you considered the claim my grandfather made that *he* was the rightful Crown since his older brother died?" Mark asked.

So, the kid was finally broaching the subject. Eli turned back toward Mark, took a sip from his glass of wine, and glanced briefly at the crown on Mark's head. "By de facto bestowing that right to yourself, no doubt?"

"Naturally," Mark said.

"Is that your intention? To challenge the throne?"

"What are your thoughts on the subject, Your Highness?" Mark asked.

"The claim has merit." Eli hesitated. "You would have an uphill battle, that's for sure."

"I am wearing *the* crown," Mark stated, raising his brows.

"I'm aware of that," Eli said through clenched teeth. "Boldly, I might add."

"Thank you." Mark lifted his chin.

"I'm not sure I intended that as a compliment," Eli said. Mark's grandfather had taken his older brother's official crown, the one bestowed upon the crown prince at his coronation. Mark's brazen display of the adornment at this reception was enough to cause contention and division among the royal family. "I'm undecided."

"Understandably."

"I will tell you this," Eli said, looking Mark in the eye, man to man, cousin to cousin, prince to prince. "I would stand at your side should you make that choice."

"I would welcome your support," Mark said with sincerity, all haughtiness gone from his countenance.

"You would be a far better ruler than my brother, and more honest." Eli sighed and glanced around the throne room as if he were a stranger evaluating those in attendance at the reception. "I fear for the future of our country if Princess Nimrah gains any more power than she already possesses."

"Let's discuss this again in a few days after I've taken a full assessment of the situation," Mark suggested.

"I look forward to that report," Eli said, nodding thoughtfully.

Just then, the young caller announced that dinner was ready to be served.

"Your princess awaits," Eli said with a chuckle, not envying Mark's predicament.

"Wish me luck," Mark grumbled.

Watching from across the table as Mark charmed the princess was comical. Eli was embarrassed how well the attention was working. He nodded at his cousin once, acknowledging his perfect acting skills.

Dinner was followed by entertainment back in the throne room, which had been transformed into a dance hall with colorful lighting, Zaffa drummers, Egyptian dancers, and a Middle Eastern Dabke dance number. The palace staff had gone to great lengths to welcome the visitors from America.

Eli was glad this wasn't a regular occurrence because he was annoyed at the spectacle. After he participated in the tribute dance honoring their great-grandmother and queen, he feigned a yawn and retired for the night.

As he strode down the hall toward his suite, his phone lit up with an incoming text. *Aced my midterms, packed and ready to board the plane. See you in the morning.*

Travel safely, my love. Eli hit send and knew he'd lay awake in anticipation of holding Savannah in his arms the following day.

Chapter Thirty-Two

The Future of Our Monarchy

E li didn't want to wait for Savannah to fly commercial, so he'd sent the Sayid family's jet to Jerusalem to retrieve her. Six months at her university had been too long to be apart. She was right. They needed to get married. Immediately. Forget an engagement. He wanted the coronation. And the honeymoon. Today preferably.

Savannah appeared in the doorway of the plane, her flawless copper skin and flowing ebony hair sent his blood racing. She slipped a pair of sunglasses onto her face, shielding her eyes from the brutal desert sun. Eli could tell the minute she saw him because she bounded down the stairs and raced across the tarmac, throwing herself into his arms. He fell back against the side of the limo, and their lips connected.

Forget asking his grandma for the pretty ring in her jewelry closet. He almost got down on his knee right there on the hot pavement and begged for her hand. But he didn't want to pull his hungry body away from hers for that long.

After a minute or two of kissing—he completely lost track—she pulled away just long enough to gasp, "Air conditioning."

Eli pulled open the door to the limo, barely interrupting their kiss long enough to climb into the Hummer. She scooted over on the seat, tossing her sunglasses aside, and pulled him down on top of her.

"Um, Your Highness?" Their driver cleared his throat. Eli looked up at their driver with a sheepish but unrepentant connection in the rearview mirror. "Need I remind you that in this particular style of limousine I will be able to see and hear everything you do. Not that I'll judge your behavior, but this may not be the best time or place for that... um... activity."

"Ugh," Eli moaned and lowered his head to Savanna's shoulder, burying his face in her hair, still almost completely on top of her, having not even closed the side door yet. "Probably for the best anyway," he mumbled low enough that only she would be able to hear.

"Later," Savannah whispered back.

"I need to marry you first."

"Ugh, you're still insisting on that?" Savannah rested her head against the seat and stared up at the ceiling, lifting her hands into her raven curls and pulling gently.

"Yes, ma'am." Eli sat up and pulled the door closed, extricating himself from her legs wrapped around his waist. When did that happen? "I *will* hold to my principles."

"Fine, call up the king and tell him to draft a marriage contract, and we can be married an hour from now."

Eli pulled her to a seated position and laughed, knowing she was only half-joking. "He's entertaining my cousin today. Let's wait until after the funeral tomorrow and Mark heads back to America."

"You call him Mark?" Savannah's jaw dropped. "Does he call you Eli?"

"Only in private," Eli said. "We're quite good at shifting cadence when in the company of others."

"I can't wait to meet him."

"You won't have to wait long. The king has instructed me to be available later this morning when he brings Prince Marcos around to informally meet the princes away from the pageantry of the throne room and banquet hall and royal family and court."

"What's he like?" Savannah sounded excited. Eli wondered if he should worry about her flirting with him like every other woman at the reception last night. Mark had made it clear he had a girlfriend back in America. Good. Maybe that would keep him there for now.

"I don't know. Calculating. Smart. Young. You'll have to judge him for yourself and tell me what you think."

"Was he seriously bold enough to wear the crown last night?" Savannah's avoidance of calling the crown *his* crown wasn't lost on Eli.

But who *should* wear the crown? Eli's father, Omar? His brother, Jared? He shuddered at the thought. Eli was reminded of his conversation before dinner the night before; how he had all but pledged his allegiance to Mark. The kid was world-traveled, knowledgeable about international affairs, had connections in Mexico and the United States, and most importantly, Mark loved Madain Saleh. How? Why? Eli wasn't sure. The land called to

Mark just as it called to Eli. He'd make a better king than anyone in the entire royal family.

"Hey, deep thinker?" Savannah waved her hand in front of Eli's face. "What mystery of the world are you contemplating?"

"The future of our monarchy," Eli said softly, then turned to her and met her gaze. He was keenly aware of what their driver had said a few moments prior. They had an audience. Eli tried to communicate with his eyes that they'd continue this conversation later. "Yes, he wore the crown. You'll just have to meet him and tell me your opinions afterward."

"Okay," Savannah said, reaching for his hand. "Can we make out some more now?"

"You won't get me in trouble again?" He raised his eyebrows.

"I make no promises," she whispered.

He took his chances and leaned forward, matching her hunger with controlled passion. A few more days. They could wait that long. Hopefully.

Chapter Thirty-Three

My Bloodline Is of Little Consequence

As was the king's habit, he swept open the door, entering Eli's office unannounced, bringing with him Prince Marcos and his advisor, Alexander.

Eli jumped to attention, almost dropping Savannah off his lap. He caught her before she toppled over and steadied both her and himself while trying to mask a sheepish expression.

"Your Majesty, we, uh, I mean, we weren't doing anything inappropriate. I realize how this must look."

"Your Highness, you are an adult," Sayid said with a wave of his hand. "What you do with the captain's daughter is none of my concern. Welcome home from university, young Savannah."

"Thank you, Your Majesty." Savannah bowed her head respectfully and kept her eyes averted.

"She is not *just* the captain's daughter," Eli insisted, panic crushing his chest that the king would think such a thing. "I would never take liberties with your captain's daughter."

"I would hope you wouldn't take liberties with *any* girl, Your Highness," Savannah hissed under her breath.

"You know I wouldn't," Eli grumbled just as low.

"Six months was a long time to wait while I was gone."

"I've waited for you for twenty-three years," Eli said. "I think I can handle waiting a few more months."

King Sayid interrupted their quarrel, turning to Mark and Alexander with a wide smile. "Savannah's father is captain of my royal guard. The finest man I have in my employ."

"Thank you, Your Majesty," Savannah responded. "He enjoys working for you."

"Savannah, may I introduce you to my cousin, Prince Marcos, and his advisor, Alexander Cohen-Stephenson." Eli placed his hand on Savannah's lower back, guiding her forward. "Savannah and I have been friends since we were young children, playing together in the nursery. Rather than my mother care for me herself, she took me to play with the palace staff's children. Thankfully." Eli met her gaze with longing.

"These two have been playing house since they were children, and someday soon we'll watch them raise their own children," Sayid said.

"You wouldn't"—Eli gulped—"be averse to me choosing a wife who is not of royal blood?"

"You are not the crown prince," the king said dismissively. "Your bloodline is of little consequence."

Little consequence? Eli tried to hold his composure at the way the king brushed him aside but found it hard not to be offended.

First, they'd barged into Eli's office while he was having a private moment with his girlfriend and then his great-grandfather had insulted Eli and discounted his importance in the family. Way to rub salt in his wound that he would never be king. Whatever. He didn't want that stupid crown anyway. And he certainly didn't want to fight for the crown.

Notwithstanding the frustration, the king had inadvertently offered his blessing on their union. Eli decided to request his great-grandfather draft contracts that very day.

One item of business first; he had to obtain the blessing of the captain of the guard. He sighed and returned his attention to the conversations around himself. There would be time to meet with Savannah's father later.

"Tell me more about these cool linen robes you all seem to wear around here." Mark asked, stepping closer and lifting the unique fabric between his fingers. "Where can I get some of these?"

"We could take you into the city center and check out some of the vendors there, if you'd like," Eli said, appreciating the distraction from that uncomfortable conversation with their great-grandfather. "That, or you could just raid my closet."

"I'd like to buy some that we could take back with us," Mark said, then glanced at Alexander. "We'd be styling on campus at our university."

"Heck no! I'm not wearing one of those at college," Alexander said, shaking his head adamantly. Then he seemed to realize the casual way he was discussing clothing choices and straightened to his full height, lifting his chin. "I mean, unless you require that of me, Your Highness."

"Well," King Sayid said with a chuckle. "I'm going to rest awhile before the noon meal. I'll leave you young people to plan an afternoon shopping trip."

"We'll see you at lunch, Your Majesty." Mark said, bowing with respect.

After the king left Eli's office, Alexander turned toward the other three college-aged kids. "I am so sorry. I don't know what got into me. I'm still not used to playing this role."

"You're fine, Alex, relax." Mark laid a hand on his shoulder.

Eli strode over and closed the door to his office. "There, now you can be as casual as you want. It's just us *young people*, as grandfather called us."

"Where do you go to school, Your Highness?" Savannah returned to the sofa where she'd been sitting with Eli, and lounged casually, slipping her feet from her sandals and pulling her legs up onto the sofa.

"North Carolina State University," Mark said. He and Alexander sat beside one another, and Eli sat next to Savannah, tucking her feet up under his legs as if needing to keep them warm. "You?"

"Ariel University, Department of Molecular Biology, in Jerusalem," Savannah said flippantly as if she knew that was impressive.

"Molecular biology? Dang," Mark said. "You must be super smart."

"She is," Eli said, pulling her hand to his lips for a kiss. He met her gaze and wished these intrusive visitors would leave so he could have her alone again. She winked and then pulled her gaze away.

"So, um, Alex, are you related to the Cohen family who used to own a whole bunch of businesses in Jerusalem?" Savannah asked. "The library where I go to college was named by their foundation because they provided the funding."

"Yeah, Nicholas Cohen is my grandfather," Alexander said, sitting up a little straighter.

"And what are you studying in college?" Savannah asked.

"I'm learning how to become the advisor to a cocky prince who thinks the world revolves around him," Alexander said with a straight face. Mark punched him in the arm. "Kidding! Kidding. Geesh. I'm pre-law but considering public administration."

"Are you in college, Eli?" Mark cringed, and Eli knew exactly why. Here Eli had just been bragging about how he and Prince Marcos had the ability to change cadence when others were in the room, and not two hours later,

Mark had used the prince's nickname rather than addressing him with his title.

"No, I'm not... *Mark*." Eli allowed sarcasm to drip from his snarky answer. "You heard the king. My bloodline is of little consequence."

"Well, aside from not believing that for a second"—Mark coughed playfully—"if marrying outside of royal blood means you get to marry a smart and beautiful woman such as the one sitting at your side, I'd be thankful you aren't required to marry a snobby princess at the ripe old age of sixteen."

Eli couldn't have agreed more. "Speaking of snobby princesses," Eli said. "How are you doing with avoiding my lovely niece?"

"I have yet to see her since I handed her off to her father last night and fled to my suite with a migraine."

"She'll find you eventually," Eli said. "This palace isn't as big as it looks. I'm sure she knows where your suite is located. I wouldn't be surprised if she's waiting in your room right now, lounging on your king-sized bed and hoping you'll make her your queen."

Alexander pulled a key from his pocket and held it up on a keyring. "I'm one step ahead of you."

"Trust me," Mark said. "She won't sink her claws into me no matter how hard she tries."

Good luck with that, Eli thought. Princess Nimrah wouldn't be deterred by a key and a declaration. Eli felt bad for encouraging Mark into this situation. Hopefully the kid would figure out a way to drag himself out.

Chapter Thirty-Four

You Have My Blessing

"**O**kay, after I pull your father away," Eli said, "spend some time with your mom. I really don't want the captain to see you before I have a chance to talk with him."

"Don't take too long." Savannah wrapped her arms around Eli's waist. "I don't want to be away from you."

"If all goes well, hopefully this is the last night we have to sleep apart." Eli gazed down, brushing her hair away from her face, and was tempted to press his lips to hers again. He forced himself some restraint, knowing he wouldn't want to stop. He needed to see her father with a clear head and without swollen lips. The thought brought out a tiny smile. "Now go hide around the corner while I retrieve your father."

"Okay, okay." She lifted onto her toes to plant one tiny kiss on his mouth and hurried into the next hallway.

Eli took a deep, steadying breath and stepped forward, ready to get this over with. He reached up and wrapped his knuckles on the thick, ornately carved wooden door.

Captain Robert Dumont, of the king's royal guard, opened the door to his apartment with his usual stoic, confident expression. One of the few people in the kingdom not required to greet the royal family with a nod or bow, the captain held his chin aloft. "Your Highness, welcome."

Robert stepped aside, holding the door open. Few doors in the palace were closed to the royal family, and turning away a prince would never occur to even the captain of the guard.

But Eli didn't enter the elegant apartment reserved for the captain and his family.

"Captain, if you would, I'd like to have a word with you alone," Eli said with reverence and respect, in no way demanding an audience. "Would you be willing to join me for a walk?"

Glancing into his apartment where his wife, Virginia, stood with a soft smile, Robert answered with a curt nod. "Of course, Your Highness." He pulled the door closed behind himself and turned down the hall in the direction where Savannah was hiding.

"This way, please." Eli's words were a little too demanding, and he softened his tone. "If that's okay with you."

"Your Highness, you are quite literally allowed to demand me to do whatever you want." Robert didn't crack a smile but turned to follow Eli's direction.

"In that case, I demand you to think of me as a man for a few moments and forget I'm a prince."

Robert finally chuckled and relaxed. "Whatever you say, Your... uh... Elmer."

"Captain Dumont, I'll get right to the point. I'd like to marry your daughter."

"R-really? Savannah?"

"Have you any other daughters of whom I'm not aware?"

Brushing aside Eli's snarky comment, Robert asked, "When?"

"Tomorrow."

"Tomorrow?" Robert stopped short.

"Yes, sir." Eli turned to meet the captain where he had stopped.

"I believe we have a funeral to attend tomorrow," Robert said.

"Which is why we're waiting."

"Waiting?" Robert raised his eyebrows.

"Until after the funeral, yes."

"Aside from my shock at this declaration, I'm curious how you're planning to handle the logistics of her being in Jerusalem at the university and you being here in the kingdom."

"I flew her home this morning," Eli said.

"My daughter is here?" Robert turned to face Eli, then looked up and down the hall. "Where?"

"Please don't ask me that," Eli requested. "I don't wish to lie, but I would really like a moment with *just* you before you spend the remainder of the evening with your daughter and your wife."

Robert cocked his head to the side. "Why?"

130

"I know it's an old-fashioned notion, but I'm asking for your permission and blessing."

"I appreciate the sentiment, but shouldn't the permission be granted by the king? As much as you'd like me to think of you as a man and not as a prince, the reality is, you *are* a prince. There are protocols that must be followed. Have they not already chosen a princess from some far-off land to be your wife?"

"The king has already given us his blessing," Eli said. "We asked him an hour ago. But as you said, the reality of my being a prince means my wedding will include a coronation and my wife will be named a princess. I want to know you are okay with Savannah being named as my princess."

"Why would I have a problem with that, son?" In a rare show of endearment, Robert placed his hands upon Eli's shoulders and met his gaze.

"There are many responsibilities that accompany the title, and not all of them are pleasant."

"How does she feel about the prospect of marrying you?"

"She asked if we could have the king perform the ceremony this afternoon if possible." Eli gulped, not wanting to admit to Savannah's father the physical reasons why they'd like to be married immediately.

Robert suddenly leaned his head back and laughed heartily. Dropping his arms, he met Eli's gaze again and lifted his eyebrows with a knowing expression. "I see you continue your insistence of maintaining purity until marriage."

"Why is that such a foreign concept to people?" Eli asked.

"The notion doesn't exactly run in your family." Robert chuckled, then must have realized the way he had just spoken ill of the royals to whom he'd sworn his loyalty and protection. He straightened his back and raised his chin. "I mean... uh..."

"Don't worry about saying what the rest of us are thinking but aren't willing to admit out loud, at least not in my presence. You might want to keep your opinions to yourself in front of others."

"You did ask me to treat you like a man and not a prince." Robert seemed to be holding his breath, waiting for reprimand.

"I did indeed," Eli said, then continued. "I'd like you to spend some time with Savannah this evening and decide for yourself if she's in love with me and if you're okay with her marrying me. Then, if you feel so inclined, I'd love to have your blessing."

"I don't need to spend time with her to know your character, Your Highness. I've known you since before you were born. My son is your advisor. My daughter has been your playmate all her life. But most importantly, I know that you love her unconditionally and have her best interests in your heart."

"I do, Captain." Eli gulped and nodded.

"Then you have my blessing, Your Highness," Robert said with reverence.

"Thank you, sir." In an unprecedented move, Eli threw his arms around Robert and hugged him as he would a father, if his own father wasn't a stuffy and cynical man.

Robert hesitated and then returned the hug.

Eli suddenly pulled away from his future father-in-law with a renewed excitement. "I'm going now to have the king draw up the proper paperwork, and ensure that Savannah's crown is commissioned, and to prepare my suite for her to move in with me, and I already know which ring she has picked out, and she's waiting for you in your apartment. Thank you, Captain! I'll see you at the funeral tomorrow. You won't regret this, I promise."

Without waiting for Robert to answer, Eli hurried down the hall toward his great-grandfather's office. The proper contracts, the queen's blessing, and the gift from her collection of royal jewels, were his last hurdles. That, and about twenty-four hours of tortuous waiting.

Chapter Thirty-Five

The King's Wishes

*W*as Mark brave or an idiot? Eli wasn't sure, but the king had insisted. He asked Prince Marcos to stand to his right as he led the funeral procession from the palace to the royal family's mausoleum near the edge of the city center. Mark held his head high with confidence, and Eli fought the urge to sneer.

With one symbolic move, King Sayid had announced to the world his chosen successor.

Eli's father, Prince Omar walked to the King's left, the meaning of which was not lost on anyone. His mother, Princess Nijah stood to Omar's left, with Queen Salaina to his right, grasping Omar's right arm. She seemed to be barely holding herself together. Eli wished he could comfort his great-grandmother, but the public show of affection would have been frowned-upon and shown the queen as weak.

Prince Jared and his wife walked to the right and behind Prince Omar, and Eli to his left, Kadin at his shoulder. At that moment, Eli wished he had taken the time to marry Savannah the day before because she would have been at his side as they made their way to the tomb.

The funeral procession was formal and attended by most people in the kingdom, who seemed there out of curiosity or to be reveling in the pageantry rather than grief for a prince none of them had seen in forty years. Many of the people in the kingdom had never met Prince Marcos, and his American grandson was just a novelty.

The internment was solemn and formal. The only noise was Queen Salaina crying in the arms of her grandson, Prince Omar, who also was sobbing. Eli was at a loss how to comfort his father. The man had always been cold and stern, showing little emotion and even less affection. Omar's uncle, Prince Marcos, must have meant more to Eli's father than he ever allowed the world to see.

The pallbearers slid the ornate casket, in which Prince Marcos would forever rest, deep into a tomb that had been carved from rock. The heavy stone placed in front of the tomb already bore his name and the stone to his left read the name of his brother, Eli's late grandfather, Prince Jared Sayid of Mada'in Saleh.

Eli had never met his grandfather, Jared, but believed in his heart that he had been an upstanding crown prince and would have made a great king.

If King Sayid were to pass away, the throne would be highly contested. The king's wishes had been made clear. But would the kingdom honor his selection? Eli doubted that would be the case. He couldn't envision Jared stepping down, or Princess Tayma allowing him to step down. His brother would be a terrible king. Jared would be a puppet with a crown. Eli shuddered at the prospect.

He silently willed King Sayid to stay alive as long as he possibly could.

Chapter Thirty-Six

Destined to Be Your Princess

"My love, we must tread softly. The queen is mourning her son." Eli paused outside Queen Salaina's suite and lifted Savannah's hands in his. "Even if she is not able to provide us with that elegant piece of jewelry, I don't want to wait."

"I don't want to wait either," she said. "I don't need a ring; I just want to be with you."

"You have to make me a promise," Eli said.

"Anything."

"Promise me you'll return to college after your spring break and finish your degree, no matter how much I beg you to stay." Eli chuckled.

Savannah lowered her gaze and blushed a soft pink. "I promise."

"Serving as a princess is not easy."

"Will I sleep beside you every night?"

"If sleep is what you desire," Eli teased.

"There are lots of things I desire." Savannah's voice lowered.

"I hope by this evening I'll legally be allowed to fulfill your every desire." Eli leaned closer and whispered near her ear.

Before Eli could pull away from Savannah, the queen's door opened, and a young woman stood with her arms folded.

"Your queen would like to inquire why you're standing outside her door rather than coming inside."

"We have no reasonable excuse," Eli said, extracting himself from Savannah's arms. "Have we permission to enter?"

"Of course, Your Highness." The woman stepped aside and held open the door.

Elegant as ever, Queen Salaina perched on a perfectly sized sofa strategically placed in the sitting room to greet anyone wishing an audience.

Her flowing black dress had been draped across her lap as if her lady had smoothed it that way prior to her opening the door. The queen was staged in much the same way as the room. There was no outward indication of the sobbing she'd displayed earlier in the day.

"Your Grace, may we have a moment of your time?" Eli bowed respectfully to his great-grandmother.

"I've been expecting you, my dear." Salaina raised her hand to invite them forward.

Eli leaned down to kiss her hand, and Savanna curtsied.

"Please have a seat." The queen gestured toward the low sofa to her right. "Might I be the first to offer you congratulations on your intent to be married."

"Thank you, Your Grace." Eli nodded.

"I already know why you have come," she said.

"You do?"

"I have known the two of you all your lives. You have come to play in my suite many times over the years."

"You do keep a nice collection of toys and books and puzzles up here." Eli glanced to the far corner where a little play area was provided for when her grandchildren and great-grandchildren came to see her. He and Kadin and Savannah loved to come play under the loving attention of the queen.

"How else do I expect to draw young people into my life?" She chuckled.

"Indeed." Eli laughed softly.

"Let me speak to Savannah a moment." Queen Salaina turned her attention to the beautiful woman holding Eli's hand.

"Would you like me to leave the room, Your Grace?" Eli leaned forward, prepared to rise if she requested.

"No, my dear, you need to hear this as well."

Eli settled into his seat again, suddenly anxious.

"Princess Savannah, you will serve as a princess for longer than I will be alive on this earth." Salaina's gaze penetrated the small space between her chaise and the sofa where Eli and Savannah sat. Eli loved the way the queen had already paired his bride's title with her name. "Shortly after my death, you will be asked to serve a much higher calling."

A chill ran down Eli's spine. What did she mean by that? He felt Savannah's shoulder rest against his as if she were leaning closer for safety.

"I have faith that you are prepared for that challenge, or at least you will be by then. Learn all you can. Your education will be the driving force in your ability to succeed."

Savannah nodded and gulped but didn't respond with words.

"Now, Your Highness." Salaina turned her attention back to Eli. "You also will be required to serve in ways you never dreamed necessary. I have already requested that the king appoint you as ambassador to the United Nations."

"You have?" Eli sat back against the sofa cushions as if someone had pushed him.

"But I must ask a favor." She leaned forward with a conspiratorial note of humor. "Allow His Majesty to pretend the idea was his."

Eli chuckled and nodded. The queen winked at Savannah.

"Always let the men think your ideas were theirs. They don't have much purpose in this life, and it makes them feel better about their inadequacies."

Savannah giggled and glanced up at Eli. He leaned toward her and kissed her lightly on her lips. He couldn't help himself.

"Now, for the most important item of business." The queen glanced over at her lady who was still hovering off to the side of the room. "Could you bring me the boxes I asked you to retrieve?"

"Of course, Your Grace." The young lady left the room briefly and returned with two velvet boxes, one nested upon the other. Eli knew exactly what items were inside.

"Princess, when you were too old to play with the toys in the corner, you continued to come visit me. I welcomed your attention and humored you with tea parties and dressing up in my dresses and makeup and jewelry. And when my eyes grew tired, you read me stories."

"You always had the newest releases long before the palace library." Savannah shrugged as if that explained her reason to visit.

"Every little drawer had to be opened. Every pair of shoes tried on. Every scarf, every necklace, every ring." Salaina lifted the smaller of the two velvet boxes. "There was always one particular ring that you had to try on each time you played dress-up."

"The chocolate diamond," Savannah and the queen said at the same time.

Eli's heart pounded. The queen already knew which ring Savannah wanted before he even had to ask. He leaned forward in awe as his great-grandmother ceremoniously opened the little velvet box to reveal the hundred-year-old chocolate pear-shaped diamond with the thick band that Savannah had requested.

Instead of handing the box directly to Savannah, the queen handed the box to Eli. "I trust you know what to do with this?"

Eli took the box with shaking hands and turned to Savannah, who had streams of tears down her cheeks. This was a moment he'd dreamed about for years and couldn't believe it was finally here.

Was he really going to propose to Savannah in front of his great-grandmother? Why not? She had loved them both all their lives, watched them grow up, and had gifted them the perfect diamond ring. He couldn't think of a more appropriate place to ask the most important question of his life.

Lowering himself to one knee beside the sofa, he rested the ring box on Savannah's knee and gazed up into the most beautiful, mysteriously colorful eyes he'd ever seen. Taking a deep breath and letting it out slowly, he spoke from his heart.

"My first love. My only love. I promise to cherish you forever and be yours forever. Will you marry me? and be mine forever?"

"Yes, forever and ever, yes!" Savannah almost bounced with excitement.

Eli carefully removed the priceless diamond ring and set the velvet box aside. He slipped the ring onto Savannah's finger just as the door to the queen's suite burst open.

"Did I miss it?" King Sayid leaned over and rested his hands on his knees. "Oh, thank goodness. I'm not too late. I hurried as soon as Deborah sent me that text."

"Your Majesty." Eli hurried to his feet and bowed to his great-grandfather.

"You know I wouldn't do this without you, darling," Queen Salaina said. "I would have found a way to stall them."

"S-stall us?" Eli glanced down at the ring he'd just placed on Savannah's hand. "I'm sorry. I didn't know you wanted me to wait."

"Oh phooey, that's merely a ring." The king waved his hand dismissively. Regaining his composure, Sayid stood to his full height and strode across the room to take his place beside his wife. In a rare show of affection, he leaned closer and kissed her with a love and devotion Eli hadn't realized they shared.

Eli had a hard time grasping how a man could love his wife yet allow another woman to steal him from her bed. Still, it wasn't his place to judge.

The king had chosen to marry Princess Tayma for reasons Eli may never understand.

"Would you like to do the honors, Your Majesty?" Salaina handed the larger velvet box to the king and folded her hands in her lap.

"Thank you, Your Grace." Sayid turned to Eli and Savannah. He took a calming breath and spoke directly to Savannah. "Princess, this has belonged to you for many years."

"This was the one item of jewelry I never let you try on." Salaina smiled knowingly.

King Sayid opened the velvet box to reveal an elegant and simple band of gold inlaid with dozens of jewels and intricate carvings. A crown befitting a princess.

Savannah gasped and held her hand to her chest. She turned to Eli with wonderment. "That's for me?"

"What's a coronation without a crown?" Eli asked softly.

"All I need is you," Savannah whispered.

"Sorry, we're a package deal. If you choose to marry me, you are choosing to become a princess. If you're having second thoughts..."

"Shut up, Eli, I've known all my life that I was destined to be your princess." She chuckled and leaned forward to kiss him. Eli had to force himself to break away. A few more hours to wait.

"Well, do you have a dress, my dear? Or would you like to raid my closet for that as well?" They all chuckled at the queen's jest.

"Yes, Grandmother, I have a dress." Savannah rose from the sofa and crossed the distance to reach for a hug from Salaina. Afterward, she threw her arms around the king as well. "Thank you both, so much."

"Hey, I have ulterior motives," the king said, holding Savannah at arm's length. "I expect great-great-grandbabies out of this union."

Eli coughed lightly and stood. "On that note, I think it's time to prepare ourselves for our wedding." He reached for Savannah's hand and helped her to her feet, pulling her into his arms.

"This evening we dine in honor of your new life together," Sayid said. "Thank you for helping lighten this day that started so dark. Here's to new beginnings."

"Thank you, Your Majesty." Eli leaned down to hug his great-grandparents, forgetting all conventions. In that moment, they were not the king and queen. They were family.

Chapter Thirty-Seven

A Higher Calling

"Congratulations, Your Highness." Mark spoke softly, coming up behind Eli where he stood at the base of the grand staircase, waiting for other family members to join him. Although not taking time to plan a formal wedding, they had spread the word throughout the palace that Prince Elmer and Princess Savannah would be signing marriage contracts that evening in the grand foyer. Many people were already milling about, standing in little groups talking amongst themselves.

"Your Highness?" Eli startled to see Mark and Alexander in full formal robes, similar to his own, having changed out of their black mourning attire into something more festive, more fitting for a wedding celebration. "I thought you had already left to return to America."

"When I heard you were planning to marry your princess this evening, I delayed my departure. I couldn't miss the chance to see my cousin voluntarily committing to a life of servitude."

"Very funny." Eli chuckled and accepted a hug from Mark. How quickly the two had become friends. "If a life of servitude means I get to sleep in the arms of my lovely Savannah, tie me in chains and shackle me to the bed."

"I hear you. Waiting for Hazel to be legally allowed to become my wife is torture."

"What's holding you back?" Eli creased his brow.

"She's only seventeen"—Mark glanced at his watch in gest—"for another two months."

"Shoot, that wouldn't stop anyone here in the kingdom. At seventeen she would have brought forth your first son by now."

"Well, she's an American, and perhaps a year from now, you and I both will be celebrating our first sons."

"I sincerely hope so, my cousin."

A movement caught their attention at the head of the grand staircase, and Captain Robert Dumont stepped into view in full uniform, wearing his usual stoic expression. On his arm was an elegant woman Eli hardly recognized.

Her raven curls had been tamed into cascades of waves draping across her shoulder like a cape. The top of her head was uncovered by a veil and ready for the crown that would be placed there in a few short moments. Her dark hair paired with her flawless copper skin, and hauntingly mesmerizing eyes contrasted with the white gown that rivaled any Saudi princesses' he'd ever seen. She must have commissioned the dress months or years ago to have something so elaborate available in less than two days' notice.

A tiny smile played on her lips when she noticed him standing at the base of the staircase. Eli straightened. Chills ran down his spine. The grand staircase curved around an open atrium, pulling light from the three-story cathedral ceiling, the color a soft pink from the setting sun.

The captain stepped down first and offered his hand to his daughter, always remaining one step below her as if to prevent her from falling should one of her feet slip on the marble staircase. When they reached the bottom step, Robert lifted Savannah's hand and placed it symbolically into Eli's. They met one another's eyes, man to man, and Eli promised without an exchange of words that he would care for and serve Robert's daughter. He nodded once and took a step back, leaving Savannah in Eli's protective embrace.

With very little pageantry but an abundance of solemnity, King Sayid recited the oaths Eli and Savannah were committing to one another by signing the marriage contract. They agreed verbally and then were invited to come forward and sign those sacred documents.

The first signature read *Savannah Shaia Dumont Sayid*. After the coronation, and for the remainder of her life, her signature would include her title and remove her surname. Eli stepped forward and with confident strokes wrote *Prince Elmer Sayid of Mada'in Saleh*. Below their signatures, were their two witnesses, *Captain Robert Dumont* and *Prince Omar Sayid of Mada'in Saleh*.

The final signature, and the one with the official power to complete the contract was *King Sayid of Mada'in Saleh*.

"Princess, are you prepared to accept the responsibilities, rights, and duties of your title?" the king asked.

"I am, Your Majesty." Savannah nodded reverently.

King Sayid lifted Savannah's commissioned crown from where it rested on the table and floated the gold band with inlaid jewels toward her. She curtsied and bowed her head with vulnerability, offering herself to accept the crown.

The gold band seemed to meld into the crown of her head, symbolically becoming one. Eli understood the feeling of wearing a crown, almost as if a weighted blanket were draped across his shoulders and the world was complete when that gold band was fitted to his head.

Savannah rose from the curtsy and gazed up into the eyes of her king. Tears spilled down her cheeks. King Sayid turned her gently toward Eli and his breath caught. No princess had ever been more elegant or regal.

Eli had a strange flash forward moment, envisioning Savannah wearing his great-grandmother's crown. A queen. A higher calling. Almost as quickly as the vision materialized, it vanished, and his princess once again stood in place of his queen.

The shock nearly caused Eli to stumble. He was not Crown. He would never be king, which meant Savannah would never be queen. That had to have been a manifestation of an alternate reality brought on by his great-grandmother's strange prediction.

With the wedding and coronation complete, Eli was invited to kiss the lovely woman before him, and he dutifully complied. He was glad they had not prepared a reception because he had no desire to be surrounded by friends and family a moment longer.

He remembered the words of the limousine driver suggesting the backseat of his limo was neither the time nor place for that particular activity. Now was the time, and he could hardly wait to carry his bride up that grand staircase.

Chapter Thirty-Eight

Keeper of the Crown

"In all the years I've been assisting you with the removal of your crown, I never dreamed I'd someday be instructing my sister on the proper procedure." Standing behind his prince, Kadin rested his hands upon Eli's shoulders and met his gaze in the mirror with an amused grin.

"Oh, come on, Kadin," Eli teased his advisor. "You've known we were in love since we were little children." Eli winked at Savannah, who was standing beside her brother.

"I certainly never connected these particular dots." Kadin stepped aside and invited Savannah to come forward. "Your Highness, you may do the honors—okay, that sounds really weird calling my little sister by that title."

"Little sister? I am older than you," Savannah teased. Eli could see in the mirror how Kadin was almost a head taller and understood the reference.

Eli had grown up loving Savannah's spunk and fire, her willingness to slide down the bannister of the grand staircase and run down the palace hallways, chasing a soccer ball because the desert heat discouraged outdoor play. He loved the early teen years when she had been awkward and chunky and insecure. He loved the way she blew them all away in math and science and could write poems and love stories and read historical fiction while acting out the voices and lifting her chin like a graceful lady at court in an English countryside.

And then she grew up and became a lady.

And then a princess.

The jeweled crown that rested on Savannah's ebony hair sparkled in the mirror. Her eyes sparkled with excitement. She was elegance personified. Sheer white lace and beading danced across her bosom, subtly concealing her graceful neck and full figure.

This new and exciting chapter beginning for the two of them was better than any romance novel ever written. The love story playing out in his mind would make their great-grandmother blush. He could never read this story out loud. And yet tonight, they could act out the scenes in vivid detail. There was no need for imagination. But there was the need to get her brother out of the room.

"Could the two of you hurry this process along?" Eli asked. "I'd really like to remove that white dress along with her crown, and I *know* you don't want to be here for that."

"I'm restraining myself from holding a knife to your throat for even suggesting such a thing with my sister," Kadin said in jest. "But seeing as how you have a marriage contract and the blessing of the monarch legally allowing that, I'll let the comment slide."

"I'm also legally allowed to order you from my suite," Eli teased right back. "Now get this crown off my head so I can kick you out of here and make love to my wife."

Kadin made a gagging noise and closed his eyes with a shudder. Turning to his sister, he offered instructions. "The removal of the crown should be performed with reverence. Stand behind your prince and meet his gaze in the mirror."

All three of them erased the lighthearted banter from their countenances as Savannah stood behind Eli and they almost seemed to breathe as one for just a moment.

"The velvet and mahogany box should already be resting on the dressing table, and open, before you begin the ceremony," Kadin said, nodding toward the table. "We've already prepared that. Now, with both hands, clasp the sides of his crown and lift the band in one sure movement and carry it over to rest in the box."

Barely breaking eye contact in the mirror, Savannah did as she'd been instructed and laid the symbolic adornment within the box and slowly closed the lid. Nothing in his life had ever felt more provocative. He'd had his crown placed and removed dozens of times since his coronation years ago, but this was a new experience.

"Now His Highness will remove your crown, princess," Kadin said, no longer teasing his sister but addressing royalty. And not just any royalty—the wife of his prince. Until Kadin married, his sister was now the most important woman in his life.

Eli rose from the settee, and Savannah took his place. Standing behind her and gazing into the mirror, Eli wanted to lower his face and kiss her. He restrained his desire for a moment more.

Kadin didn't need to use words to offer Eli instructions; he merely needed to wait.

Eli lifted the crown from Savannah's head and carefully placed the band of gold in the velvet box. Nesting the box on top of his, he placed them both in the leather bag where they would stay until needed again.

In another symbolic gesture, Eli lifted the leather bag from the dressing table and handed the bag to Kadin, who stepped over to the closet and tucked the bag into the safe that sat just inside the door. Without another word, Kadin bowed to his prince and princess and quietly left the room.

Chapter Thirty-Nine

Where Does Your Allegiance Lie?

"I have a confession, Your Highness," Kadin said after closing Eli's office door behind him. He strode confidently into the office and stood before his prince. "I've been acting as a double agent."

Eli was confused. Savannah had left to go back to college, and Eli was getting caught up with his advisor. Although he'd barely left his suite the past week, he thought this would be a quick briefing. He thought he could walk into his office and pick up with the work he'd left before his uncle passed away, before his cousin came to visit, and before he got married and flipped his life upside down. "W-what?"

"I've been learning things I would not have learned otherwise if you were by my side."

"I'm not following you," Eli said, leaning against his stately desk and crossing his arms. Eli's office was masculine and sophisticated rather than ostentatious like his brother's and the king's, or stuffy and sterile like his father's. He was comfortable here.

"There is talk among the staff and dignitaries." Kadin paced the sculptured carpet in front of the bookcases.

"About?" Eli raised his eyebrows, waiting for his advisor to explain.

"A murder plot." Kadin shrunk back and cowered slightly.

"Who?"

"Your father."

"My father wants to murder someone?" Eli felt his jaw go slack.

"No, Your Highness. Someone wants to murder your father."

Eli's stomach dropped. "Why would anyone want to murder my father?"

"To gain the Crown."

"Shouldn't they be plotting against Prince Marcos?"

"They don't recognize your haughty American cousin as Crown." Kadin held his hands in surrender when Eli narrowed his eyes at him. "Their words, not mine."

"Who all is involved?"

"Mainly your brother, Jared. But he has gained the favor of many of the staff and dignitaries, at least he thinks he has."

"Including yourself?" Eli felt sick.

"He *thinks* he has my allegiance. I have even promised to spy on my prince."

"You have promised to spy on *me?*" Eli choked on the words.

"Yes, Your Highness." Kadin held his chin high. "Until we discover what is really going on, we have to pretend that you don't know that I'm a double agent. We have to pretend that I'm spying on you and feeding bits of information to them."

"What information?"

"You need to learn all you can from your father and from the king, then I need to feed them just enough to make them think I'm double-crossing you."

"Or to make them think I'm in on the plan as well..."

"Hmm... interesting angle."

"You and I are going to have access to the world soon," Eli said. "We will be traveling to and from America and probably other countries in our new role as ambassador to the United Nations. Let them think we're bringing information back to my brother as part of the plot to kill our father. They will open up to you, and we will gain information even quicker."

"Good plan," Kadin said. "I'll quietly share the message that you're on board and that we'll be working together toward the ultimate goal. To assassinate your father, the Crown Prince."

Eli wanted to share with his advisor his allegiance to his cousin but hesitated. How much could he really trust Kadin? What if Kadin slipped and told someone that Eli was faithful to Prince Marcos and now recognized him as Crown? Eli made a snap decision to keep that information within his own thoughts. "So, what's the next step?"

"Meet with your father. Learn all you can. Let him think you want to learn how to run the kingdom. Let him think you need information in order to serve in the UN."

"I kind of do anyway, don't I? This would be believable because it's plausible." Eli gazed out the window at the sturdy date trees that grew in the courtyard. They represented one of the kingdom's primary exports. No better dates grew anywhere in the world than those in Madain Saleh. He turned back to Kadin. "What information would I share with you to feed to them?"

"I don't know. We'll have to think about that. For now, trust no one, and assume everyone in this palace is on board with the plot. Yet do not show any outward sign that you are, or that you know the plan exists. I'll continue my role as double agent, feeding them just enough information that they think I'm fully in their corner, and serving as your eyes and ears within the secret group."

"Kadin." Eli hesitated, wondering if he really needed to ask this question or if he should. "Where *does* your allegiance lie?"

"With *you*, my prince." There was no hesitation. Either he was a good liar or was indeed still loyal to Eli. For now.

"Are you sure?"

"Do you even have to ask?" Kadin's countenance changed. He was hurt by Eli's question.

"You said, 'trust no one.' Does that include my most trusted advisor?"

"Your Highness, I have been loyal to you my entire life. You're married to my sister. My heart is broken that you would even question my loyalty." Kadin's shoulders slouched. His eyebrows creased, and his gaze fell to the floor.

"Come here, my friend." Eli pulled Kadin into his arms, and Kadin rested his head on Eli's shoulder. "You are my brother. More so than my own flesh and blood."

"That's not saying much." Kadin chuckled, almost through tears. "Your brother's kind of a cockroach."

"True, but he may be our king someday, so we need to figure this out."

"You can trust me, my prince." Kadin pulled away and stepped back a foot, lifting his chin with confidence. "I am *your* servant, not theirs."

"No, you are my brother," Eli said. "We're in this together."

"Thank you, Your Highness."

Chapter Forty

Who Is in Charge?

"Your Highness, may I have a word?" Eli stopped in the entryway to his father's office, preferring to be invited rather than barge in unannounced.

"Come in, son." Prince Omar glanced up from the memo he'd been writing and removed the small, round reading glasses from his nose. His business suit was pristine, as if he were expecting a meeting with dignitaries, not working in his office. His dark, bushy hair showed a sprinkling of salt-and-pepper gray, lending an air of sophistication as he pushed into middle age. At forty-eight years old, he was living in his prime, honed, trained, ready to take over as leader of the kingdom should the king pass away. He was the epitome of a crown prince. If Eli worked strategically, he could learn a great deal from his father. "What can I do for you?"

"Have you spoken to the king about my new assignment?" Eli stepped tentatively into Omar's workspace. There was nothing comforting or inviting about this room. Where Eli had elegant bookshelves of leather-bound volumes, Omar had filing cabinets. The carpet was durable Berber when most of the palace had sculpted plush carpeting or marble. Omar's furniture had been shipped from an office supply catalog, and Eli commissioned his furniture from expert craftsmen who carved and polished and perfected each piece. Eli wanted his office to be an extension of his home. Omar's was designed for business. The business of running a small country.

"We're aware of your intended appointment to the UN." Ahmed answered the question intended for Prince Omar. Eli startled. He hadn't realized Ahmed was sitting in the corner at his desk. "That's quite a tall order the king has tasked you with." Tall was something Ahmed knew very well. He had several inches on most everyone in the palace. Lanky and towering when he stood in front of a person, Ahmed had shoulders that hunched forward as he looked down with beady eyes and a straight, thin nose.

"Ahmed, I am an adult, and a prince," Eli said, holding his chin in the air, refusing to allow his father's advisor to intimidate him. "I would suggest you start treating me as such."

"I've watched you grow from a little boy as I've served my charge, and I find it difficult to think of you as anything less than the pest who was always underfoot." Ahmed rose from his desk chair and crossed the room slowly sneering with disdain.

"My father is not your *charge*," Eli said with confidence. "He is your *prince*. And you are his advisor. You might want to remember your place."

"Gentlemen," Prince Omar interrupted. "I'd suggest you *both* remember your places. You are in my office and have requested an audience."

"My apologies, Your Highness." Eli bowed reverently to his father and noticed with disappointment that Ahmed stood in front of his desk and leaned back, defiant rather than submissive or apologetic.

"How can I be of assistance?" Omar asked. His pinched lips and creased brow showed his annoyance at having been interrupted. Eli decided he'd better make this meeting brief.

"I'd like your tutelage as I prepare to fulfill my responsibilities with the UN."

"Have a seat," Prince Omar said, sitting formally on a low sofa in front of his desk.

Eli mirrored his father's stance, sitting on the opposite sofa, leaning forward, intentionally engaged.

Ahmed, on the other hand, slouched into one of the adjacent sofas and spread his arms across the back, one leg crossed over his other knee, showing a complete disrespect toward the two members of the royal family present, including his own prince.

Omar ignored him and continued talking to Eli. "One of the most important things about serving on the UN Security Council is that you are not only there to represent the interests of our kingdom, but also to help maintain international peace and security. Every decision you make, every discussion you are involved in, should be within the framework of protecting human rights and upholding international laws."

"That sounds straightforward enough." Eli nodded.

Ahmed scoffed. "Do you think it's going to be easy?" He rolled his eyes and turned his head in mock superiority. "You've got a lot to learn."

"Such as patience in dealing with obnoxious individuals who disrespect their superiors?"

"Are you calling yourself my superior?" Ahmed sat forward in an offensive posture.

"That is up for debate," Eli said. "But your prince is most definitely your superior."

"I think that's enough for one day." Omar rose from his seat, effectively ending the conversation.

"Thank you for your advice, Your Highness," Eli said, rising quickly and bowing to his father.

"You're welcome, Your Highness." Omar stood and lifted his chin. "Perhaps you'd like to come have dinner with your mother and me this evening. I know the princess would enjoy your company."

"Thank you, Father, I'll do that." Before Eli could leave the room, he glared at Ahmed, sensing he'd won that showdown having been invited for an informal meeting at Prince Omar's dinner table.

Eli didn't address Ahmed as he strode from the room, wondering why his father kept that vile man around.

Chapter Forty-One

Positive Role Models

Eli greeted his mother with a hug, thankful the private dining room in his parents' suite was empty and the table set for three. Both princes had dismissed their advisors for the evening and the princess her lady. Other than the kitchen staff coming and going—who Eli knew he couldn't trust—there would be few interruptions. Eli didn't want to know state secrets; he just wanted to learn how to run the kingdom.

"My son, how is married life treating you?" Princess Nijah returned Eli's hug.

"I dare say I'd enjoy married life better if my bride hadn't returned to her university after our short-lived honeymoon." Eli chuckled.

"Unfortunate timing," the princess said with a knowing smirk, then pulled her face into a more serious expression. "But I'm proud of you for marrying her rather than allowing your lust for her to cause you to do something you'd both regret later."

Eli coughed at the uncomfortable shift in conversation. "Mother, I've wanted to marry Savannah for years. That had nothing to do with lust."

"You think that, but the truth is you could spend every waking moment together without signing marriage contracts, but the difference between her becoming your lover or your wife is that official document."

"I would *never* take a lover," Eli said through clenched teeth, offended she would even suggest such a thing.

"Exactly." His mother had won the argument. She leaned closer to offer one more thought in a controlled whisper. "You are possibly the only man in this royal family who insists on that level of purity."

"Even father?" Eli choked on his whispered question.

"I have no proof," she said, raising her eyebrows, still with a lowered voice. "But ours was an arranged marriage at a very young age. Whether or not love has grown over time, that is certainly not the reason we signed contracts. Your father is a cold man with little in the way of affection. Whether or not he's sharing his affection with another, he certainly isn't sharing it with me."

"I thought I was the only one who received a cold shoulder from father," Eli mumbled.

The door to his suite opened, and Prince Omar swept into the room, with a confident presence that demanded attention of those present. Still wearing his pristine business suit, he appeared ready to attend a council meeting or give a keynote address at a convention.

"Your Highness." Eli stepped away from his mother and bowed his head in respect to his father.

"Good evening, Your Highness," Omar said to Eli, barely acknowledging his wife. "Is the meal prepared?" He removed his suit coat and opened the coat closet near the door. After hanging up his coat, he loosened his tie and transitioned into a relaxed evening mode. Eli knew this was a façade. If called upon to leave again, a quick tightening of his collar and slipping his suit coat back over his shoulders and he'd be out the door with as much professionalism as when he left for his office that morning.

"We were merely waiting on you, Your Highness." Eli's mother didn't bother nodding to show respect. She was one of the few people in the kingdom not required to do so. "The staff will bring our food as soon as we are seated."

"Thank you, Your Highness." Omar almost seemed to notice the princess for the first time since arriving. "I trust you found the inclusion of our son a welcome addition to your evening."

"We were just catching up on life since his wedding and the unfortunate departure of Princess Savannah having returned to her university."

"Ah, yes, that was brave of you to let her out of your arms so soon after your marriage." Omar strode over to the table and held out a chair for his wife.

Princess Nijah was always dressed as if she'd returned that afternoon from a shopping trip. Her maroon slacks perfectly complemented the tiny flowers on her top, and the simple jewelry at her wrists and neck pulled the look together with sophistication. She accepted her husband's gesture and straightened her fashionable blouse over her lap as she pulled herself to the table.

"I'm thankful to report that your mother and I cannot relate to your plight," Omar continued, moving over to his own chair and sitting. "I don't think the princess and I have spent a single night apart in all thirty-one years since we signed marriage contracts. Am I remembering that correctly, Your Highness?" He creased his brow.

"Thirty-two years, actually, Your Highness," Nijah corrected Omar with humor carefully shrouded under respect. "And if I remember correctly, I spent several nights in the hospital when having your sons."

"I can't think of a more honorable reason to spend the night apart." Omar offered a rare smile, then leaned closer to his wife. "Although, you may not be aware, I technically never left the hospital the entire time you were there. I refused to leave your sons alone. The hospital staff had to drag a portable bed into the nursery. Most uncomfortable bed I've ever slept on, but worth the missed sleep."

"You never told me that you stayed at the hospital..." Nijah's jaw was slack, a hint of wonder in her countenance.

Omar pursed his lips and shrugged. "The subject never presented itself."

"I find it interesting that you both referred to your son's as belonging to the other," Eli said, leaning forward and resting his elbows on the table, intertwining his fingers.

"Out of respect to your mother," Omar said. "She is the person who had to endure the pain of delivery. I only participated in the more enjoyable aspects of bringing children into the world."

Nijah coughed, choking on the water she'd just swallowed. After the discussion she and Eli had prior to the prince walking in the door, Eli wasn't sure how to interpret his mother's reaction.

"You married quite young," Eli said. "I'm not sure I could have handled an adult relationship at the age of sixteen."

"That's why we sign marriage contracts for life, son. Perhaps by the time I die, I'll have figured out how to be a husband and father. Growing up without my own father, I didn't exactly have a good role model."

"What about your grandfather? Shouldn't the king have been a role model?" Eli asked.

"I lost respect for my grandfather the day he began sleeping with my mother." Omar's face was a mask lacking emotion. "I may not have been a good father or husband, but no one could ever accuse me of being unfaithful to my princess." He lifted his chin and pursed his lips.

"Perhaps you've been a better role model then you realize," Nijah said. "I was just complimenting *our* son for having married his princess before taking her to his bed."

"Indeed," Omar said with a nod, glancing first at his wife and then back toward his son. "That is commendable."

"Well, uh, thanks for being a good role model, Father." Eli had rarely thought of Omar that way. As his mother had described, he was cold and dismissive. Ahmed had described Eli earlier as being a pest who was always underfoot, but that hadn't been the case. Eli discovered at an early age that his father wanted little to do with him. This evening's was the longest conversation he could remember. Still, Eli couldn't think of a time when any rumor had presented an appearance of indiscretion.

"You're welcome, son." Omar leaned closer and stage-whispered. "Now I just need to figure out how to be a good husband."

"Maybe you and your princess could discuss the subject later this evening, you know, without one of your children in the room," Eli said, winking at his mother. "Shall we talk more about my United Nations assignment? I assume that's why you invited me to your table."

"That I did." Omar leaned back to allow one of the kitchen staff to set down a china bowl, which contained some exotic fish soup that smelled delicious. "You'll have to come to dinner frequently if I'm to instruct you how to run this kingdom."

"I welcome your tutelage, Father." Eli lifted his spoon and smiled. The upcoming months without his wife suddenly didn't look quite as bleak.

Chapter Forty-Two

Urgent Phone Calls

Your Highness, we need to talk. Can you call me? Savannah's text concerned Eli. He wondered if she'd heard whisperings about his involvement in the murder plot and secret society her brother had mentioned. He needed to set her mind at ease.

Let me discreetly excuse myself from my audience with the king, and I'll call you when I'm back in my suite. Eli paused and backspaced to change that last phrase. *... in our suite.* Eli sent his text message and rose from his seat, not waiting for permission.

"Your Majesty, I have urgent business I must attend to."

"What business, Your Highness?" Suspicion laced through King Sayid's question. Eli had been the one to request an audience and leaving in the middle of the meeting was insulting and disrespecting the king.

"Her Highness, Princess Savannah, would like a word with me." Eli held up his cell phone.

"There is nothing more important than your wife," the king said. "Go with haste, my son."

Eli loved it when his great-grandfather called him his son. He bowed briefly to the king and quickly left his office, hiding a tiny smile until he was no longer within view.

He hurried to his suite, excited to talk to Savannah. They usually spoke each evening, talking late into the night, and sometimes falling asleep while still on the line. Eli would awaken in the morning with a dead battery.

Having had a one-week honeymoon was not enough. He wanted her in his arms every night. Falling asleep with the phone to his ear, listening to her breathe as she drifted into her dreams satisfied an emotional need for closeness. Physically, he was aching for his wife.

Five weeks apart was five weeks too long. He'd been thinking of flying to Jerusalem for a long weekend, stealing her away from her dorms, taking her to a resort for a couple of days, and ordering room service.

When he was still a few doors down from his suite, he couldn't wait any longer and tapped his screen to start a video chat with Savannah. What he saw broke his heart.

Tears streamed down Savannah's cheeks, and she was choking back sobs. "Eli? I'm so glad to see you."

"Darling, what is the matter?"

"I can't stop throwing up. This is horrible."

"What did you eat? Do you need me to call for an ambulance?"

"I think I'm pregnant."

"Pregnant?" Eli stopped short, aware that if anyone was in this hallway or near the door to their room, he had just announced his wife's condition to the entire palace. "We're gonna have a baby? Are you sure?" He kept walking and reached into his pocket for his key when he arrived outside his suite.

"No, I'm not sure. I don't have a test. I just woke up this morning sick, and I'm lying here on the bathroom floor crying."

"Where is your roommate?"

"In class, I think."

"Can you ask her to buy a test on her way home?"

"Will you just bring me one when you come here?"

"How do you know I'm coming there?" Eli tried to hide a grin but failed.

"You're packing as we're talking. You're in your closet right now."

"Guilty. I'll be there in a few hours. I'll take you to the Villa and hold you in my arms for days until you feel better."

"You're going to hold me for nine months?"

"If my calculations are correct, we only have seven and a half months to go."

"Ugh... not again." Savannah tossed her phone aside and all Eli could hear was her retching into the toilet. He almost gagged from the sound. How was he going to handle holding her head while sitting next to her? In sickness and in health as the old saying goes. She was bringing him an heir. How could he complain? Finally, she picked her phone back up. "You did this to me."

"I'd apologize, but you'd know I'd be lying, seeing as how I can't wait to become a father," Eli said. "I am sorry you're sick though. I'm going to get off the phone now so I can call for a helicopter to take me to the airport, and order the jet to get fueled, and make all the other arrangements. Try to get a little rest, okay?"

"Okay... I can't wait to see you."

"You too. I love you."

"I'll love you more when I'm holding your son in my arms and he's no longer gagging me every ten minutes."

"See you in a few hours."

Eli disconnected the call and selected the second name on his contact list.

"Your Highness?" Kadin answered. "How can I be of service?"

"Call for a helicopter, order the private jet to be waiting on the tarmac, make arrangements for a few week's stay at the Villa Ba'Moshava, and send someone to the market for a pregnancy test. Oh, and get packed. We're going to visit your sister in Jerusalem."

"Whoo hoo!" Kadin called out in excitement. "I'm gonna be an uncle!"

Eli had to pull the phone away from his ear.

"I'll get right on that, Your Highness." Kadin disconnected the call before Eli could even say goodbye.

Eli opened a search window and found a deli near Savannah's college that offered delivery service. He tapped his screen to make the international call. "Greetings, do you have a vegetable soup you could deliver to my wife's dorm room? Along with some saltine crackers and sparkling water?"

By the time Eli provided instructions for delivery, and his credit card information, his suitcase was packed, and he was locking his suite. That night he would fall asleep without a phone to his ear.

Chapter Forty-Three

Take Me Home

"Thank you for rescuing me." The vulnerability in Savannah's eyes as she gazed up at Eli from the crook of his arm was endearing. "Amazing how much better a person can feel when they're eating right and getting enough sleep."

The Villa Ba'Moshava was the perfect escape for the two of them. Kadin dutifully tucked himself in the suite down the hall and waited for days while Eli nursed his wife back to health. Room service and housekeeping kept them wanting for nothing.

Whether Eli was holding Savannah as she curled on the floor of the bathroom or spoon-feeding her soup and eventually heavier foods, he never complained. There was nothing he wanted more in his life than to be by her side in whatever way she needed him.

"I won't pressure you to explain to me why you were letting your health suffer so much, but if you ever want to talk, I'm here."

"I promised you I'd finish school before coming home to live in the kingdom," she said. "And I promised the queen." Her multicolored eyes shone from within her copper skin, finally sparkling with energy after days of furrowed brows and a dull pallor.

"Finishing school can be done over time and through the computer," Eli said, leaning down to place a kiss on the end of her nose. "And learning is a lifelong endeavor, not a four-year degree."

"Can I come home?" Savannah asked, as if he'd ever deny her. "I want to lie by your side every night, and I want my mom to come visit me without having to take an airplane."

"She will simply walk down the hall of the palace." Eli chuckled.

"I want to know everything that's happening in the kingdom. I want to serve by your side."

"I want you by my side," Eli whispered. "Forever."

"Will you make love to me?"

"What? Right now? Aren't you sick?" Under normal circumstances, Eli would have jumped at the chance, but he worried he would hurt her or the baby.

"Your Highness, people have sex during pregnancy all the time." She was either chastising him or laughing at him. He wasn't sure which.

"You threw up two hours ago..."

"I'll brush my teeth."

"That's not what I meant. I mean, yeah, that probably would be a good idea, but I'm more worried about hurting you."

"I've kept down lunch quite well, don't you think?"

"You tell me."

"I feel fine. I could get up and do yoga right now. I'm just taking advantage of the fact that you're here and holding me and I have no desire to get out of bed right now."

"I have no desire to get out of bed either," Eli admitted, his voice lowering.

"So... is that a yes?"

"You're sure I won't hurt you or the baby?" His stomach fluttered with a combination of nervousness and anticipation.

"I promise."

"Okay, if you can handle walking to and from the bathroom, under the condition that you promised you'd brush your teeth, then I will say yes."

She giggled but did as he suggested and returned to bed with a new glow and excitement. As much as he wanted her to finish school, he was ready to have her home and in his arms.

The breeze blowing in from the balcony cooled the afternoon mugginess, and the billowing comforters and pillows offered a relaxing respite from the frustrations of life, the secret meetings and murder plots back at the palace, and the illness that ravaged her body and announced the awakening of life.

Eli was able to forget everything when wrapped in Savannah's arms. They spent the afternoon reuniting after five weeks apart. Never again, he vowed. No matter where he went, he wanted her with him, every day, every night, for as long as he was alive.

Chapter Forty-Four

Secrets to Keep

"There are things I need to tell you." Eli twirled a lock of Savannah's ebony hair around one finger as he lay in bed, the approaching dusk casting shadows across the hotel room. The open balcony offered fresh air and the sounds of the city outside.

Savannah sat up and rolled onto her belly, meeting his gaze in the waning light. He tucked the hand he'd been using to play with her hair behind his head and searched her eyes, wondering if she would still feel safe coming home after what he had to tell her.

"Your brother and I are involved in an underground secret society plotting to murder my father."

"What?" She pulled away with disgust. "Why would you want to murder your father? Why would you want to murder anyone?"

"We *don't* want to murder anyone," Eli explained. "We just have to play our part, letting them *think* we're on board with the plan."

"Whose plan?" Her suspicion hadn't diminished.

"We think the primary instigator is my brother, Jared, but there are more moving parts, and we need to investigate."

"Your brother wants to murder your father? Why?"

"He wants his crown," Eli said, matter of fact.

"Isn't Prince Marcos the Crown?" Savannah's question hung in the air, and Eli hesitated.

"Depends on who you talk to."

"I'm talking to *you*. Who do *you* think is Crown?" Her husky voice led him to believe he could be honest with her. If Eli could be honest with anyone in the world, his wife needed to be that person.

"Mark," Eli's whisper was apprehensive.

"I agree."

"You do?" Eli turned to Savannah, with relief and excitement.

"Without hesitation," she said.

"Me too!" Eli let out a relieved breath. "I was afraid to tell you."

"Why?"

"I don't know. I haven't told your brother."

"Wow, your most trusted advisor? I never thought I'd see the day when you'd hide anything from Kadin."

"He's too entrenched in the underground society. It's not that I don't trust him; I just don't want to risk him slipping and telling someone else."

"Do you guys attend some sort of secret meetings or something?"

"I don't," Eli said. "I'm not sure whom he talks to, who the organizers are, who's in charge."

"Does he share details with you?"

"A few. But it's best if I know as little as possible," Eli said. "We plan to feed bits of information back to the group based on my meetings with my father and the king. The longer we can stave off their designs, the more likely we can stop the crime."

"What about you being implicated as part of the group plotting the murder?"

"I've thought of that. That's one of the reasons I want as little involvement as possible. I want to trust your brother, I really do. But the more involved he becomes, the more I fear he'll be swayed by their cunning words."

"I'll help keep an eye on Kadin," Savannah promised. "Now, can we order room service? We burned a million calories this afternoon, and I'm starving. I'm eating for two now, remember?" Savannah rolled over and rested her hand on her abdomen. All her natural curves and mounds and valleys were still in the same places they were five and a half weeks ago when he'd seen them for the first time.

Eli rested his hand on top of hers, sealing a connection between his wife and their baby. Never had he felt this much peace and contentment.

He closed his eyes and took a deep breath, filling his lungs with the heavenly fragrance surrounding him. A combination of essential oils, incense burning on the bedside table, pheromones and a hint of perspiration leftover from an afternoon of lovemaking mixed with wafting aromas of meals cooking at the nearby restaurants and the light breeze of spring.

He leaned forward to kiss Savannah's lips one more time, then pulled away and smiled down at his wife. "Yes, let's order room service."

Chapter Forty-Five

Come to America

"**W**ould you kindly join me in America, Your Highness?" Prince Marcos Sayid asked over an international phone line.

Eli rose from his seat on the sofa in the king's office to answer Mark's call. He suspected there was only one reason Mark would invite him to the United States. "Are you planning a wedding by any chance?"

"Already planned," Mark corrected him. "We're practically eloping we pulled things together so quickly. It's amazing the doors you can open when the daughter of a senator wants to marry a prince."

Eli laughed heartily along with Mark, keeping his back to the group of men waiting for him, suspecting they could hear everything he said. "When's the big day?"

"July fifteenth, if all goes according to plan."

"Geesh, you don't mess around." Eli stared out the window at the dry landscape beyond the edge of the city. The rocky terrain of the desert burned, waves of heat rising like an endless mirage, with his little kingdom oasis tucked in the center.

"Look who's talking, Mister I'm-getting-married-tomorrow."

"We would have gotten married the day she came home from Jerusalem if the choice had been Savannah's."

"Speaking of, how is your lovely bride?"

"Pregnant," Eli said. He had to pull the phone away from his ear because Mark whooped so loud it reminded Eli of the day he'd told Kadin.

"Geesh, who's messing around now?" Mark teased.

"We are," Eli said. "Frequently." Eli's eyes glazed over as he thought of their nights together with fondness. And afternoons. Mornings weren't quite as much fun. His mind floated back to earth as he remembered the phone still to his ear.

"Jealous," Mark said.

"Worth waiting for."

"Good answer," Mark said. "Hey, how's the king doing? Do you think he'd be up for a trip across the Atlantic? I'd love to have him officiate at our wedding."

"You can ask him yourself," Eli said, turning around and striding back to the group of men sitting around the low sofas in his great-grandfather's ostentatious office. He lowered himself to the sofa again. "He's sitting right next to me. I'll put you on speakerphone."

Eli touched the screen of his phone.

"Okay, Your Highness, you are now officially in a meeting with three members of the royal family and our advisors, since we were just convening when your name showed up on my caller ID."

King Sayid leaned close to the phone. "Greetings, Your Highness."

"Greetings, Your Majesty," Mark answered. "Who else is in the room?"

"Hello, Your Highness, this is Prince Omar. My advisor, Ahmed, my son's advisor, Kadin, and the king's advisor, Damian, are also in attendance."

"Well, gentlemen," Mark said. "I'd like to extend an invitation to visit Washington D.C. and meet Senator Alejandro Cohen as he graciously hands his daughter into my care for safekeeping till death do us part."

There was a general mayhem of congratulations as everyone in the room spoke at once. Eli waited and then reminded Mark, "Did you have something you wanted to ask the king?"

"Oh, yes, thank you for reminding me. Your Majesty, if you're feeling up to an international expedition, we'd be honored to have you officiate at our wedding."

"I think I might be able to fit that into my schedule." King Sayid winked at Eli. "Can you arrange a meeting with your president while I'm there?"

"P-president?" Mark stuttered. "As in president of the United States?"

"That is where you live, isn't it?" Sayid creased his brows. "You didn't move back to Mexico did you?"

"No, Your Majesty, we're here in the United States, very close to the capital actually. It's just that most people don't request a meeting with the president."

"Most people are not a king..." Sayid shrugged as if Mark could see him through the phone.

"Good point. I'll ask Senator Cohen if he can help make the arrangements."

"Very good. I'll look forward to visiting." The king nodded his finality.

"Let me know how many people will be coming and the status of sleeping arrangements," Mark said. "I want to make sure I have enough hotel suites reserved."

"We'll get back with you in a few days, Your Highness," Eli said.

"Thank you, Your Highness. I'll look forward to hearing from you."

Eli touched the screen of his phone to end the call and shrugged at his father, great-grandfather, and their three advisors. "Who wants to fly with me to America?"

Chapter Forty-Six

International Relations

A merican weddings were nothing like weddings in Madain Saleh. Eli thought he was attending a royal reception but with church pews and flowers everywhere and ribbons and pageantry. When Mark said he'd managed to pull things together quickly, Eli was expecting a few dozen people in a small room with a champagne toast and a cake.

There were hundreds of people in attendance. Women dressed in pastel colors, and men with sports coats that they draped over the backs of their chairs as soon as they entered the ballroom. Eli half expected Zaffa drummers, Egyptian dancers, and Dabke. Instead, there was a small orchestra in the corner, playing soft dinner music.

Several distinct groups of people became evident. There were Senator Alejandro Cohen's friends from the United States democratically elected congress; the royal family from the kingdom of Madain Saleh; the elite Cohen family members who'd flown up from Mexico, practically royalty in their own right; and then the college-aged and teenaged crowd—to be expected when the bride graduated high school weeks prior and the groom was a university student. Everyone attempted intermingling but would fall back into their groups after a little while.

The wedding itself was a mixture of cultures, including a religious prayer or blessing offered by one of the elder Cohen family members from Mexico, cliché American wedding vows, and, of course, a coronation to crown Princess Hazel as Mark's bride. That was a part of the ceremony Eli could relate to. He wrapped his arm around Savannah and leaned over to kiss the top of her head.

There were no formal contracts signed as there would have been in the kingdom, but they referred to a marriage license that sounded like a similar document. Eli had a lot to learn about customs outside of Madain Saleh if he was going to serve on the UN Security Council.

Mark was pulled in a million directions and yet handled each interruption with grace and dignity. Eli was reminded again how much he supported his cousin eventually taking over as king. He seemed to fit in and complement each separate group as if he already belonged with them even though they didn't all belong with each other.

Hazel was every bit as playful and eccentric as Mark had described. Mature for her eighteen years, she handled the spotlight on Mark's arm as if these events were normal. Perhaps they were normal in her world. Perhaps growing up as the daughter of a senator, she'd had to endure fancy parties and smiling for cameras.

From his standpoint, seated at one of the round tables, Eli took inventory of the royal family. They were easy to spot because most were wearing crowns and formal robes.

The king and queen seemed enthralled with the legendary and dignified Nicholas Cohen, who was apparently Hazel's grandfather and had been best friends with the late Prince Marcos Sayid.

Jared led his daughter, Princess Nimrah, around to introduce her to anyone and everyone he thought she needed to know. His wife, Princess Linah, was left seated at the table beside a woman Eli thought was one of Jared's lovers. Neither of them looked comfortable, Linah with her crown and expensive diamond ring, the other woman with a smug expression and eyes that rarely strayed from Jared.

Prince Omar and Princess Nijah were on the dancefloor, cheek to cheek, with soft smiles and renewed affection. Eli couldn't help feeling a little prideful for having pushed his parents closer together. They deserved some happiness.

Mark's father, Prince Benjamin Sayid, had flown up from Mexico, along with his wife, Princess Nisha, although neither of them were wearing crowns. They fit in better with the Cohen family than the Sayid family.

"Oh, little Ethan just kicked me," Savannah said out of the blue, distracting Eli from his contemplative state. "Put your hand right here."

Eli did as his wife suggested, resting his hand on her rounded belly. A little nudge bumped against him and Eli startled. "Fascinating." Another member of the royal family to add to the group.

He smiled and leaned over to kiss Savannah. Her second trimester had seen welcome improvements from the early days of illness, and she was finally enjoying being pregnant. Eli was looking forward to becoming a dad.

What kind of world would Ethan witness? Murder plots against the royal family, a contested crown, a kingdom surrounded by desert that is holding on to the last-ditch effort of its monarchy. Poor Ethan might someday shoulder the responsibility of running the kingdom, depending on who was chosen as the next king.

Eli glanced over again to where King Sayid laughed heartily with Nicholas Cohen and hoped his great-grandfather held on to this life as long as he could.

Chapter Forty-Seven

Interesting Developments

"**A**hmed is in on the plan," Kadin announced, barging into the sitting room of Eli and Savannah's suite. He immediately halted his entrance and lifted his hand to his face, shielding his eyes. "Oh my gosh, are you guys fully dressed?"

"Yes, we're dressed." Savannah yanked her shirt back down, concealing her midriff from view.

"Hey, I was not finished," Eli said, lifting her shirt again. "I'm trying to have a conversation with my son here." He and Savannah were lying together on the sofa, enjoying the way baby Ethan kicked every time Eli poked him in various locations around her belly. Every time Eli pressed against the taut skin, Ethan would kick, almost as if they were communicating.

"I can come back." Kadin inched toward the door.

"Stay, you're fine." Eli barely looked up. "You've seen your sister in a swimsuit before, right? She's not showing anything you wouldn't see on the beach."

"Yes, well, she's never been that *big* while wearing a swimsuit," Kadin said. He closed the outer door to the suite and hesitantly crept closer to the opposite sofa with wide eyes.

"Hey, it's not like I'm fat or something," Savannah said. "I'm eight and a half months pregnant. That's all baby." She patted the other side of her belly.

"I still can't believe my little sister is going to be a mom," Kadin said, a tone of awe in his voice.

"And I can't believe after being on this earth for twenty-two years you haven't figured out yet that I'm your *older* sister, not younger."

"I didn't call you younger," Kadin corrected her. "I called you little."

"Right after you called me big, as in too big for a swimsuit."

"You guys fight like brother and sister," Eli said with mock scolding. "Now tell me what you learned about Ahmed?"

"He's involved in the plot to murder your father."

"His own prince?" Eli found that hard to believe. As much as Eli hated the guy, Ahmed was faithful to his prince. He wouldn't be plotting against him.

"I also learned that Ahmed convinced them to wait until the king dies before killing Omar because *none* of them will be crowned as long as the king is still alive."

"That could be years." Eli felt hope for the first time since he'd heard the rumors.

"They also don't want to bring international attention to our little kingdom so soon after the Sayid family joined the Cohen family."

"Ah, that is an interesting development, isn't it?" Eli sat up halfway. "The Cohens and Sayids have been best friends until now. A marriage contract takes that bond up a notch, doesn't it? I think because they're halfway around the world, people forget how much power the Cohen's still have in Mexico."

"And the United States Senate," Kadin pointed out.

"And Jerusalem," Savannah added. "They may have sold off most of their holdings when they fled to Dubai, but they still throw around a lot of money for historical restorations and major donations to charities."

"Yeah, Jared would be stupid to stir that pot," Eli said. He lifted Savannah to a seated position, finally tucking her shirt down over her belly. "Let's hope all their plans fizzle between now and when the king dies. I honestly don't want to see my father killed. I rather like the man."

"He's really changed in the past few months, hasn't he?" Kadin said.

"I think he's excited to welcome a new grandchild." Savannah once again rubbed her belly.

"I know I'm excited to be an uncle," Kadin said with a smile.

"And I'm excited to be a dad." Eli leaned over and kissed Savannah lightly on her lips. He gazed into her mysteriously colorful eyes, then pulled his focus to her brother. "Although, I fear we're bringing our child into a potential warzone. There's more to this murder plot than just the Crown. I have a suspicion that this secret underground society will be the undoing of our tiny kingdom."

"For all of our sakes," Kadin said. "I hope you're wrong."

Chapter Forty-Eight

Next in Line

Eli snapped one more photograph and sent the picture by text message to his American cousin. *Please welcome Prince Ethan Sayid, born October 15th at 9:52 a.m.*

A few minutes later, a notification popped up with a text from Mark. The photo he sent was a grainy black-and-white ultrasound. *Please welcome Prince Mateo Sayid scheduled to be born April 15th of next year.*

"Yes!" Eli laughed out loud, startling Savannah where she was resting with baby Ethan in her arms, the heavy hospital blankets draped over her lap. He held the phone up to show her the ultrasound. "Mark and Hazel are going to have a baby."

"Ah, look how cute he is, the little peanut." Savannah leaned closer to get a better look. "Our little Ethan is cuter."

"And bigger and, ya know, breathing oxygen," Eli pointed out. "And no longer injuring my wife."

"That was very nice of Ethan to stop kicking and gagging me," Savannah said. "I hope his behavior inside my body is not an indicator of how he'll behave as a little boy."

"How quaint," a sadistic voice preceded Princess Nimrah as she stepped in the doorway of Savannah's hospital room. "Aren't you the happy little family."

Eli stood and maneuvered protectively between Nimrah and Savannah. No way was he letting the conniving teenage princess near his new baby prince. "What are you doing here, Your Highness?" Eli nearly choked on his words, knowing he'd hear from his older brother if he didn't address his spoiled daughter by her title.

"Can't I pay a social visit to meet my new baby cousin?" she asked in a sugary sweet voice. Her skinny jeans and high-heeled shoes revealed her immaturity in the way she was trying to dress like an adult. In reality, she looked like a little girl who had raided her mother's closet and cosmetics drawer.

"No... that's not in your nature. What do you really want?" Eli asked.

"What did you name the little prince?" Nimrah tried to step around Eli to get a closer look, a complete lack of tenderness in her countenance.

When Eli shifted to keep her several feet away from the bed, she took a step back and crossed her arms, glaring up at him. She had nerve coming here under the pretense of meeting her cousin. "Out with it. What are you doing here?"

"I wanted to *remind* you that just because your baby is a boy doesn't change the fact that I was born first and am still next in line." She continued to insist that the kingdom was ready for the first crown princess. At seventeen, she was technically old enough to have a husband chosen for her. If she had been born a boy and was the designated next in line, they would have already planned a wedding by now.

"We don't need a reminder," Eli said through clenched teeth. "We are aware of your intentions."

"Good, just so we have that straight." Nimrah started to turn to walk out the door but hesitated and twisted back around to offer one last threat. "As a precaution, you might want to train my little cousin to sleep with one eye opened." Princess Nimrah flipped her high ponytail off her shoulder and strode from the room.

Eli felt a chill run down his spine.

Chapter Forty-Nine

This Was Her Idea

"They're getting married!" Kadin barged in the door of Eli's suite, out of breath. He must have run from whatever meeting he'd attended. He leaned forward, resting his hands on his knees.

"Who is getting married?" Eli had barely left his suite in months because all he wanted was to spend time with baby Ethan and Savannah. He came down to his office every day to get a few things done but always returned quickly with a longing to be there for every little milestone. He knew his idyllic world would be shaken soon because he was planning his first trip to New York City to meet with the UN Security Council. But that was weeks away.

"Jared is involved in some twisted plot to marry off his daughter, Princess Nimrah."

"Okay... she's of marrying age," Eli said. "What's the problem?"

"She's marrying Ahmed." Kadin sneered.

"But... but he's old enough to be her grandfather." Eli's stomach churned with disgust. He strode to the door of the suite, glanced both ways down the palace hallways to ensure they were alone, then closed and bolted the door.

"Do you believe me now that he's involved in the plot to murder your father?"

"I never doubted you." Eli felt the lie as it fell from his lips. "Okay, maybe a little. How does the princess feel about this?"

"One, she doesn't have a choice. If her father wants to give her to some creepy old man as a bride, she will do as he says." Kadin stood to his full height, finally gaining control of his breathing. "But here's the strange part. The marriage was her idea."

"Why?" Eli shuddered at the thought of a seventeen-year-old wanting to marry a man as old as Ahmed.

"She wants to help her father get closer to Prince Omar in order to take down the monarchy. What better way than to go through his advisor."

"And has Ahmed agreed to go along with this plan?"

Kadin snorted. "Who wouldn't? Have you looked at the princess lately? That girl is officially a woman, if you know what I mean."

Eli folded his arms across his chest and scowled. "Maybe I should start attending these meetings with you."

"Your Highness, I would appreciate that. I can't be this go-between. I forget what information I'm supposed to know and what I'm not supposed to know and who I'm supposed to tell what. You're the prince, not me."

This was exactly why Eli had never shared his opinions about Mark with his advisor. He hated keeping secrets from the man who was supposed to be his confidant, but if Ahmed could so easily turn on Omar, who's to say Kadin might not turn on Eli.

"When's the next meeting?" Eli's low voice was almost a growl.

Chapter Fifty

Pledge Your Allegiance

"I had a difficult time maintaining composure during our council meeting this afternoon," Eli muttered under his breath, his voice low enough he was sure no one else could hear.

"What a coincidence," Ahmed answered, his voice just as low. "Neither could I."

They stood together in a dark alcove to the back of the cramped meeting room deep in the underground bunker of the palace. The oppressive desert heat from the surface was replaced by a damp chill from standing water.

Brilliant location for a secret meeting. No self-respecting member of the royal family would slink this far.

Yet, here he stood next to Prince Omar's advisor, watching his brother, Prince Jared, relay a passionate speech about the outdated views of the monarchy and the importance of changing the Crown before the king dies.

"I'm not sure what disgusts me more about this," Eli grumbled. "Her desire to marry you, his willingness to go along with the plan, or your sadistic desires to take a little girl as your bride."

"The princess is old enough to choose a husband." Ahmed's whisper made Eli's skin crawl. The salt-and-pepper gray in Ahmed's thinning hair and the fine lines creasing his forehead were a reminder that the princess should be choosing someone her own age.

"What's the matter? Been in my grandmother's bed too long? Needing younger stimulation? You're a sick man."

"And yet the ladies fall at my feet." Ahmed chuckled.

Princess Nimrah's beauty was unmatched in the kingdom. She could snap her fingers and have any man she wanted. Why she wanted Ahmed was a mystery. "There's more to this story, and I intend to get to the bottom of it," Eli said.

"I highly doubt you'll succeed." Ahmed didn't turn to Eli, but his menacing words sent chills down Eli's spine. "Three years from now, you'll look back in wonderment at what I've accomplished."

"What *you've* accomplished? I thought this was Jared's plan."

"Do you honestly think your brother is smart enough to come up with this elaborate scheme on his own?"

Definitely not, but Eli didn't vocalize his agreement, just grunted and listened with more interest to the words falling from Prince Jared's mouth.

"Which side of history will you be on?" Jared paced back and forth across the front of the meeting room, calling out to his enraptured audience. "Who will you follow into the next millennium? Who will be your leader?"

He stopped and pointed to a man in the front row, one of the palace guards. Eli wondered whether his father-in-law, Captain Dumont, was aware his guards were down here.

"Will you hold onto the idealistic dreams of an old man as he passes the mantle to another old man? Or will you embrace the new way of organizing this kingdom?"

Jared looked up again, and his gaze swept the audience. He raised his fist in a powerful gesture of solidarity.

"*We* are the young and the strong. We are the ones who have seen what the future holds and can grasp that future. Who here is ready, *right now*, to pledge their allegiance to *me* as your king? Who is ready to stand beside me as we take down the old ways and bring in the new?"

The men in the room stood and cheered as one voice. Eli turned on his heel and exited through the back tunnel, not willing to stomach one more moment. As he escaped into the dark, he wondered where Kadin was hiding within that audience, and more importantly, to whom he was pledging his allegiance.

Chapter Fifty-One

A Little Prince

*M*y heart is broken, my cousin, Mark's text read. *I'm texting from the hospital where sadly my little Prince Mateo was stillborn this morning.*

I'm so sorry, Your Highness, Eli texted back. *Is Hazel okay?*

She's had better days. Physically, she'll be fine. Emotionally... we'll see. The doctor said we should get pregnant again in a few months and that will help her fill the emptiness in her heart. After experiencing twelve hours of grueling labor, during which she repeatedly blamed me for her condition and warned me never to touch her again for as long as we are married, I'm not so sure she'll let me get her pregnant again.

Eli felt heartbroken for his cousin.

How are wedding plans coming along? Mark asked. *Your skin still crawling?*

Princess Nimrah is the bride from Hades, Eli said. Although Eli still couldn't stand looking at Ahmed, at least the murder threats were on the back burner while the royal family prepared for the wedding. There was an underlying thread of tension and suspicion whenever Jared or Ahmed was near. But when the princess walked in the room, they both jumped into action to fulfil every one of her commands.

Eli continued his text to Mark. *We never should have allowed her to see what American weddings are like. Now she wants something bigger and better. She's insisting on inviting royalty and dignitaries from as far away as China and India. Oh, and some princess in Hawaii. Do they even have a princess in Hawaii?*

Probably from the Polynesian royal family, Mark answered. *Have they set a date?*

Almost exactly two years from right now, Eli said. *May first.*

I'll be sure to add that to my calendar so I can come wish my little cousin the best of luck in her sham of a marriage.

I wonder if my grandmother will be jealous, Eli texted.

Okay, I just lost my appetite.

Eli threw his head back in laughter. *Are you still planning to meet me for lunch in NYC next month when I come from the UN Security Council meeting?*

Of course.

Sorry again, man, seriously, Eli texted. *Give Hazel a hug from me.*

Thanks, Your Highness, Mark said. *See you in about four weeks. Give that little Prince Ethan a hug for me.*

Will do, Your Highness. See you next month. Eli tucked his cell phone back into the pocket of his sport coat and got back to work.

Chapter Fifty-Two

Betrayal

P rince Marcos did not return to the kingdom for Princess Nimrah's wedding because Hazel was newly pregnant again—for the fifth time. They'd waited the minimum six weeks after Prince Mateo's stillbirth to get pregnant for a little girl. Sadly, Princess Avellana only lived through eight months of gestation. Hazel lovingly announced that her family in heaven would be much bigger than her family on earth, waited another six weeks and thankfully hadn't miscarried again.

Prince Aaron was six weeks old when she conceived Prince Owen, and six weeks after Owen was born, she was pregnant again. Mark refused to leave Hazel with two babies and morning sickness just to attend the wedding of his spoiled second cousin, royalty or not.

The wedding was perfect. Princess Nimrah was elegant. Guests traveled from all over the globe. Champagne flowed. Delicacies were prepared and served in abundance.

And the murder was planned for that evening.

No one knew who the murderer was... except everyone knew who the murderer was.

Plans had been set in place years prior. Meetings had been held. Troops rallied. Allegiances bought and sold. But no matter how many times Eli tried to warn his father, Prince Omar refused to be concerned.

Prince Jared placed Princess Nimrah's hand in Ahmed's in a time-honored tradition of a father giving his daughter to be married. The smirk he gave Ahmed was almost as telling as the gift. Eli still couldn't understand what Prince Jared stood to gain from the arrangement. There had to be some backroom deal he didn't know about.

Ahmed bowed before King Sayid as a crown was placed atop his head and his coronation was complete. He posed for countless photos beside his nineteen-year-old bride, his new father-in-law, who was fifteen years his junior, and his prince, Omar, the man he planned to murder. The man who had been his best friend almost as long as Eli had been alive.

Eli was helpless. He'd warned his father repeatedly, but Prince Omar refused to have his advisor arrested. Omar insisted that Ahmed would never hurt him, regardless of the evidence against him.

That night, Omar escorted his wife, Princess Nijah, to their suite, with a confident swagger, and Eli's heart ached, wanting to protect his parents.

The following morning, nothing had changed. The only people who didn't come to brunch were the bride and groom, as would be expected.

There was an eerie calm throughout the palace, eyebrows raised, shoulders shrugged, no one wanted to ask the question on everyone's minds. What happened to the plan?

Eli didn't want to complain. His father, after all, was still alive, and all was normal in the kingdom. The palace staff gradually returned the throne room and reception hall back to their normal splendor and elegance, showing no signs of a royal wedding. Guests who had been visiting gradually left to return to their own lands, international relations strengthened.

Business meetings resumed, imports and exports discussed, water shortages remedied, skirmishes between tribal communities resolved. Trips throughout the Middle East as well as to Europe, Mexico, and the United States were planned.

Mark and Eli had made several appearances together over the previous two years as Eli traveled the world representing Madain Saleh on the UN Security Council. The world knew Crown Prince Marcos Sayid was living in America to be with his wife and that was an acceptable excuse.

The king and Prince Omar gradually laid more and more responsibilities on Eli's shoulders even as Jared continued to insist he was next in line. He was preparing his daughter, Nimrah, to become Crown Princess with her husband Prince Ahmed prepared to lead the country as king. Their extravagant lifestyle, traveling the world and partying, drew negative attention as if they were Hollywood celebrities that were tolerated because they spent money and threw lavish parties in Dubai, Hong Kong, and Los Angeles.

Ahmed frequently traveled back and forth to the kingdom, meeting with his former prince, and Prince Omar's new advisor, Kurtis. Eli was comforted when Ahmed was away, and on-edge when he was in-kingdom, still suspecting he was plotting Omar's demise.

Three months after the wedding, Jared began holding secret meetings again, rallying his troops, openly stating his son-in-law, Ahmed, intended to murder Prince Omar.

Eli warned his father, again, and his father ignored the warnings, again.

Then one day, a scream was heard throughout the palace when a maid entered the main foyer to find a man lying in his own blood, having fallen from the upper balcony to his death with a dagger to his chest. The dagger belonged to Prince Ahmed.

The murdered man was Prince Jared Sayid.

Chapter Fifty-Three

You Will Never Be King

"**D**id you honestly think I would betray my prince?" Ahmed snarled. No sooner had Prince Jared's body been discovered in the foyer did Ahmed pull Eli into his office to chastise him for thinking he was planning to kill Prince Omar.

"I don't know what to think anymore." Eli got right in Ahmed's face, not controlling his anger. "You have kept me paranoid for years while you toyed with everyone, leading us to believe you intended to murder Prince Omar. I don't know whether to be thankful that my father's still alive or angry that you killed my brother."

"Your brother was plotting against your father," Ahmed said, his rancid breath causing Eli to cringe and take a step back. "He had to be stopped."

"He was your son-in-law. How could you kill him?"

"No, he was my *father*-in-law," Ahmed reminded Eli. His thinning gray hair and pallid, wrinkled skin made that statement difficult to fully grasp, even though Eli knew the truth. "Your brother was openly threatening my prince. I held him off as long as I could, making excuses, delaying what he thought was inevitable. But he was getting impatient, and impatience is dangerous."

"None of this makes any sense." Eli paced his spacious office, his hands in fists. Eli couldn't understand how anyone could kill another person, much less family.

"Your dysfunctional royal family makes no sense," Ahmed said, settling into a cocky posture, leaning against the door frame, arms crossed and a sneer on his face. "That's why my plan worked so well. I have stood beside the crown prince his entire adult life, learned all that he learned, manipulated his son into giving me his only daughter, convinced the king to crown me a prince, and gotten away with murder. I am going to be the most powerful king this sorry excuse for a kingdom has ever encountered."

"You are wrong on so many levels. You have no idea." Eli shook his head. "You will never be king of Madain Saleh."

"I have proven that anyone who stands in my way becomes disposable, Your Highness." Ahmed stood to his full height and towered over Eli. "Don't test me."

"I have powerful friends across the world, Ahmed. I believe it is *you* who should not test *me*. And I think it's time you realized that you have *never* stood beside *the* crown prince."

"If you're referring to your haughty American cousin, you are sadly mistaken. He wasn't even born in-kingdom. He knows nothing about this country."

"Blood runs deeper than the location a person was born. This is the land of his inheritance, and this is the land where he will rule. Mark my words, the next king of Madain Saleh will be a direct descendent of King Sayid, not a murderer who manipulated those you *thought* were in power. You may wear a crown, but you could never be a prince, and over my dead body will you ever be king."

"*That* can be arranged." Ahmed narrowed his eyes, turned on his heel, and confidently strode from Eli's office, slamming the door behind himself.

Eli picked up his phone and dialed his cousin in America. "Your Highness, your presence is required."

Chapter Fifty-Four

The Crown Prince

F rom his throne on the lowest platform of the marble risers, Eli could see his cousin, Prince Marcos, step into the doorway, his advisor, Alexander, at his right side. They seemed to be whispering to one another, and Eli felt a sense of déjà vu. Many things had changed since the first time they entered this throne room, and yet much was the same.

The royal family on the marble platforms held almost the same people as the first time Prince Marcos arrived five years prior, but there was no grand reception. Most of the room was empty, including the throne where Eli's brother, Prince Jared, would have sat.

Eli was disgusted at the morbidity of leaving Jared's throne on the platform. They'd also allowed Ahmed to enter this room as a member of the royal family, knowing he murdered Prince Jared.

Eli fought the need to narrow his eyes at his father's former advisor, who now sat at a place of honor beside his young bride, Princess Nimrah.

Mark maintained a stoic expression as Alexander fell back from his prince's right shoulder. No fanfare or caller announced their entrance. Prince Marcos and his wife, Princess Hazel, stepped forward, her hand tucked in the crook of his arm. Mark carried their baby, and Hazel held the hand of their little three-year-old, who lifted his chin with confidence as if he'd been coached.

Hazel was every bit the elegant princess. Her hair piled high in cascading curls perfectly complementing a golden jeweled crown. Her dress was high-waisted and pleated to enhance and celebrate the growing life within rather than attempting to conceal her extended belly.

Mark wore a very formal suit and his full crown, and his boys wore little matching suits. Their progress was painstakingly slow, keeping pace with Prince Aaron's little legs.

Alexander was accompanied by a beautiful woman in a tastefully elegant evening dress. He tucked the woman's hand in the crook of his arm, leading her into the throne room like a lady and gentleman entering a formal ball.

A photographer hovered to the side, waiting to capture a rare multi-generational photo of the entire living royal family.

As Mark approached the marble steps to the stand, Mark handed his baby to Hazel and gently brought little Aaron to his side. Prince Marcos lowered to one knee and helped his son lower to his knee. They'd likely practiced that move ahead of time.

"Your Majesty and Your Grace," Mark called out in a clear and confident voice. "May I present His Highness, Prince Aaron, and His Highness, Prince Owen, along with my wife, Her Highness Princess Hazel. I am also joined by my advisor, Alexander Cohen-Stephenson, and his bride, the lovely Krystina Clark."

"Welcome," King Sayid called out, holding his hand out formally, inviting them to join him on the stand.

Mark helped Aaron to his feet and rose from his knee. Before they ascended the stairs, he lifted baby Owen out of Hazel's hands and offered her his arm to help her up the stairs.

They made their way to the top of the marble stairs, Alexander and Krystina a few steps behind. Mark bowed to the king, as did little Aaron, then kissed Queen Salaina's hand and coached Aaron to kiss his great-great-grandmother's hand. Mark held out baby Owen for the queen's inspection, and she took his little hand in hers, making funny faces at the little prince.

Hazel and Krystina each curtsied to the king, and he kissed their hands, then they curtsied to the queen, and she spoke quietly to the ladies. Eli couldn't hear what was said.

Mark held out his hand to help Hazel down a step to her place of honor on a throne directly to his left, and Prince Aaron stood to his right, one hand on the arm of his father's throne, chin lifted like a confident little gentleman. Mark continued to hold baby Owen on his lap as he lowered himself to sit beside Aaron.

Alexander helped Krystina back down the stairs and led her to one of the chairs near the edge of the room, then ascended the stairs again and took his place behind Prince Marcos's throne to the right of his shoulder.

With no more preparation than that, the entire royal family faced forward as the photographer took many shots from different angles, requesting minor changes here and there. One person needed to turn their head just so, another needed to move a hand to an arm rest or fold it neatly in their lap. Finally, after dozens of shots, the photographer left the room and the mood in the throne room shifted.

King Sayid was the first to rise to his feet, and he leaned down to help Queen Salaina from her throne. From somewhere off to the side, an assistant quickly approached to work with Sayid to help her down the stairs where Salaina was immediately lowered into an ornate wheelchair that was quite literally fit for a queen.

As soon as his wife was comfortable, the king turned to the rest of the group and called out, "Let's adjourn to the dining room, shall we?"

Sayid shooed aside the assistant and took the handles of his queen's wheelchair, personally guiding her into the dining room.

Prince Marcos, Hazel, and their boys followed closely behind. Alexander retrieved his bride and took his place behind his prince, ahead of everyone else.

Eli's father, Prince Omar, turned and met his gaze, shoulders slumped in resignation as once again the king had made his wishes known to everyone in the room.

No matter who had claimed the title of Crown, the message was clear. Prince Marcos Sayid was recognized by the king as his successor.

Chapter Fifty-Five

A New Princess

I f Eli thought his and Savannah's wedding had been planned in haste, Alexander and Krystina had taken wedding planning to a new extreme. Mark's advisor had only known Krystina a few months, had discussed the idea of marriage just days prior, and had gotten engaged that afternoon. When they arrived in the kingdom, King Sayid insisted they allow him to draw up marriage contracts. They decided to wait until after dinner with the family. At least Eli had known Savannah all their lives, had been planning to marry eventually, and waited until the following day.

Eli listened from just outside the door of the king's executive secretary's office where Alexander and Krystina were having a video chat with her parents back in the United States. They hadn't been preparing for a wedding. No one had.

Krystina's father wasn't happy. Her mother was confused. They were both in disbelief that somehow their adult daughter from the mountainous forests of New York State was standing half a world away in the deserts of Madain Saleh, which they'd never heard of, in the office of a king, with several princes and princesses, announcing that she was about to marry an advisor to a prince *right now*. Eli was confused, and he was standing right there. He felt bad for her parents.

There wasn't much space in the tiny office, so Eli and Savannah stood just outside in the hall, waiting for Eli to serve as a second witness to the signing of their marriage contracts. They were still dressed in formal attire, complete with their crowns, as was everyone else in the royal family crowded together for this joyous union.

With very little formalities, and a few simple vows, Alexander and Krystina made their marriage official. Then Hazel and Mark carried two sleepy little princes in their arms and said a quiet goodnight.

Eli led Savannah toward the grand staircase to head up to their suite where their son Ethan slept under the watchful care of his nanny.

Before ascending the stairs, Savannah paused on the bottom step and turned to face Eli, a soft gleam in her eyes. She reached up and touched Eli's face affectionately. "Can I tell you something?"

"You can tell me anything, my darling." Eli reached his hands up and placed them on Savannah's hips, loving the way the fabric of her dress pulled tightly against her ample waistline. She represented the epitome of how a woman should look after bringing a child into the world, soft curves in all the right places. He loved her more and more every day and couldn't imagine how life could get any better than this.

"I kind of liked the way Prince Marcos and Princess Hazel juggled two little boys, and a third on the way."

"Would you like to have more babies sometime soon?" Eli's heart raced, and he couldn't help a smile spreading across his face. He'd been waiting for her to choose when she was ready. He didn't want to pressure her.

"Yes, I would like another baby," she whispered. Eli fought the urge to jump up and down and cry out in excitement. "I'd like another baby in about seven months."

Eli's jaw dropped. Did she just say what he thought she said? "Are you? Are we?" He reverently moved his hands from her hips to her belly in wonderment. He'd just been thinking how he loved the way the fabric of her dress pulled tight against her waist.

His gaze moved up along her torso, appreciating every curve, loving the copper skin of her elegant neck and bosom, the way her raven curls tucked up and around the intricately engraved jewels of her crown, and finally met her multicolored eyes.

He said the only thing he could think in that moment. "You're beautiful."

Tears of happiness fell down Savannah's cheeks, and he kissed them away. He grabbed her in a hug and spun her around before resting her back on that lowest step.

In an excited whisper, as if they had any control of such things, he asked, "Can we have a girl this time?"

Chapter Fifty-Six

The Fall of Madain Saleh

Trust no one. That was the underlying message Eli whispered to his cousin as preparations were made for Prince Jared's funeral.

The best thing Prince Marcos and his family could do was get out of the kingdom as quickly as possible and leave the day-to-day operations in Eli's capable, if only limited, hands.

Once again, the king boldly requested Prince Marcos stand to his right during the formal funeral proceedings, nearly shoulder to shoulder, with Eli to his left but one step behind. That alone was enough to send a clear message to the kingdom and the world that Mark would be his predecessor should anything happen to the king.

The entire free world was aware that Prince Elmer was ambassador to the United Nations, and Marcos Sayid was Crown Prince. Anything less than full cooperation among the royal family would likely cause a civil war. Eli shuddered at the prospect. Mark would be returning to America. Eli would be here to try to hold their kingdom together. If that were possible.

Eli didn't mind. He'd rather be standing here in the front beside his cousin than behind his father and to the left of his brother. Kadin stood behind and to his right shoulder, with Princess Savannah to his left and the two of them holding hands with little Prince Ethan.

Behind Prince Marcos, his advisor, Alexander stood to the right, with Princess Hazel to his left, and little Prince Aaron in between, holding each of their hands. Alexander's wife, Krystina walked immediately behind them, carrying baby Prince Owen.

The queen was not healthy enough to accompany the funeral procession, but the king's second wife, Princess Tayma walked a few feet behind the king with her son, Eli's father, Prince Omar, one step behind and to her right, along with his wife, Eli's mother, Princess Nijah and his father's new advisor, Kurtis. Princess Nimrah was at Tayma's left shoulder, along with her husband, the known murderer, Ahmed. Eli refused to even mentally add his title.

The one notable exception to this otherwise standard processional, was Prince Jared's widow, Princess Linah, clinging to the king's arm and faking tears like an award-winning actress. Eli wondered how much she knew about the plot to kill her husband—if she knew that her husband had been planning to kill his father; if she knew why her daughter, Nimrah, had married Ahmed; if she knew about the secret underground societies. He suspected she did.

As fate would allow, his cousin had the perfect excuse to board their private jet and leave the country since one of their business partners had been arrested in the United States, not to mention Princess Hazel's delicate condition and the impending arrival of Prince Hayden.

Eli had a private meeting the morning before the funeral with the king, Kadin, Mark and his advisor, Alexander. Everyone knew Ahmed killed Jared, yet no one could prove his guilt. The entire household had an unspoken agreement of secrecy. The only thing keeping Eli and the king alive was the assumption they were in on it too. Murder investigations were only effective if there was a way to punish the murderer. For now, they were at a loss as to what to do.

Kadin served the unique position as eyes and ears among the staff and dignitaries. The information he shared with Eli was held close to the chest, but Mark needed to be kept in the loop.

The assassination didn't make sense. If Ahmed was trying to overthrow the monarchy, why hadn't he killed the king? If those who were part of the secret underground society in the kingdom thought of Omar as their crown prince, why did they kill his son? Why not kill the Crown? Since Eli was ambassador to the United Nations, why not kill him?

There was some underlying reason Ahmed had killed Jared, and Eli needed to learn the truth. For that, he needed to stay open to the whisperings and pretend to agree with their tactics. In the process, he was watching his kingdom crumble.

Eli had the sneaking suspicion that Madain Saleh was slated to be absorbed into their host country as a bygone kingdom that had outlived its purpose. Saudi Arabia would soon be the proud owners of a very nice artesian spring that provided the highest-quality water source in the Arabian peninsula, some historically significant ruins, and a state-of-the-art modern palace built by a wealthy and snobby royal family who couldn't get along well enough to govern themselves.

Madain Saleh would fall.

Chapter Fifty-Seven

You are the Crown

"Your Highness, you know it's the best course of action," Mark said, his international line offering clear connection.

Eli knew in his heart that his cousin was right. They'd worked together through the years, leaning on one another's expertise as they'd pushed through the myriad of challenges inherent with running a small country. They'd watched their children grow into young adults and felt the sting of rejection as their young princes chose more worldly pursuits rather than following in their fathers' footsteps. Now they were faced with choosing a successor to be king of Madain Saleh.

"But I'm *not* next in line." Eli's throat tightened again for the hundredth time since learning of their great-grandfather's passing early that morning.

"Says who?" Mark asked. "An outdated tradition that has been contested since your grandfather died sixty-five years ago?"

"The king wanted you as his successor," Eli said, feeling the lie as it left his mouth. Eli had sat beside King Sayid for years, learning from him, comforting him when Queen Salaina had passed, and when Prince Omar had passed, and when the old man was lonely or scared or sick. Their great-grandfather had held on to life for one hundred and six years, always claiming the waters of Madain Saleh were the fountain of youth.

Eli had lived in the kingdom his entire life, while Mark continued to reside in America. They both loved Madain Saleh, but Eli's allegiance had never been torn between two nations. He knew every little town and village on the outskirts, he'd watched their people struggle through droughts and wars and illnesses, and eventually dwindle into a tiny oasis tucked into the rocky desert.

Their great-grandfather had been the only thing holding this kingdom in existence. The Saudis humored the dying old man. The land would be absorbed into the desert until all that remained were the palaces, tombs, and hieroglyphs no one could translate. Madain Saleh would be a memory.

"Stay and maintain the dignity that has been our homeland for centuries," Mark said. "As long as there are still members of the royal family willing to claim the throne, Madain Saleh will survive."

"But you are the rightful heir. You are next in line. You are the Crown."

"I will continue to be Crown with you as my king." Mark was now the one whose voice faltered with unshed tears. "At your coronation, I will pledge my allegiance to *you*."

"What about your sons?" Eli asked.

"They don't want that crown any more than your son or your daughter."

Mark spoke the truth. Prince Ethan had already moved to America to attend a university and had expressed the desire to stay. Princess Miranda intended to follow her older brother once she completed her secondary school.

No one else cared who claimed the throne. Eli's niece, Princess Nimrah had taken a lover in Dubai years ago and her sham of a marriage to Ahmed had ended when he died of mysterious causes a few months later. Eli hadn't heard from Nimrah in ten years or so.

He knew his cousin was right. The time had come for Eli to rule in place of all the others who had been the likely successors. He, who'd been told all his life that his bloodline was inconsequential because he would never be king, was now the only person left to claim the throne, the only person left who loved their kingdom enough to stand within her borders as they crumbled around him.

"Will you be the one to perform the coronation?" Eli asked, hearing his own vulnerability as his voice cracked.

"Of course, Your Highness. My family and I have already begun packing and will be there with you before the end of the week."

"I look forward to meeting your young princes," Eli said. He hadn't seen Aaron and Owen since they were babies and had never met Hayden or Augustus. They planned to hold a press conference that afternoon formally abdicating all rights to the throne, opening the way for the world to recognize Prince Elmer Sayid as the new king of Madain Saleh.

"My young princes look forward to meeting the lovely Princess Miranda," Mark said with a chuckle.

"They'd better keep their hands off my daughter," Eli warned in a teasing growl.

"Ah, my friend. It will be good to see you." There was love and compassion in Mark's endearment.

"You as well, Your Highness. Travel safely." Eli found hope in his heart for the first time in days.

Chapter Fifty-Eight

King of Mada'in Saleh

"The Kingdom of Mada'in Saleh will live on in the memory of King Sayid." Eli paused to choke back emotion, then pressed forward through the remainder of his prepared eulogy. "We were fortunate to have had him serve our people for many years.

"Since before any of us were born, his throne has been contested. So much so that even now we are unclear who claims the right to the Crown.

"All of our sons or daughters, who may attempt a claim to that right, have declined. Should any one of them later challenge that right, I fear a civil war would begin.

"For this reason, my wife, Princess Savannah, and I will maintain the throne as king and queen of Mada'in Saleh as we assist the Saudi government to absorb our tiny kingdom. We will serve until we are taken from this earth.

"I have fought all my life for this kingdom, that we might have peace here. I have fought to uphold laws where there was no punishment for crimes. I have watched my kingdom be destroyed by men and women who thought themselves to be above the law.

"I desire that this kingdom should be a land of peace, that all who dwell here will enjoy freedom and liberty, that all people will be equal, that all people will abide by the laws and be punished if they will not.

"King Sayid was my great-grandfather. Prince Marcos Sayid and I are his closest living relatives. As has been agreed upon, Prince Marcos will perform the sacred duty of placing our king's crown upon my head as a symbolic transfer of power. I will then place Queen Saliana's crown upon Princess Savannah's head, naming her as my queen." Eli stepped back and bowed regally to his cousin.

Prince Marcos, wearing the crown that had been his since his coronation at the age of twenty, the crown that represented the king's successor, stepped to the front of the marble platform. Eli lowered himself to one knee and bowed his head. With his eyes closed, he felt, rather than saw, his cousin remove the crown from his head and in his mind's eye envisioned the crown being placed in its velvet and mahogany box to remain forever.

Eli visualized Mark lifting their great-grandfather's crown from its nest of velvet and felt certain this is what the king would have wanted. All his life Eli had been told his bloodline was inconsequential because he was not the Crown Prince. And now, in the end, the named successor was irrelevant. The mantle now rested on the man least likely to have been given this honor.

"By the power vested in me by the Kingdom of Mada'in Saleh," Mark said with conviction. "I do hereby pronounce Prince Elmer Sayid, *King* of Mada'in Saleh until his body is laid to rest."

King Sayid's crown was heavier than that which Eli had worn all his life, and yet the weight felt right and true. Without Eli realizing it, emotion had broken through his carefully maintained façade. Eli felt a tear fall from each of his eyes as he lifted his gaze to his cousin. Mark also had moist eyes, but neither of them wiped their faces. That would show a sign of weakness.

"Arise, Your Majesty," Mark whispered. "And crown your queen."

Eli rose from his knee and lifted his chin with confidence. "Thank you, Your Highness." Eli turned to face his wife.

Savannah stood before Eli with a confident yet humble expression, ready to begin this next phase in their lives. Eli was simultaneously reminded of Queen Salaina's prediction that Savannah would take on a higher calling than princess, as well as his vision during their wedding of Savannah wearing the queen's crown.

"Princess Savannah, are you prepared to take upon yourself the title of queen and are you prepared to accept the responsibilities, rights, and duties of that title?"

"I am, Your Majesty," Savannah whispered. She lowered her head, presenting her crown to her husband and closing her eyes. In one confident movement, as he'd done countless times, Eli lifted Savannah's crown and placed it within its velvet and mahogany box for the last time. He clasped Queen Salaina's crown, noting the difference in weight, just as he'd noticed the difference in weight when the king's crown was placed upon his head.

"By the power vested in me as king of Mada'in Saleh, I do hereby crown you, Princess Savannah, *Queen* of Mada'in Saleh." Eli lightly rested the crown on his wife's head, and the ring of gold seemed to fit perfectly as if it had been fashioned for her. He took one step back. "Arise, Your Grace."

Savannah lifted her gaze, and Eli fought the need to pull her into his arms and kiss her with power and hunger and passion and life. Oh, what the heck. He was king. He could do whatever he wanted.

Eli pulled his wife forward and took her in his arms. She wrapped her arms around his neck, and their lips came together in a kiss that rivaled that which they'd shared at their wedding. The solemn crowd erupted in cheers and catcalls, a celebration of this new age of their kingdom and their new king and queen.

Reluctantly, Eli pulled away from Savannah and joined in the celebration, hugging his cousin, Mark; his son, Ethan; his daughter, Miranda; his advisor, Kadin; and anyone else who was brave enough to come forward in congratulations.

The funeral and coronation shifted into an evening of music and dance and celebrating. The young princes from America flirted and danced with Princess Miranda under the watchful eye of her older brother, Prince Ethan. The adults laughed and hugged and smiled as they celebrated the promise of youth. All was well in the kingdom. At least for one night.

Chapter Fifty-Nine

Until We Meet Again

"My son, the time has come," Eli said, taking Ethan by the shoulders with a piercing gaze.

"What if I'm not ready, Your Majesty?" The vulnerability in Ethan's pale face pulled at Eli's heart, almost to the point of backing out of their plan. Ethan's hair had grown out since ending the chemotherapy, and he'd gained weight. The fight was over. His multi-colored eyes, so similar to his mother's, shone with unshed tears.

"You are ready, Your Highness. But more importantly, the world is waiting." As hard as it was to watch his son leave, Eli knew he needed to provide that last bit of encouragement.

"I will not be returning to the kingdom," Ethan said, his voice hitching. "Ever." At thirty years of age, Ethan had already finished his education at a private business school in New York City and had plans to accomplish great things with his life. Cancer wasn't part of the plan.

"Invest what time you have left exploring the world and sharing that which is now rightfully yours."

"This is a large sum of money, Your Majesty. You and mother will be destitute."

"We have sufficient for our needs to see us through the remainder of our lives."

"What about Princess Miranda?" Ethan was grasping, delaying his departure.

"Your sister is married to a prince nearly as wealthy as you. She will want for nothing."

"You're sure you don't mind me giving it all away?"

"I don't see this as giving the money away," Eli said. "I see you investing in the lives of others, using riches that have gathered value for decades and are now liquidated. You have conducted careful research and will make good choices."

"You're right, Father," Ethan whispered. "I'll do my best."

"While you're out distributing the money, travel to see the world. Visit the Grand Canyon, Niagara Falls, Lake Victoria, the Mayan ruins, stand on a glacier, go to the top of the Eiffel Tower, and the St. Louis Arch, float the Amazon River and go on an African Safari."

"I'm not going to live long enough to do all those things, Father. But I'll do as many as I can." Ethan pulled Eli into a hug and allowed tears to fall unabashedly. "Take care of Mother for me."

"I promise," Eli said, pushing his son gently out of his arms. "Now go, before I beg you to stay."

"As you wish, Your Majesty." Ethan bowed and then lifted his chin.

Eli held his son's gaze for one last long moment, then Prince Ethan Sayid turned to go pack and begin this new adventure.

His heart broke as Eli watched his son walk away. The next time he saw Ethan would be the day he was laid to rest.

Part Three: The Last Prince
Prince Ethan Sayid

As told by Prince Ethan Sayid, son of King Elmer Sayid, grandson of Prince Omar Sayid, great-grandson of Crown Prince Jared Sayid, great-great-grandson of King Sayid, who was in his one hundred and sixth year at the time of his passing...

Chapter Sixty

Decimated Royal Bloodline

P rince Ethan Sayid of Madain Saleh had every intention of walking into the attorney's office and stating, "I'm dying, and I need to give away all my money."

But when the beautiful, young lawyer looked up from her desk with eyes that sparkled like emeralds, he choked. He disguised his accent and changed his approach.

"I need help preparing a will," he said.

"You've come to the right place." She rose from her desk and stepped forward with her hand raised. "Estate planning is my specialty."

"You're perfect," Ethan said, then shook off his awe as he clasped her hand in greeting. "I mean, that's perfect. I need an estate attorney."

"I'm Natalie Dolan. It's nice to meet you, Mister..."

"Ethan Sayid."

"Salad?" She raised her eyebrows and bit her lower lip. Was she laughing?

"No, Sayid, like sigh-eed." Ethan cringed. "It's a traditional middle eastern name that is not widely used in American culture."

This was why he didn't want to use his real name anymore. But his attorney would need his full legal name if she was going to help him. She didn't need to know his full title or lineage, however. At least not yet.

"Please, just call me Ethan unless you're filling out legal documents."

He was a prince in name only and the last of his family. His tiny monarchy had been swallowed into the deserts of the middle east and the royal family splintered. When his great-great-grandfather, King Sayid of Madain Saleh had died at the age of one-hundred and six, Ethan's parents had remained in their homeland to take their rightful place as heirs, but the country had now been absorbed into Saudi Arabia.

Ethan had heard tales of how his uncles and father had fought over what was left of their grandfather's power until all that was left was the money. A monarchy without a kingdom is merely a very wealthy family. Now that his parents had signed over their fortune, Ethan was the sole heir to just over a billion dollars.

And he was dying.

The trouble was cancer didn't know who was rich and who was poor, who was young and who was old, who was the last of a decimated royal bloodline, or who was the first-generation in a newly created interracial family with all the promise that ensues. No, cancer didn't care.

"I'm sorry, I didn't mean to offend you," Natalie said with a barely contained hysteria. She collapsed back into her leather swivel chair. "It's just been one of those days. I think I need an evening of binge-watching old episodes of The Big Bang Theory and eating chocolate ice cream."

"I'm rather fond of chocolate ice cream myself," Ethan said, sitting cautiously in the seat across her desk.

"What about old sitcoms?" She chuckled.

"Is that an invitation?" Ethan leaned forward and couldn't help his voice dropping to what he imagined was a sexy, smoldering huskiness. Other than a few casual flings during college, he'd never invested the time to pursue a woman before. This was unfamiliar territory.

Natalie seemed momentarily distracted and speechless, then cleared her throat and shook her head as if to refocus. "I don't date my clients." She gulped.

"My apologies," Ethan said. He pulled back his stance and resumed an air of professionalism. "Shall we discuss a more appropriate topic? Help me with my estate planning. I'm a billionaire prince with no throne or heir, and I'm dying of cancer."

"You're so funny, Ethan." She opened a drawer in her desk and pulled out a packet of forms, obviously assuming he was joking. "Here is the stack of paperwork needed to get started. With something so important as estate planning, I prefer to have paper copies in the client's own handwriting, as well as computer files, and printed copies with signatures. Do you have in mind who will be your named beneficiaries?"

"I have very little in the way of physical possessions, other than a very large trust account controlled mostly by myself and a few carefully chosen trustees, none of whom I fully trust. I have done a great deal of research into charitable organizations throughout the world and have determined approximate dollar amounts I'd like to leave to each of them. I have the list here."

Ethan pulled from his briefcase a fifty-seven-page single-spaced, twelve-point font document that represented his years of research narrowed down to a bulleted list of the names of charitable organizations.

"I have computer files backed up on multiple servers as well as paper documentation for each of these organizations in my nondescript home in an undisclosed location. Given my recent prognosis, I am concerned that my wishes will not be carried out if I don't take action quickly. I have researched your father's law firm here in the middle of the United States of America where I have determined that your firm has no affiliation with any of my trustees nor any of these organizations. I apologize for not being forthcoming as to my intentions upon walking into your office, but I must admit I was taken aback by your beauty. I will attempt to maintain a level of professionalism from now on." Ethan finally stopped, feeling as if he had already overwhelmed the poor girl. He was right.

"I thought you were joking," Natalie whispered.

"Not in the least, Ms. Dolan," Ethan said. "My research has shown that you conduct a great deal of your business pro bono for the less fortunate in your community and that you don't seem to be persuaded by the prospect of becoming wealthy from your work as an attorney. But I dare say the large sum of money I will offer you to take on my case will assist you in providing a great deal of service long after my departure."

"You're kind of freaking me out right now, Mr. Sayid." Natalie rose from her chair and began pacing the floor of her small office.

"Again, I apologize. I had hoped to handle this differently but was momentarily caught up in a youthful fantasy of actually meeting a woman who would care about me for my charm and personality rather than my crown and wealth. It is unfortunate that I finally meet someone worth pursuing days after receiving the news that my cancer is inoperable and will likely be my demise. Not that I'm a stranger to adversity, mind you. I've had a price on my head since the day it was determined that I was a male and potential heir to the throne in a highly contested battle for the last semblance of power in my country of origin."

"I think I need a drink," Natalie said.

"I think you need to stick to the chocolate ice cream and binge-watching old sitcoms," Ethan answered. "I need you at your highest mental faculties if we are to accomplish this task in the limited amount of time I have left."

"Okay," she squeaked out.

"Okay, what?" Ethan asked.

"Okay, I'll take your case," Natalie said.

"Thank goodness." Ethan lowered his shoulders in a relieved sigh. "I don't have time to do any more research."

Chapter Sixty-One

Do I Look Handicapped to You?

"**I** was the first-born to Prince Elmer Sayid," Ethan said, sitting straight in the chair across from Natalie's desk, all business and ready to give her a full explanation. "Ten years ago, when my great-great-grandfather died, my father was crowned king of the tiny kingdom of Madain Saleh, which was recently absorbed into Saudi Arabia. My mother and father still reign as king and queen, although we are no longer considered an independent sovereign nation-state."

"Do you still have contact with your parents?" Natalie asked. She had begun taking notes, a simple pen in hand and a spiral notebook. The blotter on her desk was stained in several places where a mug had created a condensation ring and scribbles where she'd tested an old pen or marker. There were crayon drawings facing Ethan, showing stick figures and cartoons. Ethan could picture a small child, kneeling on a chair beside a harried, frustrated parent, leaning over the desk with a crayon to stay busy while waiting for their mom or dad to be done with this boring appointment. Natalie didn't seem bored, so Ethan continued.

"They are aware of my intentions, but we have said our goodbyes. I don't want anyone, other than my attorneys, to know who I am giving the money to." Ethan nodded toward Natalie. "There are instructions in my notes to have my body returned to my parents so that I can be interred with the rest of the royal family."

"And you don't have any other family members who could make a claim against your estate?"

"I have some cousins and a sister, but they are not privy to my location nor diagnosis," Ethan said. "They are all extremely wealthy and don't need my money, but I have written each of them a letter to be delivered after my passing."

"I'm assuming their contact information is in your notes?" She didn't look up from her notetaking.

"Of course. Please, I need you to recognize that everything I do between now and when I die should be confidential between you, me, and your father. Are you comfortable with that?"

"Yes, Mr. Sayid—I mean, Ethan—I'm comfortable with that." She finally met his gaze.

"How much would you like as a retainer?" Ethan pulled out his checkbook and clicked open a pen.

"Well, the first half hour consultation is free." Natalie looked up at her clock. "We haven't quite reached that, so—"

Ethan cut her off. "I'll just write the first check for $5,000, and we'll go from there." He leaned forward and began writing the check before she could protest.

"I was going to say $200," she whispered and sat back in her chair. The wheels creaked as the momentum pushed her a few inches away from her desk. She clasped her hand over her chest. Her cheap, department store blouse hid behind a faded cardigan sweater with one button missing.

Ethan couldn't help thinking she'd look beautiful in one of the hand-woven overwraps his sister, Princess Miranda, had purchased in India last year. He had the sudden desire to introduce Natalie to his sister but knew that wasn't an option. In order for this plan to work, no one in his family could have knowledge of where he was or who he was working with. A lump formed in his throat and he had to look away.

"You... can't possibly... realize." A broken sob escaped from the startled attorney, and Ethan whipped his gaze back to her.

"What is it? What have I done wrong?" Ethan leaned forward in concern.

"No." Natalie held her hand up to stop him. "Not wrong. I haven't taken a paycheck in weeks because our budget is so tight. I've barely had any paid clients in months. This town is so destitute. You are an answer to my prayers."

Natalie lowered her head into her hands and broke into tears. Ethan set his pen and checkbook on the desk and came around to her side, dropping to his knees in front of her and pulling her into his arms. He didn't speak, just held her while she rested her head on his shoulder and cried.

Suddenly she pushed away from him and scrambled to get out of her chair. "What are you doing? What am *I* doing?" She hurried to the other side of the room, grabbing a tissue from the box on the corner of her desk.

Ethan used what strength he had left and hoisted himself from the floor, closing his eyes and counting backward from ten. He had trained himself to snap out of any pain by the time he reached one. Some days the technique worked better than others. He opened his eyes and blew out a long breath.

"Are you okay?" Natalie took a tentative step forward, not quite reaching out to him, but fighting the natural instinct to want to help another human.

"Maybe we should be done for the day." Ethan lowered himself back into the chair in front of her desk and finished writing her check, reminding himself to sign his name without his full title. That would take some getting used to.

He realized in that moment that international travel would not be in his best interest now that he was maintaining a low profile. His passport and identification were diplomatic documents designed to allow him access throughout the world. Even getting pulled over by a local police officer would draw unwanted attention.

"Where are you staying? There are no hotels between here and Omaha."

"I've reserved a room at the bed-and-breakfast on First Street," Ethan said, still trying to catch his breath.

"That's not exactly handicap accessible," Natalie said, pacing again. "They don't even have a main floor suite. You'd have to climb all those stairs. There's a Holiday Inn up in Columbus but that's a half hour drive."

"Do I *look* handicapped to you?" Ethan glanced at his Italian made Sutor Mantellassi shoes and Dolce & Gabbana cashmere suit. Everything about him screamed success, other than his pallid skin and the sheen on his forehead.

"Yes," Natalie said, handing him a tissue which he used to wipe his face. "You do look handicapped, and I don't like the idea of you climbing all those stairs."

As Ethan was contemplating the need for a wardrobe change in order to blend in with society, Natalie's father swept in the front door with a bag of Chinese takeout and a cheerful smile.

"Whose Lincoln Continental is that out front?" Miles Dolan asked, not having noticed Ethan yet. "I need to get me one of those when I become rich and famous." He snorted, laughing at his own joke.

Ethan rose from his chair and offered Miles a subdued grin. "Or I could just leave you that beauty in my will. She purrs like a kitten and rides like a cloud."

"Well, hello there. I didn't realize we had company." Miles set the bag of food on the folding table in the corner of the sparsely decorated office and turned to Ethan.

"Hello, Mr. Dolan, I'm Ethan Sayid." He extended a hand. "Your daughter and I were just discussing me hiring your firm to draft some estate planning documents."

"Welcome, Mr. Salad." Miles clasped his hand and cocked his head to the side. "Where are you from? Your attempt to disguise your foreign accent isn't working."

"Please, just call me Ethan." He chose not to point out the complete mispronunciation of his last name, but Natalie jumped in with a correction.

"It's pronounced sigh-eed, Daddy." Natalie helped him out of his coat and hung it on the coat hanger in the corner. "He's from somewhere in Saudi Arabia, right?" Natalie turned to Ethan and raised her eyebrows.

"Madain Saleh, yes." Ethan tucked both hands in his pants pockets, feeling better after having rested a minute. Dropping to his knees so quickly and then leaning over to push himself off the floor had messed up his equilibrium.

Miles creased his brows, all friendliness gone from his countenance. Natalie didn't seem to notice her father's reaction.

"Would you care to join us for lunch, Ethan?" Natalie began pulling containers out of the bag and spreading them on the table. She opened a container of white rice, fried rice, egg rolls, noodles, and orange chicken.

Ethan's mouth watered and stomach rumbled at the heavenly aromas. "I wouldn't want to put you out."

"Oh please, we have plenty." She waved away his concern. "Daddy always buys enough for lunch and dinner."

"Well, I insist on buying you both dinner this evening to make up for your willingness to share your lunch." Ethan sidestepped Miles, who seemed to need a minute more to absorb the situation, and joined Natalie at the small folding table.

"You're on," she said, handing him a paper plate. With each helping of food she scooped onto her plate, she added a scoop to his and her father's. "Come on, Daddy, let's eat."

"I've heard of people like you." Miles didn't try to hide his suspicion as he joined them at the table. "You prey on unsuspecting young ladies, claiming to be a Jordanian prince and convincing them to send you money to some overseas bank."

"Prince Rashid is a very nice man," Ethan said, ripping open the clear wrap around the plastic fork and napkin provided by the Chinese restaurant. A little packet of salt fell out, and he set it aside. Chinese food was usually salty enough on its own. "My father served with him on the United Nations Security Council a few years ago, I think." Ethan carefully lifted a bite of food onto the fork and leaned over his plate to avoid spilling.

"Who—what?" Miles shook his head in confusion.

"The Jordanian prince," Ethan said, hiding his mouth behind a napkin to avoid talking with his mouth full of food. "They're one of our primary trading partners."

"Would you rather have chopsticks?" Natalie handed a pair of bamboo sticks to Ethan. "Those little forks are so hard to use."

"Oh, thank goodness, yes." Ethan gladly took the chopsticks and expertly lifted the next bite of food with ease.

"How long have you lived here in America, Ethan?" Natalie asked before sitting across from him. She separated her bamboo sticks and picked up a clump of rice and a piece of orange chicken.

"We have a penthouse in New York City for the family to use when my father was serving in the UN, and my sister and I both stayed there while attending Pace University. She remained in the States and married one of Prince Marcos's sons, and I returned to the kingdom after business school."

"Who's Prince Marcos?" Natalie seemed completely at ease now that they were chatting over lunch rather than discussing legal affairs. Ethan wondered if her demeanor would shift back to her stoic professionalism once they were sitting across from each other at her desk again.

"My father's second cousin, which would make Prince Hayden my sister's third cousin... I think." Ethan took another bite of food.

"Far enough removed by anyone's standards, I'd say," Natalie said.

"They met at the king's funeral of all places." Ethan chuckled and shook his head, remembering with fondness how the young princes had fallen all over each other to gain favor with Princess Miranda.

"I thought your father was still alive?" Natalie cocked her head to the side.

"Yes, my father's coronation was on the same day as my great-great-grandfather's funeral. Confusing, I know."

"Would the two of you please explain to me what you're talking about?" Miles had yet to take a bite of food and seemed to grow more agitated the longer Ethan and Natalie spoke.

"How about if Natalie tells the story, and I'll fill in the missing details," Ethan suggested, nodding to her. "That will help you to understand things better anyway. I know my story is very complicated, and we don't have many months left to get things taken care of."

Ethan pushed his chair back and reached into his briefcase for a money clip and drew out several hundred-dollar bills. He slid them across the table along with the check he'd written.

"Also, I'd like you to keep this, at least until my check clears. I don't want you to think I'm trying to swindle you out of the retainer. Sorry I don't have five thousand in cash, but four hundred is at least more than the original two you had anticipated."

Miles Dolan's jaw dropped, but Ethan pulled himself forward again and picked up his chopsticks, letting the father and daughter team gape at the exorbitant amount of money on their cheap folding table. Maybe now they'd believe him.

Chapter Sixty-Two

Bed-and-Breakfast

"Let me get this straight," Miles stopped them again. Ethan was forcing himself to stay patient. "You're dying of cancer and want our help to give away all your money."

"Yes, sir."

"And you really are a prince?"

Ethan reached into his briefcase again and pulled out his passport and diplomatic papers, spreading them in front of Miles, who had finally finished his meal.

Miles lifted each document and examined it with the scrutiny of an attorney. He narrowed his eyes at Ethan. "Where do you live now?"

"I bought a small house near Omaha where I have backups of everything I'm providing to you."

"That's too far away for you to drive back there tonight," Natalie said with a panic in her voice.

"Like I said earlier, I've reserved a room at the bed-and-breakfast."

"You should stay with us," Natalie said.

"Natalie!" Miles cried. "You can't just invite a strange man to sleep at our house!"

"Why not? Momma won't mind. She loves to entertain. She'll make a better breakfast than he'd ever get over at Rachel's bed-and-breakfast."

"Absolutely not, young lady."

"Daddy, I am thirty-one years old and a professional attorney. I am most certainly not a *young* lady."

"Thank you for the offer, Natalie, but I think I'm going to keep my reservation at the bed-and-breakfast." Ethan pushed himself away from the folding table and returned to his chair near her desk. "Let's get back to work, shall we?"

"How did you sleep last night at the bed-and-breakfast?" Natalie asked when Ethan got seated across from her desk. "Were you able to handle the stairs okay?" Concern for his welfare was a welcome change after having been alone for the past several months and feeling the decline in his health.

"The suite was comfortable and quiet, with a beautiful view of the sunrise this morning. I slept like a baby." Ethan laid the stack of paperwork on her desk, which had yet to be filled out. "You were right about the stairs. By the time I hoisted myself up there with my small travel bag, I had to sit down at the top and rest for a few minutes. I think I'm going to drive home tonight to Omaha rather than stay at the bed-and-breakfast again."

"Nonsense," Natalie said. "You can stay with us. And I'll help you with the paperwork." She moved her laptop to his side of the desk and sat in the extra chair. She reached for the paperwork and pulled the stack closer.

"Your dad would throw a fit again," Ethan said. "I'll be fine driving home."

"That's almost two hours, Ethan." Natalie's jaw dropped. Her emerald eyes had darkened to a hazy jade and frustration pulled her brows together.

"More like an hour and a half. I live on the outskirts of town." He waved away her concern, afraid if she continued these passionate exchanges, he would say something inappropriate again and offend her. She was beautiful to the point of making his stomach flutter, or maybe that was the homemade pastry he'd indulged in during breakfast.

"Humph." She scowled at him and started flipping through the stack of papers. "Did you have trouble with any of these questions? Or did you just not have time to fill them out?"

"When I got to my room, I was so exhausted I prepared for bed immediately. I barely glanced at the packet. I noticed that you need tax information for my new house. I'll have to find that when I get home tonight."

"We can look up that information on the internet." Natalie turned to her computer and jiggled the mouse. The screen saver—a picture of a big family wedding—disappeared, and she opened a browser window. "You'd be surprised how many public records you can find on the internet. Hey, do you mind if I do a Google search for your kingdom? I want to know where you're from." The excited gleam in her eyes was enough incentive for him to offer her anything she desired.

"M-a-d-a-i-n S-a-l-e-h," Ethan said as she typed. Images popped up on her screen, and he couldn't help leaning across the desk to see better.

"Is that your mother and father?" Natalie leaned closer as well. "Oh, Ethan, she's beautiful. You have her eyes. And your skin tone is closer to hers than your father's."

"Her Grace is elegant." Ethan's words caught in his throat as he took in his mother's multicolored eyes. Her copper skin had aged well, and she never tried to hide her full figure. Ethan always had the impression that his father loved her curves and was often caught gazing at her across the room with love and longing in his eyes.

Ethan wished he could have a tiny bit of the passion his parents had for one another but knew that wasn't possible. Loving a dying man would just lead to hurt and loss. He would never want to do that to a woman.

"I wish I could introduce you to them." Ethan cleared his husky throat and refocused, pointing to the screen. "That's my sister, Princess Miranda, the one who's married to Prince Hayden."

"She looks more like your father," Natalie said. "And she lives in the United States?"

"Yes, they settled close to Hayden's family in the Hudson Valley a few hours from New York City."

"Didn't you say you needed to go to the city to settle some affairs?" Natalie asked. "Maybe I could come with you, and we could take a detour afterward and go visit her."

"Do you have time in your schedule to travel with me?" Ethan's heart raced with excitement. The idea of spending hours together in a car was intriguing. "Don't you need to work?"

"Work is slow right now," she said with a wave of her hand. "Have you seen any clients coming and going since you arrived yesterday? My father can handle any business we have for a couple days."

"I plan to be traveling for a couple of weeks," Ethan said. "I have a bucket list of famous places to see. I want my last few days to have meaning. I don't want to sit home and wait to die."

"What if you get sick while you're traveling?" Natalie's voice lowered with concern and compassion.

"Then I'll check myself into a hospital and wait *there* to die, hoping the duration of my stay won't be prolonged."

"Do you have a DNR?" She gulped.

"Yes, it's right here." Ethan reached into his briefcase and pulled out the legal document. "Do not resuscitate. Only palliative care."

"That's smart." Her voice caught at the end. "No reason to prolong the inevitable. Better to keep you comfortable." Did she have tears in the corners of her eyes?

"Are you okay?"

"I just need a minute." Natalie rose from her desk and grabbed a tissue on the way to stand by the window. She dabbed at her eyes a few times, then turned with a determined stance. "I'm struggling with this, Ethan. Usually when I talk to clients about estate planning, it's in the abstract, in the future, sometime far away. Not a young, handsome man who doesn't seem ready to die."

"Oh, come on, I thought I looked handicapped." Ethan chuckled and stood from his chair. He leaned against the edge of her desk and folded his arms. From where he stood, Ethan could see out the window at rolling hills in the distance. Keeping his eyes unfocused on the horizon, he mused, "You're right though; I'm not ready to die."

Neither of them spoke for a moment; then he shook off his stupor and returned to the present.

"Would you like to see my bucket list?" Ethan reached into his briefcase and pulled out a handwritten piece of paper. A few of the items had already been crossed off. He handed the paper to Natalie who sat in the chair next to his rather than moving to the other side of her desk.

"I've always wanted to go to Niagara Falls." She ran her finger down the page. She looked up at him with raised eyebrows. "Mackinaw Island?"

"I hear it's beautiful." Ethan cleared his throat and nodded to the page. "Have you ever been to the Grand Canyon?"

"No... gosh, no wonder you want to take several weeks. This is a long list."

"Running out of time, aren't I?"

"Well, let's get this paperwork started so we can get on the road." Her false enthusiasm broke the seriousness of the moment, which Ethan welcomed. He was here for business.

Getting all these emotions involved was adding confusion to Ethan's situation. Natalie had already made her intentions clear. He was a client, and she didn't date clients. Not that he'd date her anyway. He was dying with an inoperable malignant brain tumor. He had a few months left, at the most.

Chapter Sixty-Three

Baked Potatoes

An intercom beeped through the phone on Natalie's desk and a woman's voice rang out. "Nattie, I made lunch. Take a break and bring your client over to introduce me."

"Okay, Mom," Natalie called into the air, then looked over at Ethan. "Our house is just next door. Come on."

They left her law office, which was a small home that had been converted, and stepped onto a quaint sidewalk lined with maple trees. Towering over the town, the trees created a shady tunnel between her office and a modest home with a veranda porch wrapping around the front and side.

The wooden steps up to the porch creaked a little under Ethan's weight in a comfortable homey way. A sense of peace washed over Ethan as Natalie held open the door and he stepped into an elegant living room worthy of greeting formal guests yet casual enough to sit at the window seat with a novel and gaze out across the tiny town tucked into the heart of Nebraska. Forget lunch; Ethan wanted to sink into the embroidered sofa and lose himself in time.

An older version of Natalie came walking down the hall with a friendly smile. "Hello, Mr. Sayid, welcome to our home." Ethan reached for her outstretched hand, honored that she had pronounced his name correctly, and wondered if she'd been coached by her lovely daughter.

"Please, call me Ethan." He nodded politely.

"And you can call me Bonnie," she said, then turned back toward an open kitchen. "I hope you're hungry. I made baked potatoes on the grill, and they are just falling out of their skins."

"That sounds wonderful, Bonnie, thank you." Ethan opened his arm to Natalie, then lowered his voice. "I'll follow you."

As she passed him to head down the hall after her mother, Ethan fought the urge to rest his hand on her lower back. He smiled at her but silently chastised himself. *I'm her client, not her friend.*

"I have a confession to make." Bonnie giggled like a little girl. "Natalie and I spent most of the evening yesterday researching you on the internet."

"Oh, you did, did you?" Ethan cocked his head and raised his eyebrows at Natalie, fighting a full-on grin.

"Don't look at me," Natalie said. "The internet search was my mom's idea."

"Was our little search this morning your mom's idea also?" Ethan leaned against a large kitchen table that had been built in the style of a giant butcher block with just the right amount of wear to give it soft character.

The heavenly scent of grilled food and chopped green onions wafted from the kitchen island where small oval foil packets cooled on a rack. They'd been charred on the outside. He could almost taste the baked potatoes inside. He turned his attention back to Bonnie.

"What juicy details did you uncover?"

"Let's see, you made the Dean's List at Pace University."

"That, I did."

"You once dated an exotic beauty from India who attended your college."

"She was after my money," Ethan said, waving his arm dismissively. "We broke off the engagement when she complained her diamond wasn't large enough."

Natalie gasped and covered her mouth.

"I'm kidding. We were never engaged. But she was dating me for my money and the prestige of being seen on the arm of a prince."

"That's terrible." Natalie's eyes were still wide with horror as she opened a cupboard to pull down plates, and a drawer to dig out silverware.

"Here, let me help you with those." Ethan reached for the stack of plates and distributed them around the table, which felt quite normal even though he'd never sat around a family table in a real kitchen like this. Every suite at the palace had a dining area, but servants brought the meals and plated the food. The main dining hall with the whole royal family was stuffy and formal. This was exciting.

"Actually, bring those over to the island." Bonnie pointed to the spot beside the potatoes.

"Won't we be sitting at the table together?" Ethan looked longingly at the butcher block table, not hiding his disappointment.

"Of course, we will," Bonnie said softly. "But we'll dish up from over here. That way I don't have to bring over all the toppings."

"That makes sense." Ethan gathered up the plates and nested them in a pile next to the potatoes.

A door to the back end of the kitchen clunked open, and Miles Dolan stomped his feet on the rug by the door. "Do I have time to wash up before lunch? Weeding that garden took longer than I thought it would. Oh, hello, Ethan, how are you this afternoon?" Miles smiled as he stepped over to the large kitchen sink and turned on the faucet.

"Get out of my kitchen with those filthy hands," Bonnie scolded him. "Go use the utility sink in the laundry room."

"Yes, ma'am." Miles saluted Bonnie playfully, then turned to Ethan. "See what I put up with around here?"

"You lead a tough life, Mr. Dolan," Ethan called after him as he disappeared around a corner in another hallway off the back of the kitchen.

"Natalie, why don't you and Ethan dish up first?" Bonnie lifted a plate off the stack and handed it to Natalie, who then handed it to Ethan and grabbed another.

"Is there a trick to this?" Ethan asked, scooting up next to her and placing his plate beside hers on the island.

"Yeah, touch as little of the foil as possible so you don't get covered in charcoal." Natalie grasped an oval foil ball by one tiny corner and shook the little packet as the perfectly baked potato rolled down from its wrapper.

Ethan followed her lead, and soon a steaming lump landed on his plate, breaking open the skin and releasing an earthy smell that made his mouth water. He watched as she spread open the skin of her potato and dolloped butter and sour cream inside before sprinkling shredded cheddar and minced green onions on top. He tried to recreate her masterpiece, and thought he came up with something pretty close.

Natalie and Ethan moved over to the table, and before she sat down, Natalie reached for a large pitcher of lemonade and poured them each a glass. "Oh, I'm sorry. I forgot to ask. Do you like lemonade? Or would you rather have something else."

"That sounds perfect actually." Ethan lifted the heavy glass she offered him, and drips of condensation already gathered on the sides. The sweet and sour combination was iced, delicious heaven as it traveled down his throat.

Bonnie hummed as she plated a potato for herself and one for Miles and joined them at the table just as Miles returned from his handwashing in the utility room.

"These smell wonderful, my dear." Miles kissed Bonnie on top of her head as he sat next to her.

They were all quiet for a moment as they ate, until Natalie glanced up as if remembering something.

"Daddy, I'm going to need you to run the office for a few weeks by yourself because I'm going on a road trip with Ethan to New York City."

She probably should have waited until her father had finished eating because he immediately choked on his food. The muffled cough that followed sounded something like, "Over my dead body."

Chapter Sixty-Four

Don't Elope While You're in Vegas

"Well... I need to go to New York City, anyway," Ethan said. "Natalie offered to come with me. I need to settle affairs with the trustees who've been handling my estate for years."

"I'm excited to travel with you," Natalie said, lifting another forkful of her food. She didn't seem to notice her father's death glare from across the table. "As long as we can take your car. Mine's a little old. Plus, I'll require a separate hotel room everywhere we go."

"Money is no object, obviously." Ethan hesitated, glancing at Miles, who still seemed to be choking and holding his anger at bay. Bonnie placed her hand on his arm, as if to prevent him from reaching across the table to strangle Ethan.

"Mom," Natalie continued with excitement. "We also want to go see Niagara Falls, and Mackinaw Island, and Ethan's sister, Princess Miranda, and his cousins, and... what was the other big thing?" Natalie turned to Ethan with a crease in her brow.

"The Grand Canyon," Ethan said, dabbing at his mouth with his napkin and trying to avoid her father's glare.

"Ooh, we should go to Las Vegas while we're over there. It's only a couple hours from the Grand Canyon." Natalie's emerald eyes sparkled with excitement.

"Gee, don't elope while you're in Vegas." Bonnie chuckled nervously, her smile faltering.

Ethan and Natalie both snorted a laugh, wrinkled their faces at each other and answered at nearly the same time.

"Mom, we're not dating."

"I'm just her client."

The room grew quiet for a moment, and Ethan leaned over his plate to shovel in another bite of potato, avoiding anyone's gaze.

Eventually Natalie broke the silence. "Mom, you should see the bucket list Ethan has. We have so many exciting things to do before he... uh..." Natalie glanced at Ethan with wide eyes and bit her lower lip, drawing his attention to them without his permission.

"Kick the bucket?" he finished her sentence and chuckled. "It's okay, we can talk about the elephant in the room. I know it's cliché, but that's why I made the bucket list. Because I'm dying."

"I guess I don't want to think about it that way." Natalie's voice lowered and shook.

Bonnie brought some humor back into her voice. "Ethan, I bet you didn't realize you'd be in such a hurry to check off that list, huh?"

"Actually, I just made the list a few weeks ago at my father's suggestion," Ethan said. "He knew what I was planning to do with my inheritance and wanted me to enjoy the last few weeks, hopefully months, of my life and not take things too seriously."

Ethan pushed the food around on his plate for a minute, then met Bonnie's gaze again.

"This newest brain tumor is inoperable, so I have two choices. Fight again, or let it win. I don't want any more chemotherapy or radiation treatments. I don't want to be sick again. I just want to drive around the countryside until I'm too tired to drive any further." He shoveled in another bite of potato, forcing himself not to cry.

"I've never been to most of these places either," Natalie said, lightening the mood. "I'm excited. This will be like a vacation for me. A working vacation, of course." She tucked her hair behind her ear and lowered her gaze.

Ethan wasn't quite sure how much work they'd be doing but he certainly wasn't going to complain. He wouldn't be alone, and that was a welcome addition to these last few weeks of his life.

"You should take grandpa's motor home," Miles said suddenly, his voice husky with emotion. "That way you can travel in comfort, won't have to worry about finding hotels along the way, and will have a traveling office. That thing's state of the art, with Wi-Fi and satellite and a full kitchen and bathroom."

"That's a great idea, Daddy." Natalie nodded with a compassionate wonder in her gaze. "You don't think he'd mind?"

Ethan suspected they all knew what she was really asking her father, for his permission.

"I think your grandfather would be very proud of you for helping your fr—client."

"Thank you." Her whisper was barely audible, and they were all quiet for a moment.

"Ethan, would you like another potato?" Bonnie asked, reaching for his plate. "We have plenty."

"Thank you, that would be wonderful." He handed Bonnie his plate and smiled shyly at Natalie, offering her a tiny wink before turning back to reach for his glass of lemonade. So far, this had been one of the happiest days of his life.

Chapter Sixty-Five

This Is What Heaven Feels Like

"**I** 'd like to buy a couple of pizzas before I head home," Ethan said later that afternoon. "Do you think Mrs. Dolan would mind if I buy everyone dinner this evening?"

Miles looked up from his typing, and Natalie looked up from hers. Ethan felt a little useless now that his part of the work was mostly complete. He'd been scrolling through business articles on his smartphone for the past twenty minutes while the two attorneys worked together to form the revocable living trust they'd use as a catch-all for his estate.

"I think Bonnie would love to have a night off from cooking," Miles said. "Why don't you walk next door and tell her your plans, and she'll help you find the phone number for the pizzeria downtown."

"Do I look that bored?" Ethan chuckled and stood to stretch his legs.

"A little, yeah." Natalie giggled.

"We won't be too much longer with this initial setup. Go ahead and order the pizza, and we'll be along in a little while."

Ethan caught Natalie's gaze as he left her office, and she smiled softly. He returned her smile and pulled the door shut behind himself, noticing the jingling of the bell that hung on the door to announce a client coming or going.

The evening summer breeze carried a subtle hint of manure from the nearby farms and someone's recently cut grass. Ethan ascended the stairs to the veranda porch and gazed out across the rolling hills, wondering if he'd already died and this was what heaven felt like.

Growing up with marble floors, crystal chandeliers, and servants to cater to his every need was different from this simple life. He hoped the riches he'd brought from his homeland would bless these good people in some way as he passed on to the next plane of existence. He'd made a good decision coming here.

The door behind him creaked, and Bonnie pushed open the screen door. "Were you planning to come inside?"

"No..." Ethan sighed. "I want to stay on this porch, gazing out at these rolling hills, until the day that I die."

"How are you feeling?" Bonnie asked, a compassionate motherly tone in her voice.

"I'm tired," he answered honestly. "But... resigned." He suspected that Bonnie understood that he didn't mean sleepy. He meant his body was fighting... and losing.

"Are you hungry? I was just about to start dinner." She nodded her head to the side, inviting him in.

"Not really, but I'd like to buy us all some pizza, if that would be an okay choice for dinner."

"That sounds great," she said. "I'll get the phone number for the pizzeria."

"Can we get some salad and breadsticks too?" Ethan followed her into the house, digging his wallet from his back pocket.

"Sure, what do you like on your pizza?" Bonnie asked.

"Whatever you guys want. I usually just get a supreme."

"That's what we like also." She smiled as she reached for the phone and dialed from a menu tacked to a bulletin board. "Hi, Rick, it's Bonnie Dolan. We'd like to order a couple of medium pizzas, supreme, with an antipasto salad and an order of breadsticks."

Just as the pizzas arrived, Natalie and Miles tromped up the porch steps and entered the house with a jovial lilt to their conversation. Ethan was quick to meet the pizza delivery boy at the front door and paid with a fifty, offering for the boy to keep the change.

They laughed and joked and made plans as they crunched on salad and the best handmade pizza Ethan had ever enjoyed. He wished there was more time left in his life because this is where he would want to spend his last weeks. He reminded himself that traveling to all the fun places they mentioned would also be fun and would be better than sitting around waiting to die.

He didn't realize his shoulders were slumped and his lids were heavy until Bonnie said, "Ethan you look like you could fall asleep right at the dinner table."

"I think I'm slipping into a food coma," Ethan joked, resting his hand on his stomach. "This was all so good."

"Oh yes, I slaved over a hot stove to reach for the phone and order you this pizza." They all laughed at Bonnie's joke.

He knew he needed to leave; he had a long drive to get home to Omaha. He sighed and wiped his mouth on his napkin, then dropped it on his plate, and pushed back his chair. "Thank you, Dolan family. This has possibly been one of the best days of my life, but it is getting late."

"I'll walk you out," Natalie said as Ethan shook Miles's hand and gave Bonnie a quick hug.

As they left the coolness of the home and stepped onto the veranda, the sunset took Ethan's breath away, and he stopped short. Pinks and grays and oranges blended together in ribbons of color sitting over the horizon. "Is all of America this beautiful?" he whispered.

"Let's go find out," she whispered back, joining him on the porch and letting the screen door swing closed behind herself. When Natalie stepped up beside him, Ethan fought the urge to wrap his arm around her and pull her close.

What was he thinking? He could not let this train of thought continue. He could not allow himself to care about her. More importantly, he couldn't allow her to develop feelings for him. He was dying. He had to keep reminding himself of that.

"Do you want to sit down on the porch swing for a few minutes to watch the sunset?" Natalie asked.

Ethan turned to where she indicated, noticing a gracefully aged wooden swing with comfortable cushions and large, painted chain links anchoring it to the ceiling of the porch. Without verbally answering her, he found himself drawn to the swing and lowered himself into the cushions, eyes still on the sunset but distracted by the hanging flower baskets and the magnetic attraction to the woman beside him.

All conversation behind them for the day, they just rocked on the swing, a gentle swaying, the mesmerizing colors in the sky blending into one soft pastel ribbon for which there was no name.

"Ethan?" Bonnie's soft voice startled him. Natalie was no longer sitting beside him on the swing but standing beside her mother, whose compassionate smile invited him to follow her request. "I want you to come inside and lie down in the guest room for a little while."

"Okay," he mumbled and cleared his throat, allowing the two women to help him to his feet. The coolness of the front living room drew him to the sofa by the lamp, but he felt gentle hands pull him toward a hallway and down to a room he hadn't seen before.

A four-poster bed sat prominently in the room, and he was guided there. On instinct he found himself sitting, and then his head was on a pillow. Someone removed his shoes, but he couldn't see through his eyelids nor did he know who rested the quilt over his shoulders. The pillow smelled of lavender...

Chapter Sixty-Six

Gone for the Night

E than rolled over and forced his eyes to acknowledge the warm sunlight filtering through the thick, lace curtains. He wasn't disoriented enough to forget where he was and who he was with, although the previous day felt somewhat like a dream. He sat up and looked around.

An open door that he thought was a closet turned out to be an attached bathroom, and he made a beeline for the facilities, chastising himself for falling asleep after drinking two glasses of soda along with the pizza and salad. A welcomed feature in the guest bathroom was a little basket with pocket sized toiletries, including brand-new toothbrushes, still in their packaging. Grateful to his thoughtful hosts, he opened one and brushed the morning breath away before wandering out to see if he was alone in this grand house, where he felt more at home than in his own palace.

He heard a soft radio somewhere back near the kitchen, where Bonnie hummed along to a country music station. Ethan didn't want to intrude but the door to a sunroom was open, and Bonnie had an easel set up with oil paints and a landscape taking shape on a large canvas. He knocked on the wooden frame and cleared his throat. "Knock, knock, mind if I interrupt your work?"

"Oh, good morning, Ethan." Bonnie turned and smiled, then set down her paint brush, and reached for the dial on the radio. "Did you sleep well?"

"Thank you, yes. Sorry if I overstayed my welcome. I don't know what came over me." He chuckled and thrust his hands into his pockets, sensing she didn't believe his lie any more than he did. He was dying of cancer. Fatigue was to be expected.

"Nonsense, all you did was fall asleep instead of getting into your car and driving home. Either way you were gone for the night."

"True. Hadn't thought of it that way." He hitched his thumb behind himself. "I'm gonna take off and head back to Omaha first thing this morning. It is still morning, right?" He looked out the wall of windows that made up the whole back end of the room, gaging the angle of the sun

"Barely, but yes." She chuckled. "Let me grab you a water bottle and protein bar for the road. We had breakfast hours ago, and it's not quite time for lunch."

"That would be great, thanks." He followed Bonnie to the kitchen, and she reached into the refrigerator as he pawed through a little basket of snack bars on the island. He chose a granola bar with chunks of dried fruit and a label that promised to curb his hunger until lunchtime. Just what he needed. "Are Miles and Natalie next door? I'll poke my head in and make sure there's nothing else they need from me before I head out."

"Yes, they should be in their office." Bonnie handed Ethan a cold water bottle, and he strode down the hallway to the front room.

Pushing open the screen door, he glanced toward the porch swing that had been his demise the previous evening and chuckled. "Thank you again for your hospitality. I'm sure I'll see you in a few days."

"Anytime. Drive safely."

Ethan bounded down the porch stairs with a spring in his step and realized his illness was easy to forget when in such a peaceful environment. He glanced up at the tunnel of trees over the sidewalk between the Dolan's home and the little house next door that had been converted to the Law Offices of Dolan & Dolan. He pushed open the door, and the hanging bell chimed.

"Hello, sleepyhead." Natalie's face lit up when she saw him, and Miles removed his reading glasses and stood from his desk.

"How are you feeling this morning, Ethan?" Miles truly sounded concerned.

"Actually, I feel really good. I think I must have needed a good night's sleep." Ethan shuffled his foot, poking the toe of his shoe into a swirl on the pattern of the industrial carpet that covered the floor. "Plus, I think the work you're doing for me has taken a load off my shoulders, if you know what I mean."

"Planning for your future naturally brings a feeling of security," Miles said. Ethan wondered how many times in his life Miles had said those exact words to his clients. He was honored to be one of them.

"Is there anything else you need from me before I take off?" Ethan asked, laying his hand on the stack of paperwork he'd left on the corner of Natalie's desk. "I can come back in a couple of days and bring you whatever else you need."

"I need *you* to come back and take me to New York City," Natalie said, a gleam in her eye. She held up her fingers to make air quotes. "This 'work' vacation is going to be the highlight of my adult life."

Ethan chuckled, suspecting this trip would be the highlight of his adult life as well, what little he had left. "You're the one I dumped my mess on. You tell me when you're ready to leave, and I'll be ready to go. I'll pack this afternoon."

"Lucky for Natalie, her father is an attorney," Miles said with a teasing tone. "I'm going to make this case my priority while you two head out into the great unknown, and we'll converse using modern technology as you travel."

"You're sure you don't mind us using your motor home?"

"I've already called my mother and told her to clean that baby up and stock the fridge and fill the gas tank." Miles stuck his chest out with pride. "They're too old to be taking cross-country trips anyway. In a way, it's good to get that monstrosity out of the pole barn and drive it a couple times a year."

"Please let them know I'll reimburse them for the cost of gas and everything," Ethan said, then pulled out his wallet. "On second thought, here, just give them a couple hundred dollars now. I'll bring more cash to cover the rest. I know those things cost a fortune to fill with gasoline." He handed Miles his last hundred plus two fifties, leaving himself with only a few twenties after handing over four hundred the day before. He was heading home. There was no reason to need cash between here and Omaha.

"Thank you, I'm sure they'll appreciate that." Miles nodded, taking his money.

"Okay, then, I'm going home to get ready for our adventure."

"I'll start packing tonight," Natalie said.

"Shall we maybe plan on leaving the day after tomorrow?" Ethan raised his eyebrows, glancing nervously between Miles and Natalie, still incredulous that Miles was resigned to watch his daughter drive away with a strange man for an indefinite amount of time. "That will give me all day tomorrow to get some last-minute errands run and wrap up a few things."

"Sounds good to me." Natalie had a full out grin on her face and was almost bouncing on her toes. Ethan decided he'd better leave before he did something stupid like take her in his arms and swing her around in a circle with excitement.

Before he left, Ethan turned back and grinned. "Hey, Miles... would you mind watching over my Lincoln for me while we're gone? You know, take her out for a spin every couple of days, keep her gassed up and happy?"

"I might be able to fit that into my schedule." Miles's grin was almost as wide as Natalie's, and Ethan clicked his key fob as he strode over to his car. It really was a pretty car.

Ethan climbed in and purred the engine to life, pulling away from the Dolan's home with a smile on his face.

Chapter Sixty-Seven

Does She Meet Your Approval

"Sleeping arrangements..." Ethan stood in the living area of the luxury motor home, a travel bag slung over his shoulder. "I hadn't thought of that."

"I have," Natalie said from behind him, shoving him all the way in the door so she could join him. "You get the back bedroom, one, because you're sick and will need to be extra comfortable, two, you'll probably go to bed much earlier than me, and I don't want my late night television habit to keep you up, and three, I'm smaller and can fit in the smaller bunk."

"I can't argue with any of your reasoning," Ethan said, turning down the hall past the kitchenette, past the bathroom, and into a larger bedroom than he thought would fit in a motor home. Not that he'd ever stayed in a motor home before, but he was impressed. He turned in a full circle, taking it all in. "Natalie, this is beautiful."

"You sound surprised." Her voice was soft, but she quickly shifted from endearing compassion to flirty salesperson, telling him all the exciting things he could expect from their rolling home away from home. "This is the elite Esteem 29V Class C Motor home, complete with leather seating, stainless steel kitchen appliances, a queen-sized bed, and full shower. Roomy and comfortable, you and your family will travel the country wrapped in luxury."

"Well, considering *you* are my family for the next few weeks," Ethan said, just as playfully, "As long as you are happy, I'm happy."

"I'm happy," Natalie said, her voice soft again.

Ethan was captivated by her sparkling green eyes and momentarily forgot what he had planned to say. They stood there awkwardly for a moment, and then he remembered where he was and the importance of maintaining a professional relationship. He cleared his throat and pulled his focus away.

"Well, we'll see if you're still happy after spending a few weeks with a spoiled prince who's used to being waited on hand and foot, has a strange obsession with his own mortality, and sometimes snores."

"I've slept down the hall from my dad my whole life." She put her hands on her hips and raised her chin defiantly. "I think I can handle a little snoring."

As if on cue, her father, Miles opened the flimsy outer door to the motor home and stepped inside. "What do you think, Ethan? Does she meet your approval?"

"It's gonna be tough, Mr. Dolan." Ethan rubbed his chin playfully. "She's already getting a little feisty, and we haven't even left yet." Ethan knew Miles was referring to the motor home, but he couldn't help poking fun at his daughter.

"You jerk." Natalie pushed his shoulder playfully. "He was talking about the motor home."

"Oh! The motor home!" Ethan winked at Miles. "Yes, it's very nice. The finest motor home I've ever stood in."

"Is this the only motor home you've ever stood in?" Natalie looked at him skeptically.

"Yes, ma'am, it is." Ethan nodded.

"I have a prediction to make." Miles cocked an eyebrow and had a thoughtful, suspicious demeanor. "You two are going to fall in love by the time you're done with this trip."

They both guffawed as they'd done the other day at lunch and shook their heads.

"I highly doubt that," Natalie mumbled.

"I'm not exactly in a good position to fall in love right now," Ethan said, taking a deep breath. "Besides, do you really want your daughter falling in love with a man who's going to die before the honeymoon's over?"

They were all quiet for a moment. "I didn't say I *want* you to fall in love." Miles creased his brow. "I just predict you're going to."

"Sir, I'll do my best not to let that happen." Ethan felt his throat tighten. "If I have to, I'll act so obnoxious that she'll come running home screaming that she wished she'd never met His Highness, Prince Ethan Sayid of Madain Saleh."

That broke the tension as all three of them laughed. Natalie even snorted from holding in a laugh, then cocked her head to the side. "Is that your full title?"

"Yeah." Ethan cleared his throat.

"That's pretty cool," she said, sounding impressed.

Ethan turned to Miles. "So, were you going to teach us how to handle this beautiful vehicle?"

"Yes, of course." Miles snapped out of his inner contemplation and walked around the motor home showing Ethan and Natalie all the ins and outs of the water system controls and how to maneuver the pop-outs and awnings, and the gears and gadgets.

They spent most of the morning getting acquainted with the vehicle and packing and organizing until Bonnie called them in for a nice, hearty lunch of ham sandwiches with lettuce and tomato on toasted bread.

The itinerary was simple. Take two or three days to get to New York City, spend a couple days at his family's penthouse there, and then head west toward Niagara Falls. From there the wide-open road was the limit. Now that they had a motor home, they didn't need to worry about finding hotels and restaurants. They could simply drive.

After lunch, they said lots of goodbyes, exchanged hugs, and shed a few tears, and then Ethan climbed into the driver's seat, with Natalie beside himself.

"You sure you're up for this?" Ethan asked with a grin before putting the truck in gear.

"I'm sure... Your Highness." She bit her lower lip with a teasing grin.

"Very funny," he said, shifting out of park and pulling away from the curb.

"I thought so." Natalie threw her head back and laughed, then rolled her window down, and called out the side. "Bye, Mom and Dad! Don't wait up!"

"Drive safely!" Miles said.

"Have fun in Vegas!" Bonnie called out. Natalie giggled as she pushed the button to close the window.

"She was just kidding," Natalie said.

"Of course, I knew that." Ethan gulped as they increased speed to leave town. *Vegas.* He tried to hide a smile.

Chapter Sixty-Eight

Happily Ever After

"**I**f you don't mind, I'd like our first destination to be my home in Omaha." Ethan glanced to the side, keeping his eyes mostly on the highway. "I know I just left there this morning, but in a few days you will officially have my power of attorney, and if I never come back here, ya know, for whatever reason, you need to know where everything is."

"Do you really think it could happen that soon?"

"I have no idea, Natalie. You saw me the other night. I went from happily eating pizza with your family to passed out for fourteen hours." He used his turn signal to merge to the other lane. "One of these days you may find me back there not breathing. How frightened are you about that? Guess we probably should have discussed this before we left. Sorry."

"I'm not," she said. "Sorry, or worried, or frightened, or anything."

"Really?" He found her confidence strangely comforting.

"You've been upfront about your condition. We're not sticking our heads in the sand, pretending you're not going to die. We're not tiptoeing around the subject. We're confronting this head-on, talking about this like we're planning your estate. Which we are."

"True..."

"So, show me everything at your house, give me a key, tell me what real estate agent you want me to list with—I'm sure you've chosen one already. You've chosen everything else—and then we'll get back on the road and head east."

Ethan chuckled. "You know me too well already, my dear."

"My dear?" Natalie laughed. "Did you really just call me that?"

"Did I?" Ethan gasped and wondered how she'd react to his slip. "I'm so sorry."

"Don't worry about it, Ethan. Seriously, we're going to be spending the next several weeks with each other. You can call me whatever you want. Just don't call me late for dinner."

"Or chocolate ice cream and binge-watching old sitcoms."

"Exactly." She pushed his shoulder. "See, you know *me* too well already too... my dear."

"Ya know, maybe we should just take your parents' advice and get married. That would take all the pressure off the whole situation."

"Very funny, Your Highness." Natalie sat back and propped her feet up on the dashboard, then slid a paperback book from the console. "I'll take that into consideration."

"You gonna read to me?" Ethan chuckled, trying to see the cover of her book without taking his eyes off the road.

"Do you *want* me to read to you?" She lowered her sunglasses to look at him with a mock-serious expression and held up the paperback book. "It's a romance novel. This is the only romance I'm gonna get unless I agree to marry you."

"Sounds good. Broaden my horizon. I've never read a romance novel," he said. "Just think, you reading this book to me could be the only romance I get for the rest of my life."

"You are indeed obsessed with your own mortality, aren't you?" Natalie cleared her throat and held open the book with exaggerated intensity. "Once upon a time there was a dying prince who fell in love with his attorney."

"Ooh, I'm gonna like this story," Ethan said with a straight face. "I can totally relate to the characters."

Natalie snickered and continued. "He loved her so much he rode off into the sunset—uh, well, sunrise. They're heading east—and took her to see his palace in Omaha, and then to a penthouse in New York City, and then to see a princess."

"Not just any princess," Ethan interrupted. "Princess Miranda, who's also married to a real prince."

"Just like the attorney is going to be someday." Natalie snickered and continued. "Then they will sit together on a grand island and sip sparkling lemonade on the veranda."

"Don't forget the waterfall," Ethan said.

"Oh yes, the Niagara Falls. Would you like to see the Canadian side or the United States side?"

"You mean *him?* The hypothetical prince in your story? Would *he* like to see the Canadian side or the United States side?"

"Yes, yes, the hypothetical prince. Which would he like to see?"

"What's the difference between them?" Ethan creased his brow.

"For the Canadian side, they have to use their passports, and for the United States side they merely need to park their motor home."

"Ooh... no passports." Ethan cringed in mock horror. "The prince doesn't like to pull out his diplomatic papers and draw attention to himself."

"Good point. Okay, United States side it is. Moving on. Literally. After the prince took the attorney to see the pretty waterfall, they drove all the way to the Grand Canyon where he held her tight while they looked over the railing so she didn't fall."

"Is she afraid of heights?" He creased his brow.

"Maybe..."

"Okay, the prince in the story holds the attorney tightly so she'll feel safe and secure in his arms."

"This is turning into a very romantic story," Natalie said.

"You did promise me a romance."

"True." She turned a page with exaggeration. "After the prince held her safely in his arms while looking down over the Grand Canyon, he drove her to Vegas to see the lights on the strip and took her to see a show with dancing girls."

"And they found a wedding chapel where Elvis joined them as husband and wife."

"Gross, no!"

"Hey, I thought the attorney loved the prince?"

"Yes, but she *hates* Elvis."

"Ah, good to know." Ethan winked at her. "I'll be sure to remove all Elvis songs from my playlist."

"And they lived happily ever after." Natalie closed her novel and nodded once to conclude her story.

"Until death do they part," Ethan added with irony.

"Thanks for ruining the ending of my story." Natalie pushed his shoulder so hard he fought to stay in his lane, and they both laughed. "My story had a happy ending."

"Yeah, well, mine doesn't." Ethan sighed as he turned on his signal to exit the highway for the road that would lead them to his tiny palace in a middle-class neighborhood near Omaha.

Chapter Sixty-Nine

Bars of Gold and Other Treasures

"Sparsely decorated, Your Highness," Natalie said as Ethan held open the front door to his modest home in Omaha. The empty living room contained one easy chair, a lamp, and a table.

"This home has but one purpose," Ethan said, turning on lights as he moved through the living room into the kitchen. "As a storage facility for all of this." He held out his arm in a grand gesture toward the large dining room filled with stacks of documents, a computer server, a safe, filing boxes, books and ledgers.

"Oh... my... gosh." Natalie made her way over to the dining room table, glancing at files, opening and closing books, peeking into ledgers. "You're going to leave this mess for me when you die?"

"Unfortunately, yes." He cleared his throat. "But you're welcome to destroy everything once we get all the money distributed. None of this has any real value."

"You're worth over a billion dollars, Ethan." She raised her eyebrows. "I've seen your portfolio, remember?"

"Okay, so, *I'm* worth over a billion, but this junk isn't." He picked up a stack of journals. "Other than this. Don't destroy this." He handed her the stack of books.

"What is it?" She sat down on a chair, resting the journals on her lap. Opening the top flap, she read aloud. "Complete Sayid Royal Family History as compiled by Prince Ethan Sayid. You wrote this?" Her voice held awe and wonderment.

"Yeah, well, I wasn't sure if anyone else in my family had written down the old stories my great-great-grandfather used to tell me when I sat at his bedside growing up... so, I wrote them."

"This is fascinating..." After a few moments of reading she looked up. "Can we bring these with us? On our trip? Now *this* is worth reading. Forget romance novels."

"Hey, we all need a little romance in our life, right? Don't discount the romance novels." Ethan scratched the back of his neck and scuffed the toe of his shoe along the wooden floorboard.

"We can make our own romance," she said absentmindedly. "This is gold."

"You really think so?" he cleared his throat.

"This is really cool, Ethan." Natalie stood, cradling the treasure in her arms. "Thank you for sharing this with me." She reached up and kissed Ethan on his cheek.

He felt that cliché feeling of never wanting to wash that cheek for the rest of his life, and he stood there a minute, trying to catch his breath.

"What's in the safe?" she asked, not setting down her newfound stories.

"That really *is* gold," Ethan said. "Ya know, actual bars of gold. The combination to the lock is in the stacks of information I gave you." He turned the dial back and forth a few times and opened the safe to reveal stacks of gold bars.

"Oh my gosh, Ethan, how much is that worth?" Her jaw dropped open.

"I don't know." He shrugged. "A few hundred thousand, maybe half a million? Sorry I didn't take the time to liquidate that yet. We can work on that when we get home. You know what? Never mind. Let's just bring this with us. The best place to liquidate gold is in New York City. I'll get a hold of my financial advisor and see if he can make the arrangements." Ethan grabbed a canvas bag and began filling it with gold bars.

"You're going to bring half a million dollars' worth of gold in our motor home?" She took a step back, clutching the books to her chest. Lucky books. He turned back to his task.

"Who would ever look for gold bars in a motor home anyway?" He tried to lift the canvas bag and realized it was too heavy, so he grabbed another bag and took half the bars out of one and loaded them into the other. "It will only take us about two days to get to New York City, right?"

"Yeah, about two days," she squeaked.

"Dude, you look like you're going to pass out. Relax. It's just a few gold bars." Ethan stood and held one bag in each hand, testing to make sure they were evenly distributed.

"I've never seen this much money in my life." She shook her head.

"Might want to get used to being around this much money if you're going to marry a billionaire prince." He leaned forward to kiss Natalie on the cheek, causing her to lose train of thought just as she'd done to him.

"Very funny, Your Highness." She chuckled nervously.

"Come on, I'll show you the rest of my stuff, and we can get back on the road. The penthouse in New York City is calling."

Chapter Seventy

You Are Dismissed

"Gentlemen, thank you for meeting with me at such short notice," Ethan said. The men in the room nodded in assent but mostly remained quiet and alert, allowing their client, Prince Ethan Sayid of Madain Saleh to take the lead.

The executive suite of offices for his financial management team overlooked Manhattan, and the firm was one of the most well-respected in the world. Ethan was comfortable with their ability to manage his money but still didn't trust them entirely.

"To preface what I'm about to say, you need to be made aware that I have recently received a disappointing medical diagnosis and will be settling my affairs over the next few weeks."

Murmurs around the table interrupted Ethan's declaration, as he'd expected. Several people gasped or said, "I'm so sorry," or "That's terrible." One said, "What can we do to help?"

There was always one willing to stray toward the topic everyone else had on their mind: how can I position myself in a way that benefits me?

This was exactly why he didn't fully trust them, and why he had sought outside counsel to handle the final distribution of wealth and be the executor of the estate. But they didn't know about that yet, and Ethan was determined to keep these gentlemen fully invested in the outcome. He would share just enough information about his plans to hold their interest and nothing more.

"I have been truly impressed with how you have served me, and how you served my father before me, and I want you each to be financially rewarded for your hard work."

Again, there were murmurs and recognition of their firm's ability to act as masters of the universe. Ethan could just envision the posturing over the next few hours, should he allow such behavior.

"I have employed outside counsel to conduct the final distribution of my wealth and carry out my wishes as executor of my estate." That was met with lowered brows and shifting in their seats. This he'd predicted as well.

"Who have you hired, Your Highness?" The feigned concern earned the man a pointed glance from Ethan, complete with narrowed eyes and lowered brows.

"That is not your concern," Ethan said firmly. "After careful research, I have found a group unaffiliated with this company or any of its associates. I intend to obtain a complete lack of conflict of interest. They have your names, and full access to my accounts should I step in front of a bus on my way out of this building. Any changes that are made to my accounts will be immediately disclosed to this third-party firm."

These gentlemen needed to be aware that they were no longer in control of Ethan's affairs.

"I have laid out a very specific plan that includes the exact same percentage to each of you as individuals and a separate percentage to the company as a whole. Should something happen to one of you between now and the time I die, your portion will be distributed to a charity I have already chosen. There is no incentive for any one of you to kill each other off."

That earned nervous chuckles around the room and comments like, "We wouldn't consider such a thing." *Yeah, right.* Money changes people. The prospect of gain changes people as well.

"Anyway, I just wanted to let you know where things stand and that I have made arrangements for how my affairs will be handled," Ethan told them. "If all goes well, each of the named beneficiaries will have zero knowledge of one another nor will they realize they are receiving money from a deceased billionaire prince. Other than the six men in this room, and the executors, all anyone else will know is that they received an anonymous donation."

He paused for a moment in case any of them wanted to contribute to the discussion, then nodded regally.

"That will be all, gentlemen. If you'll excuse me, I plan to take a road trip and see as much of this beautiful country as I can before I'm too sick to enjoy the landscape. Again, thank you all for your service, and good luck in your future endeavors."

With that, Ethan walked from the room with no emotion and left New York City with no intention to return.

Chapter Seventy-One

Princess Miranda

"**H**ave you told your sister that we're coming?" Natalie asked.

After two nights in the City, staying in the luxury of his family's penthouse, they were back on the road, heading north into the Hudson Valley. They had sold the bars of gold, handled all affairs with the financial firm, and taken a high-speed elevator to the top of the Empire State Building, a decision Ethan regretted immediately and had to sit on the floor for about twenty minutes to stop the dizziness before heading back down.

"Uh, hadn't thought to do that." Ethan reached into his pocket and handed Natalie his phone. "Her number is the third down in my contacts list. Put it on speaker phone so I can talk to her without taking my hands off the wheel."

"Give me a minute, and I'll sync the Bluetooth to the motor home." After a few seconds, the car's sound system blasted the ringing phone and suddenly his sister's voice boomed through the speakers.

"Ethan! How are you?"

"Greetings, Your Highness," Ethan said. "How's my favorite little sister?"

"Pregnant!"

"Again? Didn't you just have a baby?"

"Ethan, that was two years ago." Miranda giggled. "We're allowed to have more babies."

"Well, congratulations. Hey, you up for some company?"

"Sure, when are you coming for a visit?"

"In about two hours," Ethan said. "We're just leaving New York City."

Miranda squealed. "Seriously? Two hours? Wait, who's we?"

"I'm traveling with my fiancée. I want you to meet her."

"Your fiancée?" Miranda squealed again.

"Your fiancée?" Natalie mouthed.

"Yeah, we're on our way to Vegas." Ethan winked over at Natalie, and she shook her head with an amused grin. He whispered to her, "It's the easiest explanation."

"Whatever, you silly guy."

"Is that her?" Miranda asked. "Hi! What's your name?"

"Hi, Miranda, I'm Natalie."

"I'm so excited to meet you! I want to hear all about you and how you guys met and where you're from and when you're getting married. I want to hear everything."

"How about if you start by giving us your address, and we'll plug it into the GPS so we can come tell you in person?"

"Ooh, I'll give you the address to the tree house, and I'll tell the rest of the family to meet us there," Miranda said.

"The *tree* house?" Ethan glanced at Natalie, who also had creased brows.

"Yeah, that's what we call Prince Marcos and Princess Hazel's house," Miranda said. "It was built on top of a waterfall. You'll see. Just go there, and I'll get Hayden to call up his brothers and his parents, and Alex, and everyone."

"Everyone?"

"We'll have fun. I promise," Miranda said. "I'm texting you the address now, and then I'll hang up so I can help Hayden call the family."

"Okay, sis, see you in a few hours."

She squealed again. "Yay, I'm so excited!" The line went dead.

"Tree house?" Ethan said.

"Waterfall?" Natalie asked. They looked at each other with gaping jaws. "Well, this will be an adventure."

"Bring it on," Ethan said with resignation. "We did want to see a waterfall, right?"

"We sure did." Natalie plugged the address into the GPS, and the electronic voice came over the speakers.

"You are on the fastest route," the voice said. "You should reach your destination in one hour, forty-six minutes."

Chapter Seventy-Two

With This Ring

"We need to get our story straight," Natalie said as they pulled up a long driveway. Multiple cars were parked haphazardly near the house, some of them very expensive sports cars, one minivan, and a sedan. "You told your sister we're engaged."

"Well, we did talk about getting married in Vegas," Ethan teased.

"Where's my engagement ring?"

"Shoot, hadn't thought of that." Ethan pondered for a moment as they crept up the long driveway. "Hey, I've got some of my mom's jewelry in my suitcase. She gave me a ring that used to belong to my grandma. She wanted me to pass it down to my wife and children, if I ever got married."

"You want me to wear your *grandma's* ring?" Natalie raised her eyebrows.

"She was a queen, you know?" Ethan backpedaled. "It's a really nice ring."

"Really nice to you probably means something that's worth a million dollars."

"Eh, I doubt it's worth *that* much." Ethan shrugged. "Maybe a hundred thousand?"

"I'm not wearing a family heirloom worth a hundred thousand dollars," Natalie practically screeched. "What if I lost it?"

"One, you won't lose it, and two, you deserve to have pretty things. You're kind of amazing." Ethan realized his voice had grown serious. He parked the motor home off to the side of the driveway, out of the way of the other cars in case someone needed to leave sooner than them. "Come on. I'll give you the ring before we go inside."

Ethan unbuckled his seatbelt and slipped into the back of the motor home, heading straight for his suitcase. He sat on the bed and unzipped a secret compartment, then dumped a small bag out onto the comforter and sifted through a little pile of jewelry to find the elegant ring.

As Natalie tentatively approached the bedroom, Ethan held up the little diamond—okay, big diamond. "This belonged to my great-great-grand-mother, Queen Salaina of Madain Saleh."

"Ethan, I can't accept that," Natalie whispered. "It belongs with your family."

"Natalie, you *are* my family now, remember? You're my advocate, my power-of-attorney, the woman who is joining me on a working vacation to help me cross off items on my bucket list." Ethan pulled her hand forward so that she was standing directly in front of him. "You can pretend this is a fake engagement if you want, but the truth is, I want you with me until the day that I die."

"Ethan, I'm pretty sure I'm *going* to be with you until the day that you die." Her shoulders relaxed in resignation.

"Then let's make it official," Ethan whispered. He didn't go as far as asking her to marry him, but he lifted her hand and slipped the little ring onto her finger.

"Okay," Natalie whispered back, glancing down at the elegant ring.

Ethan stood and took her gently in his arms, and she wrapped her arms around his back. They held each other like that for several long seconds, and Ethan breathed in the scent of her hair, relishing the fragrance that filled his senses.

The magic bubble popped when the motor home door was flung open, and Miranda bounded up the stairs, an excited smile and gleam in her eyes. She squealed, "Oh! You're so beautiful!"

Ethan chuckled as Miranda pulled Natalie from his arms, squealing again and hugging her and squealing again. "Nice to see you too, sis."

Miranda completely ignored him as she talked a mile a minute to Natalie, explaining all the people she'd meet when they went inside the tree house.

Natalie glanced back at Ethan, with a grin, and followed her future sister-in-law down the stairs of the motor home and up the sidewalk toward the house.

Ethan pulled the door to the motor home closed behind himself and prepared to see his cousins for the first time in almost ten years.

Chapter Seventy-Three

The Tree house

E than understood immediately why they called Marcos and Hazel's home a tree house. The property surrounding his uncle's home was acres of full-sized trees, with a house that seemed to be growing out of the landscape and had been built quite literally over the top of a real waterfall.

Children were everywhere. Each of his cousins had their wives and multiple babies. He was never going to keep them all straight but grinned as Miranda introduced the adults to Natalie.

"This is my husband, Hayden," Miranda said, still with the wonderment of love in her voice after eight years of marriage. "And his oldest brother Aaron."

Aaron shook Natalie's hand, then stepped over and pulled Ethan into a quick hug. "Hey, man, how are you doing?"

"Good, you?" Ethan returned his hug.

"Living the dream." Aaron pulled an adorable Hispanic woman closer. "This is my wife, Felicia."

"Hola," Felicia said in a pronounced Mexican accent. "Encantada de conocerte."

Natalie bit her lower lip and glanced at Aaron.

"She said she's happy to meet you," Aaron translated.

"Oh, nice to meet you as well." Natalie and Felicia gave each other a hug, a universal language they could both understand.

Miranda pulled Natalie farther into the grand living room. "This is Augustus and Phoebe."

"Call me Gus," he said, shaking Natalie's hand and reaching over to Ethan for a hug. "I'm Ethan's youngest cousin. And this is my best friend, Alex and his wife, Ellen."

Alex sat comfortable and self-assured in a sleek wheelchair that seemed more a source of confidence than a handicap. Almost as if he were riding a sports car rather than a wheelchair.

After Natalie shook both of their hands, Gus pointed to his other brother. "And over there is Prince Owen. He's the only remaining bachelor."

"It's very nice to meet all of you," Natalie said graciously.

"Don't forget us," a lovely woman's voice called from over by the kitchen. "I'm Hazel, and this is Mark."

"Hey, Uncle Mark." Ethan stepped over and allowed his uncle to sweep him into a hug while Aunt Hazel focused on Natalie.

"How's your father these days, buddy?"

"He's good, Your Highness," Ethan said. "Hanging in there, I'm sure."

"How long have you been in the States?"

"A couple of months." Ethan didn't want to go into too many details and risk giving away more information than he intended. This visit hadn't been originally planned, but he was glad they'd stopped. "I have a feeling I'll be here for a while. Probably the rest of my life." He smiled over at Natalie, who coughed lightly.

"I can see why," Mark said, glancing over at Natalie as well. "You're finally settling down, huh?"

"That's the plan."

"And where are you from, Natalie? How did the two of you meet?"

"My dad's Ethan's attorney, actually." She giggled. "We fell in love pouring over estate planning documents. Real romantic, huh?"

Ethan stepped over and pulled her into a side hug. "I found the situation very romantic, actually." He leaned down and kissed the top of her head.

"Well, let me get you some refreshments," Aunt Hazel said. "You look tired from the road."

"I am tired, thank you." More than she knew. And more than he was going to tell them. "A cold beverage would be great."

"I hope you'll stay awhile," Mark said. "We have plenty of room."

"We're quite comfortable in our motor home, but thank you."

"Well, I hope you'll at least park here and hang out for the evening," Hazel said. "Or did you have reservations somewhere."

"We have no plans." Ethan looked down at Natalie. "You want to stay here tonight?"

"Sounds good to me," she said. "I'm excited to get to know your family."

"Good, then. It's settled," Mark said. "Make yourself at home with your cousins and sister and the whole brood, and Aunt Hazel and I will get some burgers ready to throw on the grill."

Natalie wrapped both arms around Ethan's waist and looked up at him. "This is the best vacation I've ever had. Thank you for bringing me here."

Ethan fought the urge to lean down and kiss her but didn't want their first kiss to be in the middle of his uncle's kitchen surrounded by kids and cousins and noise. If—when—he kissed Natalie, he wanted to give her his full attention and do it right.

He met her smoldering gaze and could tell her thoughts were heading in the same direction. He winked at her and kissed the top of her head once again. Yeah, best vacation ever.

Chapter Seventy-Four

Niagara Falls

"Kind of makes my uncle's waterfall look like a trickling brook," Ethan called over the roar of the falls.

"My grandparents spent their honeymoon at Niagara Falls," Natalie said, resting her hands on the railing overlooking the churning river below. Millions of gallons of crashing water flowed like silk over the cliff, creating a mist that fell almost like rain around them. They hadn't thought to grab raincoats before leaving the motor home.

"This sounds like a cold, wet location for a honeymoon." Ethan wrapped his arms around himself, his short-sleeved shirt providing no protection against the chill of the unseasonably cool day.

"That's what the hot tub at the hotel is for." Natalie looked up at him with a teasing grin.

"If that's the case, I think we need to check ourselves into a hotel because I'm freezing."

Natalie turned and wrapped her arms around Ethan's waist. "I'll keep you warm."

"That's much better already," he lied, loving the feeling of having her in his arms even if the gesture didn't protect his forearms or shoulders, or neck. He physically shivered but forced himself to focus on the beautiful woman smiling up at him. She awakened a warmth inside him that he had wondered was still there after having struggled through several years of chemotherapy and radiation treatments. He was tempted to pick up the conversation they'd almost had in his uncle's kitchen. The nonverbal invitation that continued in her sparkling emerald eyes. "That honeymoon sounds good right about now."

"Maybe we should skip Mackinaw Island and head straight to Vegas," she teased. Or maybe not. Ethan suspected Natalie wasn't teasing anymore.

"You're not thinking with that incredibly intelligent brain anymore, my dear." Ethan leaned down and kissed the tip of her nose.

"Probably not." Natalie leaned her head back in full, hearty laughter that was swallowed by the roar of the thundering falls beside them. She pulled herself back to a serious demeanor. "I've been thinking with my brain all my life. Maybe it's time I start thinking with my heart for a few days."

"A few days is all we'd have, Natalie." Ethan's voice was husky but frustrated.

"I know." She bit her lower lip, her own frustration showing in her countenance. "But it's fun to think about. Have you ever, ya know... thought about... getting married?"

He knew what she was really asking, and it wasn't really about a marriage contract. He wasn't sure how he wanted to answer her.

"Did things ever get serious between you and that exotic Indian princess?" Natalie tickled him playfully. "You mentioned she wore a diamond that wasn't big enough."

"I was teasing," Ethan said. "You're the only woman I've ever given a diamond."

"Really?" She seemed to like that answer.

"There was one semi-serious relationship with a girl from my university, but ours was more of an intellectual passion than the potential for long-term commitment."

"Intellectual passion? That sounds intriguing." Natalie's smile invited elaboration.

"We were in a study group together with other business majors and lived in the same building, so our relationship didn't make international headlines or cause social media scandals, like it did every time I went out with Saanvi."

"Saanvi? What a beautiful name for an Indian princess," Natalie said.

"She was *not* a princess; she just hoped to become one." Ethan sighed. "It's really easy to be turned *off* by a woman who's only dating you for your money and crown."

"Okay, no money, no crown." Natalie put her finger to her lips, feigning deep thought. "Now that I know what turns you *off*, I just have to figure out what turns you *on*."

"You," Ethan whispered. "Everything about you turns me on."

"Really?" The teasing smile left her face, and a smoldering intensity replaced the sparkle in her eyes.

Ethan lifted his hands and brushed back the tendrils of her strawberry-blonde curls that hung limp from the dampness of the spray from the waterfall. "Your playfulness, your beautiful emerald eyes, your intelligence."

"Ooh, so we're back to the intellectual passion, are we?" She laid one hand on Ethan's chest, right about where his heart pounded faster than normal. With one slow movement, Natalie's hand traveled up his chest and wrapped around his neck, providing just enough pressure to be a clear invitation.

Ethan lowered his face to hers slowly, hesitating a few inches away, allowing her the choice to close the distance and connect. She lifted onto her toes, pressing her lips to his with careful precision.

Throwing caution and reason right over the top of the waterfall, Ethan allowed himself to be caught up in her kiss, pulling her body close to his, wrapping his arms around Natalie as she wrapped her arms around him.

They were alone on a deck at the top of the waterfall, tourists forgotten, vacation forgotten, cancer forgotten, impending outcome forgotten. Ethan wanted that moment to last forever.

The wind shifted, and the mist blasted them in a shower of droplets almost strong enough to be called rain. They pulled apart in shock and laughed at each other.

"You're soaking wet, Ethan." Natalie brushed the water from his arms, and he brushed the water from her face.

His hands roamed her face, brushing his thumb against her lips, which she parted in invitation, his fingers wrapped gently around her neck and jawline, lifting her face to his for one more passionate kiss.

Ethan pulled away suddenly. "Okay, I really am freezing." He laughed and grabbed her hand to lead her back up the stairs and away from the offending mist that had interrupted their first kiss. He hoped they could continue this conversation from the warmth of their motor home.

Chapter Seventy-Five

Fever

B y the time they reached the motor home, Ethan's teeth were chattering, and his body shook, chilled to the bone. He chastised himself for allowing them to stay on that observation deck for as long as they had.

"Don't take this the wrong way, but I'm pretty much stripping in front of you," Ethan said after he'd bounded up the steps and into the living room area of the motor home. "I need to get these wet clothes off as quickly as possible."

Natalie didn't respond but didn't question his motives. The worried crease in her brow spoke volumes. "I'll make us some Echinacea tea," she said. "Getting something warm inside your body will heat you up quicker than anything."

"Sounds good." In several swift moves, Ethan's shirt was over his head, and his jeans were at his feet. He stepped out of his jeans, down to his boxers, and hurried to the back bedroom where he found a large, fluffy hooded sweatshirt and his favorite sweats.

Without waiting for the tea, he climbed into bed and pulled the blankets over himself, willing his body to stop shivering.

The microwave dinged a few minutes later and Ethan felt Natalie sit next to him on the bed. Her soft voice urged him to sit up, and he opened his eyes long enough to prop himself on one elbow. She'd thoughtfully dropped an ice cube in the tea to cool it down enough that he could gulp down a few swallows of the liquid warmth.

He laid his head back down and murmured, "Better already."

Ethan woke sometime later with Natalie in his bed. Night had fallen but he could see her eyes shining in the dark. He hoped he hadn't deliriously done something stupid like taken advantage of her but didn't think he had.

"Whatcha doing?" Ethan's voice was heavy and slurred.

"You were burning up and moaning in your sleep," Natalie said. "I hope you don't mind, but I dug through your things until I found some Tylenol and forced you to wake up long enough to take a couple. I think your fever has come down a little."

"Thanks," he said. Before falling back to sleep he remembered one important thing. "Don't let me get dehydrated."

"I won't." Natalie leaned down and placed one tiny kiss on Ethan's lips. He almost responded but wasn't sure. Darkness pulled him under again.

Chapter Seventy-Six

Can You Walk that Far?

"Can you sit up a minute and drink some broth?" Natalie asked in a soft voice. Light shone from somewhere around him, and Ethan wasn't sure if she had turned on the lamp or if he'd slept through the night.

Ethan propped himself on one elbow and sipped the cup she offered. Warm savory goodness flowed down his throat in several gulps before he pushed her away and laid his head back on the pillow, replacing the intruding light with the oblivion of sleep.

The next time he woke, the motor home was moving. Ethan was aware enough to realize Natalie must be driving somewhere. The swaying of the vehicle made him dizzy and nauseated, but he used focused meditation techniques to force his body to relax and was soon back to sleep.

All movement had stopped, and his surroundings were dark and quiet. Ethan still felt terrible but recognized the need to use the restroom. He raised his heavy arm to lift the comforter and slowly swung his legs over the side of the bed. His limbs were weak, and his head was foggy, but he managed to stumble to the tiny commode, thankful it was only a few feet away.

When he made his way back to bed, the thought occurred to him that Natalie was missing. Before lying down, he peered through the darkness and saw her bed empty. He had no idea where she'd gone or why she'd left, so he fell back onto his pillow. He was too fatigued to pull both his legs all the way up, so he left one leg hanging off the side of the bed. He tried to pull the comforter back over himself.

The door to the motor home opened, and Ethan heard Natalie tromp up the steps and into the living room area. She set something on the table, and then she was in his doorway.

"Hey, sleepyhead, how are you feeling?" Natalie leaned down and lifted his leg up onto the bed and pulled the comforter back over his body.

"Good enough to make it to the bathroom and back." He tried to smile. "Didn't want to wet the bed."

"That would be bad." Natalie chuckled. "Do you think you could walk a little farther than that? I got us a hotel room, and the door is right over there." She pointed toward the front of the motor home.

He didn't lift his head off the pillow but could envision the distance between the parking lot and a room that likely had a decent sized shower. Motivating, but still a long walk. "I can try." He didn't move.

"I'll take some things inside while you rest a minute, and then I'll help you walk, okay?"

"Okay," Ethan said, letting his eyes close again.

He awoke to the sound of a man's voice. "Are you sure you don't need a hospital?"

"No, his fever has broken. He's just very weak," Natalie said. "If he collapsed while we were walking, I wouldn't be able to hold him up, and we'd both fall."

Ethan sensed a man towering over him and felt Natalie crawl onto his bed from the other side, sliding her arm under his shoulders.

"Hey, buddy," the man's gentle voice said. "I'm Tom. I'm the hotel manager. I've got a wheelchair for you right out here. Do you think you can walk that far if I help you?"

"Sure," Ethan mumbled, recognizing Natalie lifting his shoulders from behind and Tom lifting his arms until he was in a seated position. The man helped Ethan to his feet, and he told himself that the distance wasn't far. A few more steps and he could sit back down. With Tom in front of him, guiding him and offering support, Ethan made it down the stairs and gratefully collapsed into the wheelchair. "Thanks man."

"No problem," Tom said. "Let's get you inside your room." He took the handles of the wheelchair and rolled toward the door, which wouldn't have been more than a few feet to a healthy person. It would have felt like a mile to Ethan.

Tom and Natalie repeated the process of lifting Ethan from the wheelchair and into a queen-sized bed. As he allowed the pillow to swallow his head, Ethan heard Natalie ask Tom to have room service send over some soup and crackers and whatever else they thought a man recovering from a fever would want to eat. Ethan wasn't hungry. He drifted away from the conversation.

Chapter Seventy-Seven

Will You Marry Me?

"Hi," Natalie whispered in the dark. Her face was only a few feet away, lying on the pillow beside him. "How are you feeling?"

"Okay," Ethan said. "Better."

"Better is good."

"Better is better," Ethan joked. "Good is good."

"True," Natalie agreed. "How can I help you get from better to good?"

"I should probably eat something."

"There's some vegetable soup. I put it in the fridge, but I can warm it up in the microwave."

"That sounds good." Ethan propped himself on one elbow, and Natalie quickly sat up to help him to a seated position. "I should use the bathroom again."

"Not surprising," Natalie said, helping him from the bed. "I've been force-feeding you Powerade and broth for two days."

"That explains my full bladder and the awful taste in my mouth," Ethan said, shuffling to the bathroom.

"Your toothbrush and other toiletries are in there already." Natalie helped him over to where he could hold on to the counter for support. "I'll go warm up your soup." She left him alone and pulled the door shut behind herself.

Ethan was tempted by the shower but decided to get some nourishment in himself first. He managed to shuffle back out into the hotel room, where a tiny table in the corner already had his steaming soup and a stack of crackers along with another Powerade. He pulled out the chair and took a seat, relishing the scent of carrots and celery and onions. "Thanks, this smells incredible."

Natalie sat opposite him, with her own bowl of soup, and they ate in companionable silence for a few minutes before she set aside her spoon. "You had me scared there for a few hours."

"Sorry about that." He blew on another spoonful and savored the flavor going down.

"I knew you were sick," Natalie said. "I just never thought about you *getting* sick. You know what I mean? You joke all the time about dying suddenly, but we've never discussed the possibility of you being sick."

"Should have warned you about that, huh?" Ethan smiled sheepishly.

"I'm taking you home," Natalie said. He knew she didn't mean home to Madain Saleh. She was bringing him to her parents' house.

He nodded in agreement but felt his throat tighten. "I should never have roped you into my mess."

"Nonsense," she chastised him. "This past week has been the best week of my life. I love spending time with you." She bit her lower lip, and he was momentarily distracted, remembering their kiss.

"Other than the past few days?" He chuckled.

"Including the past few days." Natalie reached across the table and laid her hand on top of his. "I wouldn't trade the past few days if it meant I got to spend a few more days with you. I want to spend the rest of your life with you."

"I want that too," he whispered.

"Will you marry me, Ethan?" Natalie asked with complete sincerity, all the previous playful joking removed from her countenance. "I want to be your wife."

"You've definitely proven your commitment to the vow 'in sickness and in health,'" Ethan said with a chuckle. "I think that earns you a proper honeymoon."

"Kind of feels like we're already on our honeymoon." She lowered her eyes with bashful innocence.

"I've kinda liked having you in my bed." Ethan pulled her hand closer and noticed the diamond ring resting on her finger. The ring that was fit for a queen. "Even if I was asleep for most of it."

"I was asleep part of the time also," Natalie said. "And I kind of liked sleeping with you."

"Do you think your dad's going to be mad at me for sleeping with his daughter before marrying her?"

"We didn't actually do anything that would make him upset."

"But I *want* to," Ethan said, rubbing his fingers along the top of her hand. "Do my impure thoughts count for anything?"

"Are you even healthy enough for that?" Natalie raised her eyebrows.

"Not right this minute," Ethan admitted. "But Vegas is still a couple days drive from here. I should be feeling better by then."

"I'll believe it when I see it." Skepticism pulled a grin onto her face.

"So, you'd be willing to marry me if I can't—you know..."

"There's more to marriage than sex, Ethan." She linked their fingers across the table. "If I only have a few more days with you, I want to hold you in my arms and be with you in every way we possibly can, whatever that means for us."

"Okay..."

"Okay, what?" Natalie asked.

"Okay, let's get married," Ethan said. "I'd get down on one knee, but I'm afraid I wouldn't be able to get back up."

"Yeah, let's not try that." She chuckled and held up her left hand. "You've already given me a ring, what more could a girl ask for?"

"Natalie?"

"Yes?"

"Will you marry me?"

"Yes, Ethan, I'll marry you." Her soft smile was encouraging.

"Since we're engaged now, can I ask you a really inappropriate question?"

"Uh... sure."

"Will you help me take a bath?"

Chapter Seventy-Eight

I Don't Want Details

"**M**r. Dolan?"

"I know from the caller ID that it's you, Ethan. You can call me Miles."

"Miles, I'll get right to the point," Ethan said. "I slept with your daughter."

"Don't tell him that!" Natalie smacked him on the arm. They were sitting on the edge of the bed, wearing clean clothes and wet hair. They had the speaker phone turned on, so she spoke directly to her dad. "We did not *sleep* together, Daddy. We just slept in the same bed while Ethan was sick."

"And we took a bath together." Ethan laughed when Natalie practically tackled him to get the phone out of his hand. He held it out of her reach, but she wound up in his arms, lying on top of him on the bed, and she couldn't help giggling.

"Daddy, we did not take a bath together," she called out.

"Okay, she gave me a sponge bath."

"You are in so much trouble." Natalie stopped struggling for the phone and gave him a seething look of mock anger.

Ethan reached up and pecked a quick kiss on her lips, the phone still in his hand at the end of a very long arm.

"Natalie, you are thirty-one years old," Miles said. "If you're going to sleep with a man, that's your prerogative, but I *really* don't want to hear the details."

"Mr. Dolan, I mean, Miles." Ethan cleared his throat. "Would you and Mom please meet us in Las Vegas in approximately four days? I'd very much like our family to witness our wedding."

Miles chuckled loudly. "Who predicted that outcome?"

"I did," Ethan said. "The minute I walked into your office and looked into your daughter's emerald eyes."

"I'm physically gagging right now," Miles said.

"Will you make all the arrangements and just text us the address?" Ethan asked, wrapping his arm tightly around Natalie. "And spare no expense. I'm a billionaire prince, and if I can't have a coronation, at the very least I want my wife to have the wedding of a princess. Oh, and reserve us a hotel suite with a hot tub."

Ethan didn't wait for Miles to answer before he touched the screen of his phone to end the call, tossing his cell phone on the floor, and rolled Natalie over so he was lying on top of her.

"I'm pretty sure I'm going to feel better in four days," Ethan said, leaning down for a quick kiss. "I'm still a little weak right now, but I'm up for a few hours of making out—okay maybe a few minutes."

"I'll take what I can get," Natalie said with a smoldering gaze, then pulled him down for a long kiss.

Ethan fell asleep in Natalie's arms a little while later, happier than he'd ever been in his life.

Chapter Seventy-Nine

Meet Me in Vegas

E than didn't feel better in four days; he felt worse. The fever had taken a toll on his body.

He rested in the front passenger seat of the motor home, refusing to lie down in bed all day while Natalie drove. He wanted to be with her. With the seat reclined, a pillow propped against the window and a blanket wrapped around him like a cocoon, he talked to her a little and slept a lot.

Each evening, they rented a hotel room and slept in each other's arms.

By the time they arrived in Las Vegas, Ethan felt as if he was dying of cancer.

From their hotel room, with Natalie's mom and dad sitting close, Ethan did something he hadn't planned to do ever again; he called his parents.

They had a video chat with Ethan propped up on pillows against the headboard, and Natalie holding the phone in a way that his parents could see both him and Natalie.

"Your Majesty and Your Grace, I'd like to introduce the woman I'm going to marry in about three hours. This is Natalie Dolan, soon to be Sayid, if she chooses to take my name."

"Of course, I will, you silly guy." Natalie leaned over to kiss Ethan's cheek. "It's nice to meet you. Your son is the most amazing man I've ever met."

"Welcome to the family, Natalie." His dad sounded as if he was choking back sobs.

"Ethan, you look terrible." His mom didn't try to hide her tears.

"And yet, she still agreed to marry me," Ethan said, turning his face toward Natalie. "You'd think she's smarter than that. She has a law degree."

"Are you nearing the end, my darling?" The second most beautiful woman in the world tried to smile into the camera, her multi-colored eyes, so similar to his own, shone with tears.

"Yeah, Mom, I'm getting close... uh, there are a couple other people I want you to meet. I'm going to hand the phone over to Natalie's parents. They have already taken very good care of me and are graciously allowing me to sleep with their daughter for the last few days of my life. Isn't that nice of them? This is Bonnie and Miles Dolan." Ethan handed the phone to his soon-to-be in-laws. "These are my parents, His Majesty, King Elmer Sayid, and Her Grace, Queen Savanna."

"We're honored to meet you, Your Majesty and Your Grace," Bonnie said with a little wave.

"Please, you're welcome to call us Eli and Savanna," the king said. "The honor is ours. Thank you for caring for our son."

"We love him like a son," Miles said, choking up. "Tomorrow we plan to fly home on a private jet, and he will stay with us..." He didn't have to finish his sentence for all of them to know what he meant. Ethan would stay with them until the day he died, however many days from now that was.

"Thank you," Savanna said, sobs escaping. "Thank you, thank you."

"I'm really glad to meet you," the king said. "But can I see my son one more time."

"Yes, of course." Bonnie handed the phone back to Natalie.

"Your Highness," his dad said, no longer hiding his emotions. "I'm so proud of you, son."

"Thanks, Dad," Ethan said. "I miss you both, every day."

"We miss you too. We're so glad you found a wonderful young lady to hold you in her arms these last few days."

"She's really good at holding me in her arms," Ethan said, turning to Natalie. "I love her so much."

"I love you too." Natalie leaned forward and kissed his lips briefly. There would be more time for that in a few hours.

"Oh, I forgot to tell you." Ethan turned back to his parents. "We drove over to see Princess Miranda and Prince Hayden, and all his brothers and their wives were there along with several beautiful babies. Oh, and Prince Marcos sends his regards. And did you know Miranda's pregnant again?" Ethan was winded but in high spirits.

"Oh! That sweetheart, she should have told her mother the minute she found out," Savanna said. "I'll have to give her a call."

"Can I ask a favor?" Ethan didn't wait for them to answer his rhetorical question. "Don't tell them about me until it's over. I've said my goodbyes to them, and I don't think I could handle my sister's tears right now."

"We'll wait," his dad said.

"And no funeral in America," Ethan said. "All Natalie's family will know is that she married a man who lived in Omaha, Nebraska, and that he died of cancer. We don't want anyone to know she was married to a wealthy prince."

"We'll bring you home to Madain Saleh for the interment, Your Highness."

"Thanks, Dad," Ethan said. "I love you."

"I love you too, son."

"Goodbye, my sweet boy," Savannah said, burying her face in her husband's chest. Ethan had to look away.

"I love you, Mamma," Ethan mumbled. "Goodbye."

Ethan nodded to Natalie and closed his eyes, turning to her as she tapped the screen to end the call. She dropped the phone beside herself and held Ethan in her arms as he sobbed and sobbed and finally fell asleep.

Chapter Eighty

Now You're a Princess

E than awoke to a cool, dark room, the shades drawn and Natalie still holding him. Her parents were gone, and they were alone.

"Hi," Natalie said. "How are you feeling?"

"Like I want to get married," Ethan said. "Did I sleep through our wedding?"

"No, my love, we waited for you." She chuckled. "Couldn't really have the wedding without the groom."

"You could have just propped me up and nodded my head for me when it was time to say, 'I do,' and then brought me back to our room and taken advantage of me."

"Nah, I'd like you to be an active participant in that part of the wedding."

"Which part?" he asked with a chuckle. "The wedding vows? Or the love making afterward?"

"Both," Natalie whispered and then leaned down to kiss the tip of his nose.

"I'll try, okay?" He heard the vulnerability in his own voice.

"Sweetheart, you don't even have to try if you don't want to."

"I *want* to. Believe me, I want to." Ethan brushed her cheek with the back of his hand.

"Me too," she said.

"Let's go get married, then, okay?"

"You want some help into your tux?" Natalie asked. She lifted him to a seated position and offered him a hand to walk with him to the bathroom.

"Is it weird for you to put this tuxedo on me only to take it back off in about twenty minutes?"

"We probably shouldn't show up at our wedding in sweatpants," she said.

"Or naked." Ethan leaned down to kiss her neck and chin and cheeks and finally her lips.

"Get dressed, Your Highness, so we can go get married and come back to our room and get naked together."

"If you insist."

"I'm going to call my dad to come help you and I'm going over to my parents' suite and my mom will help me into my dress."

"See you at the altar," Ethan said, leaning over for one more kiss.

"I'll be the one dressed in white," she teased.

"I'll be the one undressing you with my eyes," Ethan said with a husky voice.

A few minutes later, Miles Dolan wheeled Ethan down the hall to a small reception room on the same floor as their hotel room so they didn't have to use the elevator. There was less chance Ethan would get dizzy or nauseated. He wheeled Ethan to the back of the room, and Ethan rose from the wheelchair but sat on a beautiful chair decked out in white tulle, where he waited for his bride.

Natalie didn't keep him waiting long. Miles had set the wheelchair off to the side, then left the room to go retrieve his daughter. They walked in with Natalie's arm tucked in her father's. Ethan's breath caught. Her dress was simple and elegant, understated and selected in haste. A golden ring headpiece pulled her strawberry-blonde curls into an updo in a way that almost looked as if she were wearing a crown. No princess had ever looked more beautiful.

When they stepped close enough, Ethan stood, and Miles lifted Natalie's hand to rest it in Ethan's. The officiator said a few words, just enough to legally bind them as husband and wife and invited Ethan to kiss his bride.

Ethan turned to the man. "Could I have just a moment with my wife first?"

The man stepped away, hopefully out of earshot, and Natalie's parents also respectfully took a few steps back.

Gazing into Natalie's confused eyes, Ethan whispered, "Normally this would be done by our king, but I think he would make an exception due to extenuating circumstances."

Natalie cocked her head to the side with an intrigued gleam in her eye.

Ethan took a deep, shaky breath and spoke so softly the words were barely audible. "Natalie Dolan Sayid, by the power vested in me by the kingdom of Madain Saleh, I do hereby crown you *Princess* Natalie Sayid of Madain Saleh."

"Princess..." Her word was barely a breath.

"Normally I would place a crown on your head right now, but I'm fresh out of crowns at the moment."

Natalie giggled.

"Instead, simply bow your head subtly and you and I can envision the placement."

The most evocative moment of Ethan's life was the moment he imagined placing a crown on his bride's head.

"Arise, Your Highness," Ethan whispered. As she lifted her gaze, he pulled her close, more invigorated than he had been since before the fever ravaged his already weak frame. He leaned forward, and their lips met in a chaste kiss that promised more. After their kiss, Ethan placed his mouth even closer to her ear and whispered, "Let's go back to our hotel room and make love."

Epilogue—The Guest Room

Natalie Dolan Sayid

N atalie realized the guest room in her parents' elegant home was the perfect place for a honeymoon, at least since her husband was dying of cancer. She and Ethan had their own attached bathroom suite and her mom brought them meals, which they either ate at the little table in the corner or propped in bed with a tray across each of their laps.

During the day, Natalie read aloud from Ethan's journals, and occasionally Ethan would stop her and tell her a little added side story or correct something he'd gotten wrong the first time.

Natalie kept a notebook beside her to record his stories or corrections. When he would fall asleep and start to snore softly, Natalie would read quietly to herself the fascinating stories of princes and kings and contentions and famines, fleeing from persecution and settling their families in faraway lands, traveling on fancy yachts and flying on private jets to cross the globe, meeting with dignitaries and serving with the United Nations. She got caught up in the world of her husband's ancestors, drawing closer to him with each turning page.

Each night, after her parents went upstairs to bed, Natalie would help Ethan out of his clothes and they would sleep in each other's arms, skin to skin, heart to heart. Some nights Ethan would feel well enough to make love, but usually he fell asleep in her arms, and she was okay with that.

One evening when Ethan was feeling particularly good, they had a long talk, and he asked Natalie a favor she promised never to forget.

"If, by some miracle, you and I were able to conceive a child from our very brief marriage, promise me you'll raise him or her as a regular boy or girl and not as a prince or princess."

"Okay... why?" Natalie brushed his shaggy hair from his forehead and decided to give him a haircut one of these days.

"Royal families are snobby and selfish," Ethan said, and they both chuckled. "Seriously though, the money left after you distribute the gifts to all the charitable organizations will be substantial. You will be a very wealthy woman, and our child will have every opportunity known to man. But don't give them everything at once and don't tell them their father was a prince... or that their mother was a princess." Ethan leaned forward and kissed her gently and warmth traveled through her body from the top of her head to the tips of her toes.

Natalie knew that night would be a good night.

The following morning, she awoke with the sun shining in the white lace curtains, but Ethan did not.

For several long minutes, Natalie held her husband for the last time, tears staining her pillow.

They'd been married twenty-three incredible days. Twenty-three days filled with just enough passion to give Natalie the greatest gift a wife could receive: a son.

Five years passed, and Natalie climbed up beside little Ether Miles Sayid, who she'd named by combining Ethan's name with his father's name, King Elmer Sayid. A perfect little melding of names for a perfect little bundle of life.

"Read me the story about the young princes again, Mommy." Ether handed Natalie one of the many picture books her artistic mother had helped her create using Ethan's journal entries.

"Do you want to read from the middle?" Natalie asked, wrinkling her nose at his choice. "Or would you rather start at the beginning?" Natalie picked up the first book in the series and wriggled her eyebrows.

"Umm..." Ether put his finger to his chin in deep thought. "I think we should start at the beginning." He pointed to the first book.

"Good choice," Natalie said. They settled in on Ether's bed, and he pulled his blanket up near his mouth, his thumb still hovering nearby even though he'd finished sucking his thumb at least a year ago. Natalie opened to the first page of the first book. "Once upon a time there was a handsome prince named Marcos, who had a very best friend named Nicholas..."

"I like this story, Mommy." Ether snuggled in closer and closed his eyes.

"Me too, baby boy." She kissed the top of his head. "Prince Marcos and his friend Nicholas went on all kinds of adventures..."

<u>Continue reading the Royal Family Saga Book Five Billionaire's Sons</u>

Love Letter

Author Julie L. Spencer

O h, my friends, I love these characters. They are so special to me. Did your heart break for Natalie? What did you think about the selection of Eli as the king of Madain Saleh? Did you predict that in advance? I purposely left that vague throughout the rest of the series so my readers would keep guessing. Now that you know, you'll have to go back and re-read the series and see if that revelation changes how you view the character interactions.

For the final book in the series, you're going back in time to the beginning and finally hearing the story from the perspective of the illusive and distinguished gentleman known as Nicholas Cohen. What caused him to flee his homeland? Did he really murder someone? What happened with his brothers that tore the family apart?

By the way, I'm cracking up that *Billionaire's Sons* is currently touted as the final book in the series because I've now started two more stories!

Remember Alex, Jr.? The guy in the wheelchair? I started a little side story about the summer after high school when he and Ellen were pushing through the challenges of falling in love. They work through his spinal cord injury, the devasting effects from PTSD, guilt for his past sins, and the new knowledge he has that there is a God and remembering things from his near-death-experience.

I also started a little side story about Prince Benjamin and Princess Nisha. I haven't gotten far on that one. Maybe by the time I publish Billionaire's Sons, I'll be able to give you more details.

God bless you, my friends. Stay safe! *-Julie L. Spencer*

Billionaire's Sons

Continue reading the Royal Family Saga Book Five Billionaire's Sons

Four love stories, Six brothers, and the Inheritance that tears them apart.

The esteemed businessman, Nicholas Cohen, attempts to win the heart of his childhood sweetheart, Adele, despite his older brother ruining their wedding.

Meanwhile, his younger brother, Sam, impatiently waits for the girl of his dreams, Leanne, to finish her master's degree hoping to whisk her away to a far-off land to complete her PhD.

Their younger brother, Jacob, falls for the captain's daughter, Maryam, on a superyacht bound for the Caribbean, much to their parents' dismay.

One generation later, Emanuel elopes with a not-too-much-older woman, Aloise, three months after high school, less than 24-hours after they meet only to discover he's married to the enemy.

Continue reading the Royal Family Saga Book Five Billionaire's Sons

JULIE L. SPENCER

Kingston Academy

Featuring Ether Sayid

New in 2023!

Kindle Vella story: Kingston Academy – Summer Sons

They're here for the summer, and possibly until graduation. Inducted into an unofficial club of Kingston Academy royalty, the guys living in Rhinebeck Hall are the most elite of the popular kids. They're the Summer Sons. Finding love shouldn't be hard unless the local girls want nothing to do with the entitled, rich princelings. Tyrell, Jaeden, Ether, and Alejandro must navigate prep school, girls, drugs, and forbidden affairs while staying true to their values and their trust funds.

Kindle Vella story: Kingston Academy – Summer Sons

About Author Julie Spencer

Continue reading the Royal Family Saga Book Five Billionaire's Sons

Four love stories, Six brothers, and the Inheritance that tears them apart.

The esteemed businessman, Nicholas Cohen, attempts to win the heart of his childhood sweetheart, Adele, despite his older brother ruining their wedding.

Meanwhile, his younger brother, Sam, impatiently waits for the girl of his dreams, Leanne, to finish her master's degree hoping to whisk her away to a far-off land to complete her PhD.

Their younger brother, Jacob, falls for the captain's daughter, Maryam, on a superyacht bound for the Caribbean, much to their parents' dismay.

One generation later, Emanuel elopes with a not-too-much-older woman, Aloise, three months after high school, less than 24-hours after they meet only to discover he's married to the enemy.

Continue reading the Royal Family Saga Book Five Billionaire's Sons

www.ingramcontent.com/pod-product-compliance
Lightning Source LLC
Chambersburg PA
CBHW071111250626
47159CB00002B/698